Enthusiastic reviews for Lior Samson's novels —

The Rosen Singularity

"The plotting is ingenious and the characters come through strongly. It succeeds marvelously on the thriller level, but it also delivers a substantial intellectual and emotional kick."
— *Rebecca Goldstein, MacArthur Fellow, author*

"Vibrant and distinctive characters and thoughtful, yet engaging narratives and conversations, ... an exciting, pulse-pounding story."
— *Laurie Jenkins, book blogger*

Bashert (The Homeland Connection)

"Samson writes with a crisp elegance, like John Le Carré, and weaves his plot magically, sustaining suspense throughout."
— *James A. Anderson, author*

"An ambitious novel, ... moving with the speed of light between interconnected events, three continents, and a group of unique and memorable characters."
— *Avraham Azrieli, author*

The Dome (The Homeland Connection)

"Suspenseful and timely, ... I cannot say enough good things about this novel."
— *Alan Caruba, critic, BookViews*

"An excellent read, and very highly recommended."
— *Midwest Book Review*

Web Games (The Homeland Connection)

"An outstanding tech thriller—better than Tom Clancy.... This ranks up there as one of the best [thrillers] I've read in 2011."
— *James A. Anderson, author*

"This extraordinary author has the ability to anticipate events. ... You will not put it down."
— *Alan Caruba, critic, BookViews*

Chipset (The Homeland Connection)

"[A] multi-dimensional thriller that will satisfy discriminating readers who crave realistic stories populated by flesh-and-blood characters."
— *Avraham Azrieli, author*

"Lior Samson hits another one out of the park. . . . Few thriller writers can match Samson's ability to deliver a gripping story."
— *James A. Anderson, author*

Gasline (The Homeland Connection)

"Samson turns up the heat with a high-energy plot and . . . a perfect mix of techno thrill and human conflict. . . . a rip-roaring ride. Excellent!"
— *Avraham Azrieli, author*

"[A] great novel . . . high concept, flesh-and-blood protagonist, and realistic action. . . . [It] will raise your blood pressure and make you think."
— *Columbia Review of Books and Film*

Flight Track (The Homeland Connection)

"Well plotted . . . compelling and entertaining. . . . The characters are developed with dialog that provides insight . . . kept me turning pages."
— *Harrison Jones, airline pilot, author*

"Stunning, compelling, thought-provoking. To the book's broad scope and expert pacing, add three-dimensional, engaging characters."
— *M. Thornburg*

The Four-Color Puzzle

"[A]n authentic thinking person's ideal mystery; an eloquent feast of words and an excellent story. . . . [M]ay be the best [book] I have read this year."
— *Jeanie B. Clemmons, author*

"[A] fast-paced crime story that had me rooting for the hero while also feeling conflicted by his choices. The story challenges the reader."
— *Patricia O'Sullivan, author*

THE MILLICENT FACTOR

THE MILLICENT FACTOR

a novel by Lior Samson

GESHER PRESS

Gesher Press

Rowley, MA 01969

Author site: www.liorsamson.com

Gesher Press and the bridge logo are trademarks of Gesher Press.

Printed in the United States of America.

5 4 3 2 1

ISBN 978-0-9885275-7-7

Cover and book design: Larry Constantine
Set in Alegreya and Alegreya Sans
Cover painting: "Passages" copyright © 2015, Dianna Daly
DiannaDaly@gmail.com

To my Lucy—teacher, student, scientist, and singular source of surprise—
always

Teach that you may learn again, and learn that you might teach me.
—Denton Reynolds, "Teachable Moments"

Part One ~ Intercept
Chapter 1

The thick envelope, with its official Express Mail label and its metered postage askew in the corner, thudded onto the desk. "There." Gustav Holzinger was not one to waste words when actions spoke loudest. He straightened his back and neutered the expression on his weathered Teutonic face. Behind his unblinking gray eyes and text-message brevity hid the taut discipline required by his ex-officio role as head of external security for the global empire that was Biontolics Holdings.

The office was a brooding patchwork of dark wood and bright spots from recessed downlights. The small corner suite overlooking Boston's financial district was not part of Biontolics itself. The sign in the reception area said it headquartered the Berkowitz Biomedical Foundation, but that was merely the current flag of convenience for one particular vessel in the flotilla of foundations and front companies that propelled the Biontolics operation and carried out its true mission: providing a very select clientele with unique medical services.

Across the bare expanse of the zebrawood desk, Bertrand Francoise Lyon, newly renamed and freshly reinstalled as head of Biontolics, did not even blink. His botox-steady face fronting a Kalashnikov mind was the edge he used to manage the messy dealings of his long and complicated life. In many ways, he and his security chief were siblings and looked like it, the half-century difference in age notwithstanding. He took his time before sliding his tablet computer to one side, then looked up. "What is this, Gus?"

"Frau Geller. She sent these to the press, politicians."

Lyon tensed almost imperceptibly. "And?"

"And I . . . intercepted them."

Lyon spun the envelope around and read the label. "Sanger at the *New York Times*. He's good, and he can be rather dogged in pursuit of a story, especially one with geopolitical implications. How?"

"When the woman at the local post office wouldn't cooperate, I went plan B. Those Postal truck drivers are seriously underpaid. This one rather appreciated the cash bonus I offered. He pulled into a rest stop on his way to the regional sorting facility and looked away from the unsecured truck while he took a piss."

"The woman at the post office?"

"A loose end at the moment, but not for long."

"Just this one packet?"

"No, that and thirty others. I thought you might want this for reference purposes. The rest are scattered ashes."

Lyon, who in an earlier life had fully earned his nickname as The General, stood and officiously extended his hand to Holzinger. "Good work," he said, with a quick grasp and release. "Once again. I do think it might be time to consider a suitable expression of the organization's appreciation. Something with greater . . . longevity, shall we say." His hand went to the back of his head, as if marking the thought in his brain for future reference. It rested there for a moment. As Atchison Douglas Dougherty, he had favored military-style haircuts, an affectation adopted in the Viet Nam War era as a reactionary commentary on the hippie look then coming into fashion among so many of his academic colleagues; as the freshly minted French-Canadian Bertrand Lyon, he was still getting used to the shaggier locks that better matched his always untamed eyebrows.

It was training, not temperament, that made Holzinger, the former German security consultant, nearly as unreadable as Lyon. "I'll leave that to you, sir ... and the organization." He spoke as if reading lines from an email. "I just do my job."

"Yes, you do, and with quiet efficiency. What of Frau Geller, our erstwhile school teacher? Are we to expect more trouble?"

"I think not. I believe she can be ... persuaded."

Lyon nodded and sat back down, a silent dismissal. Holzinger acknowledged with a nod of his own, took two steps back, pivoted smartly, and left the office, closing the door behind him with only a barely audible click.

Lyon was thoughtfully tapping the unopened envelope as his business partner, the dapper Dr. Charles Ferguson, reentered the office from the suite's private bathroom. Ferguson, despite plastic surgery and sartorial makeovers, still resembled Llewellyn Andras Cass, the Welsh wunderkind who had helped launch their enterprise over a half century earlier. Years of life abroad and many hours of voice coaching had long ago softened his accent into an indecipherable phonetic stew, but he had originally learned English by listening to the BBC as a lad, and some words still stood out. "News?" he asked, with the first letter of the word palatalized like a Spanish enya.

"No, the lack thereof, which is all the better."

"Was that Gus I heard? What's in the envelope?"

"It was Gus, and the envelope is filled with a void, the news that is not news and never will be."

"You still speak like a professor, one leading a seminar in creative non-fiction." He craned his neck to read the label on the envelope. "The biologist's wife, I assume, trying to blow the whistle."

"Indeed, but the whistle was muffled and went unheard, thanks to our ever efficient German friend. Millicent Geller thought she was being clever, but she was no match for a professional."

Ferguson forced a grim smile and did not pursue the matter further. "Business as usual, then, I suppose. I'm off for Moscow tomorrow, but I'll make a stop in Zurich on the way back. There's a supply-chain snag at Revic, a problem with some of the precursor chemicals. In Russia, I'm being briefed at the Nichevo labs regarding their innovative work on accelerating genome sequencing."

Lyon scribbled a note to himself, tore the top sheet from the pad, folded and creased it precisely, and slipped it into his shirt pocket. "How long do you think the Russians will keep looking the other way?"

"As long as we keep paying them not to turn around."

"Perhaps, but I hear Putin wants to join The Club. His FSB has sources in Africa and our sources say, in turn, that the Russians have already guessed much of the real story behind Mbutsu's rather lengthy reign over Busanyu."

"So? The FSB is rife with rebranded KGB from the Soviet era, now older and less reliable. If Putin wants to join, he will have to apply and pay the entrance fee just like everyone else." Among themselves, their complex organization had become known as The Club. Ferguson's scattered patients were its metaphorical members, but the tens of millions required upfront to join were no metaphor. The annual fee was also very real, and the consequences for falling behind in payments were permanent.

Lyon reached for his tablet computer again. "Perhaps. But Putin? Do we want one such as Vladimir Putin becoming a one-man dynasty and pulling strings in the Russian Federation for the rest of the twenty-first century?"

Ferguson shrugged. "Let's face it, we've accepted far worse. Putin may be a conniving kleptocrat, but even at his worst he can hardly match the reign of terror our dearly departed Dr. Edgar Jabari Mbutsu managed in Africa."

Lyon sighed with impatience. "The issue is about neither ethics nor methods, but that Putin is a bully on a bigger scale. The Russian Federation is not some small West African backwater. Given enough time, Putin would take over us and half of Europe. He has already begun his post-Cold War version of a slow march westward. No, I think it is in our own self-interest to turn down his application. I would hate to lose the lab in Russia, though. An entire city with only a number and a dot on a map is advantageous in our line of work. I'm not sure where we could go to continue that sort of research and development in such splendid isolation, especially not combined with such easy access to cheap and abundant scientific talent."

"Fret not, my dear Bertrand. I am already on top of the matter. There is no shortage of alternative sites. We could take Xander Quarry up on his standing offer to move out to his ranch. The weather is certainly better in northern California than outside Moscow. And if isolation is still a priority, there's always PanAfrica Pharmacometrics. Vanderwalter has already suggested we use his estate outside Cape Town. In any case, nothing has happened yet. While I'm in Moscow, I'll put out some feelers regarding Putin's fantasies. I'll see you in London at the end of the week, then?"

"Yes, London, the new flat. You'll like it—so much like the old one, just with better security. We would not want another incident, would we, like that matter with the deranged Dutchman? I hate being shot at even more than I hate having to shoot intruders. Besides, I'm just starting to get used to being Bertrand Lyon. What a nuisance it would be to have to go through this makeover mess again so soon. My jaw still bothers me from the orthognathic surgery." His fingers traced a line along his once square jaw line and absent-mindedly scratched at his new moustache above lips that had been subtly plumped with silicone.

Chapter 2

The news story from New England had upset him when he stumbled on it among his regular news feeds that morning, but Clinton was now on stage and the show was about to start. He knew that once he actually got into it, the rhythm of his role as a teacher would take over and the knot in his chest would ease. He looked up from the notes on his laptop and scanned the seventeen faces waiting for him to begin the seminar.

"Good morning. I'm Clinton Rodrigues and this is JOUR 129, Long-form Journalism, or, as I prefer to call it, 'Writing to be Read.' Let me begin with a few basics. First, no electronics in my class, so close your laptops, pocket your smartphones, and stow your earbuds. And yes, that means you, Roger Belknap; I'm onto your tactics of texting under the table. We're here to talk with each other and learn from each other, not to swap messages with faraway associates or to surf the World Wide Web.

"Second, I draw your attention to recent reports coming out of the Big Apple about students at Columbia, who have been demanding so-called 'trigger warnings' from their professors regarding any potentially discomfiting material. Here at Sacramento State, our journalism classes are only for grownups—at least mine are—so this is the one and only trigger warning you will get from me. I fully intend to make you uncomfortable. If I don't, and you don't get to thinking about your discomfort, I will have failed in my duty as a teacher." He attempted a menacing look, but his warm eyes and gentle Hispanic features made it hard to pull it off. A few students suppressed snickers.

"We will be reading and discussing some of the best contemporary examples of long-form journalism, and this stuff is full of violence, rape, drugs, sleazy sex, poisoned food, and dirty politics. And, perhaps ugliest of all, human stupidity in all its manifold manifestations. All this material is required reading, no exceptions. If you want to be a journalist, squeamish sensitivity needs to be left at the door. We will also be writing. Lots. Every week. And we will be reading our works aloud to each other and critiquing them in class." There were the expected groans and open-mouthed silent protests from the students.

~ ~ ~

The rest of the ninety minutes passed quickly enough and ended on a sharp cadence when Clinton introduced the first writing assignment. "If you want to write to be read, you have to grab readers, get their attention, and then drag them into the story. Long-form journalism is not like simple news reporting, where the first paragraph, the 'nut graph,' tells the gist of the story in condensed form. It's actually more like writing a book, which is part of why so many of such extended narratives end up being republished in book form. Note well, this is one of the few ways journalists might have a shot at the big bucks—unless you have the looks and charisma to become a network anchor.

"So, from the outset, you need to make your audience want to keep reading. That starts with the headline or title and the first sentence and the first paragraph. I am not talking about 'burying the lede' or teasers that withhold information; I am talking about compelling, engaging writing.

"We've heard some examples of that today, so you know what I'm talking about. Therefore, for next week, I want you to start the in-depth story of your life." Rolling eyes and groans spread around the room. "I said start, as if it were the beginning of an investigative series. I want you to devise a title for your series, a subtitle for the first article, and then write the first three paragraphs. That's all. See, not so bad." He swept the room with a searchlight grin.

"And let me give you some hints about what not to do. If your first graph starts 'I was born on blah blah in East Blah-blah-blah' you will earn an automatic fail. Does anybody here know the term *in medias res*? No? It's Latin, and it's one of the best pieces of advice for storytelling. It means 'in the middle of things.' So, one way to get readers into your story is to plunge them right into the maelstrom in the middle of it. Don't start at the beginning; you can save that for later when your readers are already hooked.

"And that, my friends, is why I did not begin this first class with a long set of dreary definitions or a protracted recounting of the origins and history of long-form journalism. Boring! I've saved that stuff for next week—now that I've got you hooked."

From the back of the room a male voice called out, "That's what you think, professor." A ripple of laughter intermingled with the shuffle of backpacks and the start of conversations as the students prepared to leave.

Clinton mimed throwing something toward the back of the room. "Always ready to bust my chops, Roger. You'll get yours when we start tearing into your writing. In fact, I think next week you can go first with reading your opening lines." Roger feigned taking a blow to the stomach.

One of the students, a young African-American woman who had arrived late but taken a front row seat, waited until most of the students had left before coming up to Clinton. She wore jeans with scuffed knees and a black tee-shirt featuring an indie band Clinton recognized by name but had never heard.

"So, tell me professor, how would the series on your own life begin?"

"Not fair. I want you to be original and find your own voice as a writer. Besides, I've done this exercise many times already."

"You said this was a seminar, that we were in this, like, together. So, what would you write? Off the top of your head, like, starting in the middle of things, as you said."

"Okay. How's this? 'After teaching the same seminar year after year, I was not expecting to be thrown off guard with the first class. A student, who was new to me, was standing with one hand on her hip and the other on the strap of her sling pack, glibly challenging me to walk the walk as a journalist.' Or something like that. It could use some editing; maybe it's a tad over the top."

"You cheated! You just took what was happening and . . ."

"Hey, it's my life story, and I'm starting in the middle of things. Don't you want to hear more? Who are these people, and where are they going? Would you be protesting if you weren't already hooked?"

Her eyes narrowed in concentration, but she turned and walked away without saying anything more. At the door, she paused and spoke without turning around. "Okay, you win, professor. I'll see you at the next class."

~ ~ ~

As part of the contract faculty, the underpaid migrant workers of modern academia, Clinton did not have an office of his own. The bullpen of four desks he shared with other part-timers was not even located with the rest of his department. He unlocked the door of the office and almost stepped on the fat envelope on the floor. It was addressed to him; the return address was the *Sacramento Bee*. What would his former employer be sending him? He settled in at his desk in the far corner and opened the envelope. Inside was another envelope, this one an Express Mail packet. Clinton noted the return address and started to feel sick.

Chapter 3

From the heat of the Central Valley to the autumn chill of New England was a journey of more than mere miles for Clinton. He had agonized over walking away from his students. He had stared at his computer screen, hand shaking above the mouse, until finally he had forced his own hand by confirming non-refundable roundtrip airfare to Boston. Even discounted, the tickets would take him time to pay off. Then he had agonized over how to ask Professor Grist for help with his classes.

Now he sat in his rental car with the heater cranked up as he stalled by rereading the local story. It had been front-page news in the *Portland Press Herald* when it happened, but now the follow-up story was tucked away inside, next to a report about gravestones overturned by vandals in a nearby cemetery.

Police Recover DNA Evidence from Trailer Fire

Sheriff Douglass McAlhenny confirmed that usable traces of DNA may have been recovered from the body found in a rented trailer home after the recent explosion and fire that took the life of one resident and destroyed five mobile homes at Gibson's Seaview Mobile Home Park. The trailer in which the fire started was reduced to ashes by the intensity of the blaze, but investigators said part of a fingertip from the body had not been completely consumed. Tissue has been sent to the State Police Crime Lab in Augusta to confirm the identity of the victim by matching it against a stored blood sample from Massachusetts. Based on the rental agreement for the burned unit, the victim was earlier reported by police to be Millicent Geller, a retired teacher and former resident of Essex, Massachusetts. A firefighter, who had been on the scene, said the body was little more than a pile of ash. "I don't think I ever saw one this bad," he told this reporter. The Fire Marshal and police are still studying the cause of the fire, which is regarded as of suspicious origin. A spokesperson for the Fire Marshal's Office, citing evidence of "accelerants," promised a "continued investigation." One neighbor described the presumed victim as "some kind of scientist, I think, a nice little lady but she kept mostly to herself." Residents of the small trailer park east of town reported an explosion and fireball from Unit 14, located at a back corner of the facility. A cellphone call to 911 was logged at 6:12 am last Wednesday, and the first of three firefighting companies was on the scene within minutes. The short-lived fire was so intense that firefighters could not initially approach and instead concentrated on saving other units and preventing the fire from spreading into adjacent woodland.

Clinton tucked the newspaper under his arm and struggled to slow his racing heart as he left the car and approached the large mobile home just to the right of the trailer park entrance. He attempted to put the best calm and unthreatening expression on his swarthy face. The screen door rattled against its frame when he knocked, but there was no response. He forced himself to breathe less raggedly and tried again.

A woman's tilted face, pale and puffy, slid into view at the edge of the screen. Her gaze circled over his face with the half-buried apprehension he remembered from growing up in the WASP-y small towns of New England. The demographics of the Northeast might have changed over the years, but the social bedrock remained—ever suspicious of strangers, especially those whose ancestors had not been pale early arrivals from France or England. The woman worked her lips as she waited. Then: "Yeah?"

"Ah ... I was wondering if ... if I could see where the fire was."

The woman, big but still a few dozen pounds short of obese, squeezed through the narrow doorway of the house trailer and stepped wearily out onto the concrete blocks that served as the front stoop. "You a reporter?" She glanced down at the Nikon on the strap around his neck.

He almost said yes but then caught himself. "No, I'm just ... I was a friend of the woman who was burned."

"She weren't burned, she was cremated. You ever seen what's in those little urns what come from the funeral home? Well, I heard there weren't much more'n that: just ashes, little pieces of bone 'n' such not. Police said they couldn't even rely on dental records. You sure you ain't no reporter. Tha's some camera you got there—not a tourist-type camera. No."

"It's a hobby." He looked past the woman's bare shoulder, with its tattooed vine of green and blue winding halfway up her neck. He peered into the gloom inside the mobile home, and inspiration popped out of the shadows. "Some people do macramé; I take pictures."

"Macramé, huh. My daughter-in-law is a nut case over that, always givin' me some dang doodad all tied up like some sailor who don't know his knots and don't know when to stop tying. Got the stuff hanging ever' which way in there. I ask her whether she could tie me somethin' useful, like maybe a macramé hammock, and she jus' look at me and say, 'Amy Jane.' She keep on shaking her head and saying, 'Amy Jane.' I says, 'Tha's my name, don't wear it out.' and she laughs that big horsey laugh of hers. And ...

"Even if I shows you the spot, you can't see much, you know, 'count of the police tape. I keep askin' them when they's gonna take that dang yellow tape down and let me clean up that section, but they jus' say it's a ongoin' investigation."

Clinton nodded sympathetically. "I understand. It must be a royal-ass pain. First you get a fire, and then you can't clean up the mess and move on."

"Tha's it. Dang right. C'mere. I'll show you where it's at. Jus' don't touch nothin' or nothin', okay?"

"I sure won't. Don't want to cause any hassles with the police. You from around here? Did you know the woman?"

"Do I sound the hell like I'm from around here? No way. You don't have a very good ear for these things, do you? These people here, they's all, like, 'Ah yup. Ah don't think you can get thay-a from he-ah.' Know what I mean?"

Clinton nodded again and fell into step behind her as she led the way down the dirt road into the heart of the trailer park.

Without turning to face him, she kept talking over her shoulder. "You knew Millie Geller, did you? I was never too sure about her. Mostly kept to herself, walked to the lib'ary lots, said she was a teacher, biology. Retired, I guess. She was a bird watcher, too. One of those always with them big field glasses, you know. What did you say you do?"

"I teach, at the University."

"University of Maine?"

"No, Sacramento State."

"I've heard of that. One o' them California types, huh? Long way away. If she was a friend, you should've come earlier." She stopped suddenly, wheezing as she caught her breath. "Well, here you are, such as it is. Fire took out all these." She swept a fat arm in a half circle. "Obvious where it started, but the others is damaged beyond repair. These here were all rental units. Most o' those over there are owner-occupied, as we say. They jus' lease the pad." She finally turned to face him. "You sure I can trust you? Ain't gonna touch nothin', right?"

"Right. I'll just get some pictures and be on my way."

"Well, I guess . . ."

"Don't worry, it'll take maybe five minutes. I can find my way back out okay."

"What you say your name was?"

"Rodrigues, Clint Rodrigues."

"Clint? Well . . ." She shrugged her tattooed shoulders and ambled past him without having offered her name.

Clinton took a series of wide-angle shots from around the taped-off perimeter, then zoomed his lens all the way out to 300 millimeters to get close ups of everything in the interior. He was no forensics expert, just an ex-reporter, but his journalist's instincts were kicking in. The residue of the fire looked all wrong to him.

Most of the structure was burned out, leaving a part of the kitchen area half standing, now shored up by two-by-fours placed by the police to prevent a further collapse that might destroy evidence. At the other end, where there would have been a bed, it was burned all the way through down to bare concrete, now discolored and heavily spalled by the intense heat. Somebody had worked hard to make sure no evidence remained. They may have almost succeeded if the article in the newspaper was right. It seemed unlikely that any DNA could have survived such a fire, but Clinton figured that if they could recover DNA from long-buried Neanderthals, maybe some tiny bit of the body could yield something useful.

Clinton pushed his stomach against the plastic tape and took two steps forward, stretching the barrier by a couple of feet. Leaning inward, he raised his camera overhead to point it down at the area now outlined with little yellow evidence markers. He snapped off a rapid-fire sequence as he panned the camera in spirals above the area. Redundancy was the key. With enough shots, he could stitch together a very detailed satellite view of the entire crime scene. He knew somebody back home who might be able to make sense of it. The slick-slick-slick of the camera's continuous-shot mode slowed, telling him the buffer on his D7200 was filled. He had enough anyway. He lifted his finger from the shutter release.

In the sudden quiet, he noticed the sound of trucks and cars whizzing by on the Interstate just the other side of the rise. A gusty wind huffed and sighed through the scrub woodland that bordered the trailer park.

Clinton made one last circuit around the cordoned-off remains of the trailer. On the far side, at the very edge of the well scuffed dirt, where singed trees recorded what might have become a forest fire, were two faint parallel lines in the ground. The short lines, shallow grooves just over a foot apart, led into the wet leaves and matted pine needles of the underbrush. Something, something with small wheels or runners, had been dragged into the site or out of it.

Chapter 4

The overnight package ("Guaranteed next-day delivery by 3 pm!") had reached Clinton nearly two weeks after it had been posted from Falmouth, Maine. It had been duly logged in at the mailroom of the *Sacramento Bee* the day after it was sent, but, because it had been marked to the personal attention of Clinton Rodrigues, who was no longer on staff, the mailroom clerk had followed procedure and set it aside. Several days passed before she got around to tracking down his current address to forward it by regular mail in a plain manila envelope. At the University, the envelope sat in the mailroom for a few more days before being dropped off with the departmental secretary, who slipped it under the door of Clinton's shared office late on a Friday afternoon.

~ ~ ~

After pleas and hasty arrangements with Bonnie Grist to temporarily cover his classes, Sacramento was now a continent away, and Clinton's stalled second career as a college professor was fast fading from his mind. He scanned the contents of the envelope fanned out on the small desk in his motel room. The subtle tremor in his left cheek started again, a motor-message from the damaged nerve in his jaw now clenched in concentration. It was not the first time he had puzzled over the package with such determination. Given the list of prominent and powerful recipients stapled to the back of the brief cover letter, by the time he had opened the packet on that fateful Tuesday, headlines around the world should have been screaming with the news. But there was nothing. It seemed impossible that the news-hungry staffs of both CNN and Fox could have been silenced or simultaneously taken a pass on such a story. Either the packet was a cruel joke meant just for him, or he would have to conclude that, of the thirty-two packages listed in the appendix, his was the only one to reach its destination. The rest must have gone missing.

The story was not quite a story. Millie Geller was a biologist, not a journalist, and there were different standards of evidence and different notions of proof in science and journalism. In aggregate, the documents from Millie Geller were only an outline supported by tantalizing teasers, a drama so preposterous that Clinton's first impulse was to think his former teacher had become a card-carrying member of the conspiracy wingnuts of America.

A number of the dramatis personae listed in her summary were already dead. Geller's husband, Dr. Rosen David, had died in an isolation unit at Boston's Massachusetts General Hospital, the victim of a mysterious hemorrhagic fever like the one that had earlier struck Edgar Jabari Mbutsu, the brutal dictator of the West African nation of Busanyu. A *Boston Globe* piece linked the two deaths, claiming that Dr. David had contracted the deadly disease after mishandling biological samples sent from Busanyu for testing by the Massachusetts lab where he worked. Atchison Dougherty, head of Biontolics Holdings, parent company of the lab, had been shot in his London flat by an intruder, leaving the firm now in the hands of a French-Canadian named Bertrand Lyon. The intruder, a Dutchman named Dekker, was also dead. Bernice Quarry, wife of billionaire octogenarian Alexander Quarry, was gone. So many dead. And now Millicent Geller.

He could still picture her in her classroom, a box of tissues always within reach, the wiry little biology teacher who seemed to be allergic to nearly everything. She had been one of Clinton's favorite teachers of all time, a bright light in a dark tunnel of his life.

After his father had returned to the Azores a step-and-a-half ahead of the law, his mother lost their house in Gloucester. Sarah Toledano was too proud to go begging to her parents, who owned apartment buildings in Manhattan but had disowned her when she married a gentile. So she moved with her son into a cheap apartment in Amesbury, where she got work as a waitress and used the liberal Massachusetts school-choice system to get her bright but over-anxious offspring into the better schools of Newburyport across the river.

It had been the right move, although Clinton hated the Nock Middle School at the outset. Isolated for being from the wrong town, bullied for his too-dark, acne-pocked complexion, and teased over his name, he had retreated into a cocoon of academics. There he fell under the spell of his science teacher, who set the stage for a career in journalism by teaching him how to notice things and how to write about what he noticed. She had been a diminutive dynamo who ignited sparks in her students. And now she was gone.

He wondered why was he here, now, back East, playing at a profession for which he had a passion but was ill-suited. He could face a classroom of young adults and be at ease talking about journalism in the abstract, but to knock on doors that he had never opened before or to approach strangers for interviews sent him into tailspins of anxiety. He was good enough as a writer and sufficiently adept at online and library research that it took a while before his editor at the *Sacramento Bee* had worked out that his avoidance of direct quotations was not a matter of literary style. He was not interviewing, not talking face-to-face with people. When Clinton headed over to the State House or to the mayor's office, he would hang back, hovering at the edge before slinking away to nurse a tall latte until it seemed like the right time to reappear in the newsroom.

To him, a classroom was controllable and predictable; people on the street were not. Clinton told himself that he was not agoraphobic, yet his life had become ever more channeled into those well-traveled lanes that minimized one-on-one encounters. It had reached the point where even placing phone calls could paralyze him.

Yet, here he was, on the road, pursuing a story again, all because a former teacher had sent him a package. "This is nuts to the nth, where do I start?" He was gathering string, as reporters called it, starting with the smallest lead and fishing for the next. He looked down at the packet. "The post office, dimwit, just like you would tell your students. Go back to the beginning, to a known source or location."

He had already deviated from the ethics of journalism by not identifying himself at the trailer park. It was not like he was working for a newspaper, he rationalized, more like playing detective on a personal mission. Besides, he figured he would get nowhere at the post office asking questions as a reporter, so he fished around for some motel stationary in the desk drawer, triple-folded several sheets, and stuffed them into the one remaining business-size envelope with the motel logo and return address. He addressed the fat envelope to himself in Sacramento, grabbed his keys, and left the room before he had time to panic and change his mind.

~ ~ ~

The Falmouth Shopping Center on Route 1 had seen busier days. The parking lot was more than half empty, and there was no line of waiting customers in the small post office, which upped the ante for Clinton. He would not be able to resort to his favored tactic of hanging back to listen in hopes of catching the name of the bear of a clerk behind the counter. Around the man's neck hung a lanyard with his USPS identification attached, but the badge was tucked into the ink-stained pocket of his shirt. That probably violated protocol, but otherwise the badge would have been always spilling off the slope of his barrel chest toward one armpit or the other.

Clinton filled his lungs and exhaled. "Hi, there. I wonder if you could help me."

"Depends." The man tilted his head down to peer over his old-fashioned half glasses. "Wha' do ya need?"

"I need to send a letter to California and want to get it there as fast as possible. You know, like FedEx overnight."

"There's a FedEx office two miles south of here. This is a post office."

"Yeah, I know, but, like, how much would it cost to mail it, like, airmail special delivery?"

"What you want is Priority Mail Express. What's the zip code?"

"Like where it's going?"

"Yeah."

"Ah, 95819."

"Let's see it."

Clinton pulled the envelope from his back pocket and handed it over.

"Here. Put it in one of those flat-rate mailers over there and fill out that form. Cheaper that way."

Clinton completed the multipart form, slipped his envelope inside the stiff mailer, and returned to the counter. "I don't suppose you get a lot of rush packages to California from here."

The man scowled over the top of his glasses. "You might be surprised. Few weeks back we must've had maybe three dozen go out in one day. Not all to the Coast, mind you, but, like, lots of places."

"Were you here at the time? Do you remember who mailed them?"

"Naw, 'tweren't me. I'm just filling in as Assistant Postmaster for Hazel Shaeffer."

"Uh, she was the one here at the time?"

"Yup."

"Could I talk with her?"

"Don't think so."

Clinton was wondering how many questions it would take to get anything from the man. "Why not?"

"On account she got herself killed."

"Killed?"

"Yeah. Poor Hazel, she was headed home after work and skidded off the road into a tree. She was nearing retirement, too." He studied the screen of his terminal. "That'll be $19.99."

"Ouch, maybe I'll just send it first class."

"Your choice. Need stamps?"

"No, I have stamps. Thanks." He shook the envelope out of the flat-rate mailer and returned it to his hip pocket. "Er, when was the accident, when did the woman die?"

"Two, two-and-a-half weeks ago. I say it was no accident. I've known Hazel for decades, and she drove like a little old lady, if ya don't mind me saying. Speeding? They said she was speeding, took the curve too fast. Doesn't add up."

~ ~ ~

Clinton sat in his rental Ford in the parking lot and tried to calm himself. He was not succeeding. He was thinking that the woman who was at the post office when Millicent mailed his packet was killed shortly after. The other thing he had gotten from his visit was indirect confirmation that his had not been the only packet mailed. Something had happened to the others, but his had slipped through.

Back in his motel room, Clinton sat on the bed and tried to think about his next move. He was at a loss for ideas. When in doubt, write it out, he thought, just like he would tell students. He fired up his laptop and started writing a post for his class blog.

American education is in crisis, and the crisis deepens every time a good teacher is lost, whether to retirement, to burnout, to a higher paying job in industry, or to the nothingness beyond. The world lost one of its great teachers recently. Millicent Geller taught general science to generations of awkward and uncertain middle-school students in Newburyport, Massachusetts, but she did more than that: she inspired them to delight in discovery, to take pleasure in exploration, and to pursue the better parts of their unique potentials. She did that for me, opening doors that would take me across the continent and into new worlds. If the world were just, teaching would be one of the highest paid professions, and great teachers would live out their lives in comfort, surrounded by friends and family and former students, rather than dying alone in trailer parks. That Millicent Geller seemed to be allergic to almost everything never stopped her from being a field biologist who took her charges along on the ride. On field trips, her backpack was stuffed with guidebooks, pocket magnifiers, and extra packets of tissues. She delivered her magic between sneezes, and posed her questions punctuated by sniffles. And we loved her. I loved her. And she will be missed.

Part Two ~ Exit
Chapter 5

Ferguson gunned his nimble red-trimmed black Porsche out of the last curve and into the long straightaway heading directly toward the isolated Russian facility. There the road dead-ended at a town without a name, a gated community rescued from communism's fall. Ferguson and his friends called it *Nichevo*, Russian for nothing. There was only one way in and one way out of the Soviet-era "secret city." It had been a bargain when they bought the whole thing outright from the cash-starved Russian government during the chaos of *perestroika*. The labs, once used to design death, had been repurposed to study life. The organization had had its pick of some of the best scientists from across the new Russian Federation, and the assembled team had been churning out a stream of brilliant studies that would never be published—could never be published. The fetal stem-cell research alone was worth the many millions The Club had invested. In the current climate, it was research that could not easily be replicated anywhere else.

Stands of bare birches, like mottled white flag poles planted in mounds of early snow, flew past. Ferguson was in his prime, a perpetual forty-something with middle-age looming but kept ever at bay, a man who always stretched the rules just so. It was strictly against agreed policy for any of The Core, the four principals who steered the Biontolics ship, to drive themselves, but Ferguson kept the Porsche garaged at his Moscow apartment in defiance of policy. He supposed Bertrand knew. There was no point in even trying to keep secrets from Bertrand, whose eyes were everywhere and fingers reached into everything, but The General had bigger concerns than doctored expense reports and fudged travel logs from his partner.

Speeding down the deserted two-lane road in defiance of rules was both exhilarating and mesmerizing. For just a moment, the image of a lab technician at the compound flashed before him: Sveta, smart, sexy Sveta, with hips and breasts to match her oversized ambitions. Then he blinked. Sveta was dead. The General had decided her ambitions were too great and her loyalty too limited. Within The Core, it was better never to get involved, never to develop relationships that lasted. The life of the road could be lonely, but flying first class was some compensation. His old-style Hollywood good looks complemented by no-limit credit cards meant there was never a shortage of passing companionship.

"What the ... !?" Ferguson sprang into action as he deftly downshifted and slowed. In the distance was something in the road just ahead of the entry gate. As he approached, the dark shape resolved into the angled profile of a camouflaged armored personnel carrier. The BTR-80, with its duck-boat front and blunt rear, was angled across the road, the barrel of its 30 millimeter cannon pointed straight down the long approach. Two *Kozlik* jeep-style vehicles flanked the road. As Ferguson eased toward the roadblock, lounging soldiers straightened up and readied their weapons. A soldier manning the carrier-mounted machine gun pivoted to face the approaching Porsche.

Over a megaphone, Ferguson was ordered in Russian to stop. He was already stopped. A soldier with a Kalashnikov approached. "You cannot be here. It is forbidden. Turn around."

"What is going on?" Ferguson asked in Russian. "I want to speak to someone in charge. This facility belongs to my company, Slavic Estate Enterprises." He started to open the door to step out of the car, but the soldier used his knee to push the door closed again. "Look, I have a right to be here. Get your commanding officer."

The lieutenant ambling toward the car looked too young to be an officer, but a braided scar on his face suggested he had seen combat. "The town is closed," he said in heavily accented English. "It is being . . . returned. You had better go back the way you came before I am forced to . . . detain you."

"This is the first I have heard of any closure. It's my company, and these are our laboratories."

"I wouldn't know. I have my orders not to allow anyone into the town after the evacuation."

"Evacuation? When?"

"Yesterday, the day before—it was ordered, some emergency."

"Ordered? By whom?"

"Just ordered. We follow orders here. It is best. You should, too. Turn your car around and go back."

There was no point in arguing. The man was just a junior officer. But Ferguson would not be following orders exactly. He would not be heading back to the Moscow apartment, neither would he be going to Sheremetyevo International to catch his flight for Zurich.

He saluted the lieutenant, smartly turned the Porsche around, and drove until well around the first curve before pulling over to check his cellphone. It still had one bar from the tower that served Nichevo. He scrolled through his contacts until he found the entry for Oleg Zabrovski. "Hello, Oleg? Yes, Ferguson here. File for Hamburg but fuel for London. I'll be there within the hour."

He hesitated before dialing his Moscow office, then the extension that was a direct link to London. He realized, though, that Bertrand would need as much advanced notice as possible. "Hello, Prudence. Dr. Ferguson here. Yes, yes, I would assume Bertrand is not yet in the office, but I need you to track him down and get a message to him: 'The President took Nothing.' Got that? Yes, just those words exactly. I'll see him at the flat tonight."

He activated the app to wipe the call log and messages from his phone before slipping it back into his pocket. The tires squealed and gravel flew as the Porsche shot off the shoulder and rocketed down the empty road.

Chapter 6

The post-modern terminal at Ostafyevo Airport, with its gridded glass façade and arched roof, resembled a cross between a boxy commercial office building and a gussied-up maintenance hangar. Ostafyevo, a converted military base south of Moscow now operated by Gazprom, catered to business travelers with private jets and private agendas. Zabrovski Aviation, another Biontolics front, operated a small fleet of Gulfstreams that served as a source of revenue from Russian oligarchs and an escape route for emergencies.

Ferguson left his Porsche with the keys in it for later delivery elsewhere by a driver. As soon as he entered the terminal, an aide in the teal-trimmed black uniform of Zabrovski Aviation signaled him to follow. He was led quickly through a side door, down a long corridor, and out onto the tarmac where a G650 with a stylish blue-green Z brush-stroked on its tail was waiting. Ferguson mounted the stairs, shook hands with Oleg Zabrovski and his co-pilot, and surveyed the empty cabin before seating himself in the leather-upholstered swivel seat nearest the cockpit. A flight attendant with pixie-cut hair dyed an improbable maroon, came up from the galley with a tray. "Orange juice or champagne, Dr. Ferguson?" She was almost as tall as Ferguson but still short enough to wear heels and not graze her head on the ceiling.

He shook his head. "Drambuie, neat, thanks." He watched the sway of her hips as she returned to the pocket galley at the back. Maybe in London, he thought, before her return flight.

There seemed to be nothing special about her, but that in itself was an appeal: nothing to hook his interest, to draw him into wanting more or to stretch things out. He was thinking how odd it was that, given enough time, variety and change and newness could themselves become boring. And he most definitely had enough time, years that he no longer kept track of, years that had begun to blur into sameness despite an endless string of adventures and problems and crises that should have kept his attention. Others might envy his globe-trotting lifestyle, call it exciting and count him lucky for his very long life and unblemished health. He, however, was beginning, at times, to wonder about the path he had taken. Was it worth it? What would most people give for the extra years?

The plane started taxiing away from its hardstand almost as soon as the attendant finished raising the folding stairway and closing the door. Within minutes, they were cleared for takeoff and airborne. When they reached their cruising altitude of 40,000 feet, Oleg came back to chat with his passenger. He was carrying a brown box with a handle and a handset atop that resembled an old-fashioned car phone.

"The big boss told me to always carry this whenever I flew with you. I assume it's a secure satellite phone of some sort, but in my job, I don't ask a lot of questions."

"Wise practice. And thank you for the prompt departure on short notice."

"It's what we do. Air traffic control is already asking us some questions. Hamburg and London are almost but not quite on the same flight track. We'll be fine once we're out of Russian airspace and take a slightly more northern route over the Baltic. I'd sit tight with the phone until we're clear in about ten minutes. We've asked Malvina to join us on the flight deck, and I'll close the door behind me for your privacy. Okay?"

"Excellent. Thank you again. And thank Malvina for me. How long until we arrive in London?"

Oleg checked his watch, a flashy oversized Omega chronograph that did not look like a knockoff. "Less than three hours to London City Airport. Closer in is worth the higher fees. There will be a car waiting for you."

"Perfect."

Ferguson waited fifteen minutes before trying the encrypted phone. "Hello. It's Chas. I'm flying over Latvia at the moment, headed for London. Did you get my message?"

"I did. What the hell does it mean? What's going on? What is with Putin?"

"They have evacuated Nichevo—some kind of an emergency as pretext. It's now cordoned off by the Russian army, or three vehicles of it, I should say. It doesn't take much for a town with only one road in or out. I presume the orders came down from the top, regardless of whatever the official word might be. Putin obviously thinks he can bully or blackmail his way into The Club. Typical. Knowing this government's history, I decided it would be prudent to get out immediately. In any case, we're stuffed. We've lost the entire lab, decades of work. It's gone, in the hands of Putin."

"It's a setback, that's all. All the data and findings are already duplicated on our own servers. We can start quietly getting some of our star players out of Russia, and we can be up and running in South Africa within a month or two. Revic in Zurich and PanAfrica in Cape Town will keep up the flow of pharmaceuticals and cell strains, and you and your flying doctors will keep up the preventive health services."

Ferguson grinned. "Quarry Ranch has a bigger swimming pool than Vanderwalter's estate. Besides, California is a lot more stable and easier to reach than South Africa."

"Precisely. Remoteness and a certain amount of social chaos are good screens. Much of the research we did at Nichevo could not have been done in a more stable, more exposed locale. Imagine trying to do the fetal stem cell work in California. Now it's time to move on. This is a hiccup—a costly one, I'll admit— but just a bump in the road. We have already acquired some of the needed lab equipment at PanAfrica. We're only talking about an extra few million or so."

"What about Nichevo? The Russians now have everything: all the specialized equipment and all the paperwork. What will they make of it and get from it?"

"You still think too much like a country doctor, Chas. The Russians will get nothing. I'll see to that. They really have no idea who we are or what we are capable of. As soon as I'm off this call, I'll look into it. That's why they call me The General."

Static poured from the handset; the call had been ended.

~ ~ ~

Heavy traffic slowed the ride in from London City Airport, and Ferguson took the opportunity to get to know Malvina better. They both knew what the agenda was when he offered her a lift into the city. With the exodus from Russia behind him and Bertrand already alerted, Ferguson felt no urgency. A quick lunch was followed by a long stopover at his place before he had the limo drop Malvina at her hotel. Buoyed by a pleasant dénouement, Ferguson decided to dismiss the driver and walk the two kilometers to Bertrand's flat: the entire top floor at one of London's toniest addresses.

Ferguson deplored the ostentation that Bertrand relished. It drew attention to Biontolics and could jeopardize the entire operation. With a few notable exceptions, members of The Club led comfortable lives, quietly building wealth over the long haul and calling the shots from offstage, out of the limelight. Edgar

Jabari Mbutsu had been one of the exceptions, but he had been a necessary early compromise because it was his billions that had bankrolled the launch of The Club. Even the formerly flamboyant Xander Quarry, another of the founding underwriters, had settled down since becoming a father and losing his wife. The drug-fueled orgies for which Quarry Ranch had once been notorious were now history.

At the private elevator for Bertrand's flat, the uniformed guard nodded and used his keycard to summon the car. "Welcome back to London, Dr. Ferguson."

"Thank you, Tony." He stepped into the lift, smiled back as the doors slid shut, and waited for the stomach-lurching ride to the penthouse suite. Bertrand was waiting for him in the ivory-walled canyon that was the sitting room. A curved seven-foot wall screen mounted to one side was carrying a news feed in Russian. Lyon tapped a remote and muted the sound. "I was wondering when you would finally show. Did you catch the news on the way in?"

"I did not. I napped through the traffic, then I caught some lunch and stopped off at my place ... for a shower." On the screen, spotlights played over streets filled with rubble and dotted with smoky fires. "Where is this?"

Lyon smiled. "Nichevo."

"What? What happened?"

"Terrorists. Maybe Chechen rebels. Who knows? Lots of speculation and little specifics so far. Whoever they were, they had surface-to-surface missiles, which means they were well-funded—or well-connected. When they attacked the town at dusk, all hell broke loose. It went up, just like that. People heard the explosion clear over in Moscow, and the fireball could be seen twenty kilometers away. The media think the town housed some kind of munitions store or weapons research facility."

"But . . ."

"Of course, no one knows for sure. Maybe the former occupants of the facilities had rigged it against just such a contingency."

"You mean . . . ?"

"I mean that our Russian bad boy now knows who he is dealing with, and by letting the news out so promptly, he is effectively informing us that he knows. Look, one of us has to think like a general, anticipate, plan ahead. Your head is always buried inside your lab results, titrating treatments, monitoring patients."

"That's what's needed. The science is still shaky. It all has to be watched and tweaked or we lose someone, and then there's another mysterious death to cover up with doctored documents and a benefactor to be replaced. There are only two of us tending more than a dozen members. I also manage all of the medical infrastructure and oversee most of the research and development. I don't have time for war games."

"War games." Bertrand laughed his incongruously high-pitched snigger. "You do worry, Chas, but about the wrong things. Revenue sources are everywhere. With over two thousand billionaires in the world, nearly all of whom would probably pledge the bulk of their net worth for our services, there is no shortage of candidates for membership."

Ferguson stared, open-mouthed, at the devastation on the wall screen. "I hope the town really had been emptied."

"Or not. Either way, the evidence is gone. Of course, Putin has, no doubt, already figured out who was behind the rebels, but he will be powerless to do anything about it directly. Some rebel faction will be blamed because he cannot expose us and risk completely closing off any future prospects. One might say the livestock have already fled the barn, and now the entire farmstead has been razed. His ex-KGB heavies might try to extract information or take revenge on some of our former employees, but most of them knew next to nothing about the real mission, and some of them are already on their way to Cape Town."

Ferguson backed away from Lyon. "You really don't care about these people."

"They're just people. Ordinary people die all the time. It happens. For all but a handful of the very unordinary, it happens sooner than they would want."

"Maybe death always arrives sooner than we want, even for the ones lucky enough to be members of The Club. We still don't know how long treatment can be sustained or how long it will continue to be effective."

"As long as we want. It's biological stasis."

Ferguson shook his head sadly. "You don't read my reports anymore, do you. The real problem is not in the genetics but in the epigenetics: how the genome responds to the unique conditions each individual faces, how genes are turned off or on by circumstances. At the start, we had a method, a treatment plan that could be followed like a formula. Now we've learned that there is no plan but, at best, a template tailored to each person and constantly updated. For the oldest of our members, we are already having to up the treatment frequency just to stay even. The induced mosaicism and multiplicity of cell lines is an ever increasing challenge to manage. Even a short delay in scheduled treatment can trigger a runaway condition, a cascade of cell death."

"Enough, Chas. You are not explaining this to some grad student or new hire. I do read your reports as well as every goddamned paper our legions of research scientists crank out. I prefer to put my faith in science, and I don't mean medical science, which is really more craft and hand waving than science. We'll figure it out. I don't know about you, good doctor, but I don't intend to ever hang up my stethoscope.

"We have spawned a singularity, old friend, a discontinuity in human history. We have mastered human life, given permanence to a temporary trajectory, conquered death. Nothing is the same, all bets are off, and we will witness the outcome of the game—and the next and the next."

Bertrand reached for the remote and turned up the sound. The announcer was calling the frantic scene Armageddon in the Russian countryside.

Chapter 7

At the faux-country building housing the Falmouth Police Station, Clinton leaned on the counter like a cub reporter, reaching for all the nonchalance he could muster and trying to keep his hand steady. "So, what can you tell me about the fire over at the Seaview?"

"At the what? What fire you talking about?" The lieutenant working the desk, a beanpole with big hands, looked up from the form he was laboriously filling out on a Panasonic Toughbook, pecking away at the keys with a well-chewed Bic pen as if he had never quite completed the transition from paper forms. His pen hung suspended over the keyboard, as though he were expecting the interruption to be brief.

"The trailer that burned last week."

"Oh, you mean over at Gibson's. What can I tell you? Nothing." He looked back down and tapped away at what Clinton guessed must be a cursor key.

"I'm a reporter, working on a story." He flashed an outdated identification card.

"I don't care if you are Ernest Hemingway writing about the Spanish civil war. What I can tell you is nothing. It's an open case, possible arson."

"Okay, so that's good. Arson. You must have some good people working on it, then."

The officer gave him a dyspeptic look.

"I mean, you'll probably know pretty soon, one way or another. I can come back tomorrow."

"Tomorrow won't do you no good. The HTA expert from Seattle doesn't arrive until Tuesday. And the State Fire Marshal is handling it."

"So, you're calling in an HTA expert. Makes sense." Clinton scribbled "HTA?" in his notebook before flipping it closed.

The officer was warming to the conversation. "Yeah, I guess they had a series of these big building fires out there back twenty years or so. Took time to figure them out."

"Big buildings? But this was a little house trailer."

The officer scratched at his forehead as if uncertain whether to continue. "Well, it's about the accelerants, high temperature, you know."

"Oh, yeah." We're doing okay, Clinton thought, just keep him talking. "Do they know what the accelerant was yet?"

"No, that's why they're bringing in this West Coast hotshot."

"So, tell me, what do you think it is?"

"What do I think? I'm a detective, but I think maybe Hal Nordquist is right. He's a welder, uses something called Du-Weld, burns like hell on a stick. He says it sounded maybe like that to him: welding chemicals."

"And you,

"Me, I think she had chemicals stored in the trailer. She was some kind of science type. When the fire started, the chemicals went up and took her, too. That's what I think."

"That's a great theory. Can I get your name?"

"It's Lieutenant Sweden, Delmar Sweden."

Clinton flipped open his notebook again. "And how do you spell your name?"

"Sweden, like the country. But you can't quote me. I'm not the department spokesman; Rita Kleimer is. Spokesperson, I should say."

"And your first name, how do you spell that?"

"Delmar, just like it sounds."

"Oh, right." Clinton drew a squiggle and closed his notebook.

~ ~ ~

Northbound traffic on Interstate 95 was approaching gridlock, but southbound was not too bad once Clinton got away from the Portland area. He wasn't sure why he had checked out of his motel early and headed south. His flight home wasn't until Monday, and he had considered heading up to Bar Harbor for a break over the weekend.

The rental car's compass heading began to make sense soon after reaching Massachusetts. He crossed the Merrimack River under the baby-blue twin arches of the new Whittier Bridge and spotted the sign for Newburyport. Without thinking, he began slowing for the exit. It had been so many years that he was driving more on instinct than memory. He took the left off the ramp, then hung a right onto Low Street.

He was thinking about the crime scene and the odd residue of the fire when, near the other end of Low, he noticed girls practicing soccer drills on the athletic field while scrawny, sweaty boys in assorted tee shirts puffed around the outside track. He suddenly realized he had driven right past the Nock Middle School. He turned in at the skating rink, circled, and headed back toward the school. After slipping into the last open visitor parking space, he sat quietly in the car for a minute, thinking that it was a grim impulsive pilgrimage to a school he had hated for a teacher who was no longer there.

A new security system stopped him from simply walking in-to the building. He had to show identification and explain his reason for visiting before he could be buzzed in. "I'm a former student and . . . I was in the area. Just wanted to stop in."

By the time he reached the office, he had decided that he might as well explain the real reason to the woman working there. The scarecrow in a print dress and gray cardigan looked at him expectantly. "Yes?"

"I was a student here eons ago. I just learned that my favorite teacher died recently, and I felt like visiting the old place, maybe dropping in on her classroom."

"Oh, you must be talking about Mrs. Geller. It was so sad. And she was really quite young. She didn't come back for the start of the term this fall, you know. I think it was a family matter. She had just lost her husband, and, well … and then this. How terrible. You know, there's a tribute page started for her by former students. You'll find a link to it on the school website. Do you want me to write down the web address for you?"

"No, I can Google it. Could I just stop by her old classroom? I mean, it's not school hours."

"Mr. Collingwood, head of the department, has taken over her classes."

"Could I drop in on him anyway?"

"You have to sign in and wear one of these visitor badges. I can walk you down to the room after I finish with this form. Or I could page him and have him come to the office."

"No, that's all right. He wouldn't know me, and I'm sure he's busy. I can find the room on my own."

"I'm sorry, but visitors have to be escorted, you know."

"I keep forgetting how much schools have changed."

"Well, we can't be too careful, now can we. I mean, those school shootings and all. And we certainly can't have some pedophile just waltzing in here and roaming the halls, now, can we?"

"No, and we certainly wouldn't let kids ride school buses without wearing seatbelts, right?"

"What do you mean? School buses don't have seatbelts."

"Ah, right. Anyway, I am happy to be escorted safely to Mr. Collingwood's classroom." Do temper your sarcasm, he told himself.

"Yes, well, it will only be a minute before I'm through here."

~ ~ ~

The visit to the classroom and chat with Mr. Collingwood were both disappointing. The room looked nothing like Clinton re-membered, and Arnold Collingwood was given to droning on in response to the simplest question or the most casual comment. Clinton finally extricated himself with the excuse that he had another appointment. He stopped in at the school office to return his badge and sign out. So much for requiring an escort, he thought. Clearly, it depended on who was interpreting the rules. "Is there a place in town where I could get a burger or something. I mean, not McDonald's."

"Try the old Fowle's on State Street. Name's changed but the old sign is still there. I hear they have, like, a dozen kinds of fancy burgers now."

"Thanks, I'll give it a try."

~ ~ ~

After decades of decline, the historic seaport of Newburyport had undergone a renaissance starting in the 1970s that had transformed its downtown into a brick-sidewalk tourist mecca of galleries, funky shops, and diverse eateries. Following a stroll along the boardwalk from the municipal parking lot, Clinton settled in at the retro 17 State Street Café and began working his way through a near-perfect half-pound hamburger smothered with jalapeño barbecue sauce. Between dripping bites and quick dabs with his napkin, he was trying to figure out what to do next.

The part of him that panicked when knocking on doors or approaching strangers just wanted to fly back home and return to his quiet life in Sacramento as adjunct faculty in the Department of Communication Studies, Journalism, and Film. The part of him that loved puzzles and mysteries wanted to get to the bottom of Millie Geller's crazy story and tragic death. She had believed in him when he was just a scared middle-school misfit; she had inspired him to reach for something; and she had remembered him. He owed her at least a best try.

Somehow the very real danger that he might be getting into did not frighten him. He knew his social anxiety was completely irrational and that he should not give in to it, yet it had grown to nearly rule his life. Now here he was launching an investigation into a mysterious group that seemed quite capable of murder, and he was calmly thinking through his strategy. People are strange, he thought, and you, Clinton Jorge Rodrigues, are one of the strangest.

He wondered how much danger he was actually in? His name was on the list attached to Millie's cover letter, but as far as he could tell, none of the other packets had reached their recipients. Had they been intercepted? Lost? Destroyed? He would have to conclude, at least for the moment, that no one knew that he had received his copy.

If anyone knew, he would probably already have met the same fate as Millie and the woman at the post office. If he drew attention to himself, though, if he started poking in the wrong places or talking to the wrong people, it might not take long for someone to figure out that he had a copy of the documents. He would have to hold his cards close to the chest and play his hand with poker-faced calculation.

He opened his laptop but quickly discovered there was no Wi-Fi in the café. He paid his bill with a twenty tucked under his untouched water glass and left for the Starbucks a few doors down. The place was full, and the line for ordering was doubled back the length of the counter, past an odd assortment of mermaid paintings and carvings by some local artist, almost to the door onto State Street. When he finally reached the register, he ordered a grande latte, then squeezed into a spot at the end of the bar where he could stand while waiting for his drink. On impulse, he reopened his laptop and searched for the tribute page for Millicent Geller. He was surprised that it topped the search results and even more surprised to find hundreds of messages posted. She had touched a lot of people.

He was about to add a note of his own when he remembered about the game he was now playing. He would need to reduce his visibility, maybe go incognito. He scanned the guestbook and made note of a couple of local people who might be worth following up on. He didn't know Betsy Whitman, but her post mentioned she was now working at the nearby Crane Estate in Ipswich. He had already heard of one of Newburyport's best known and most successful graduates, venture capitalist Felix Templeman, who was now busy reinvesting his first millions at Boston's Enventia Capital.

Clinton switched over to his web-mail page. There was email from the chair of his department. Clinton realized he would have to decide soon whether he was going to teach this semester. Bonnie Grist was covering his classes for another week, but that was all they had negotiated before he left. There was also email from a student.

> *When are you coming back, professor? I read your blog about*
> *the biology teacher. She must have been good. Like you. Hurry*
> *back, that other prof is just not as good as you. I miss you.*
> *--Julia Sousa*

Clinton was picturing Julia Sousa, the pretty black girl who always arrived late and always sat in the front row. Was she trying to butter him up for a better grade? She had done fairly well on the first writing assignment and had aced the first quiz. The tone of the email seemed rather personal, but then, students these days tended toward instant familiarity, even with teachers.

After the barista slid him his coffee, Clinton stood sipping while staring at the screen and thinking about Millie's story. Was Atchison Dougherty, the former CEO of Biontolics Holdings, really nearly a hundred years old when he was killed by an intruder? Was the late President-for-Life of Busanyu even older? It was hard finding pictures of Dougherty, but there was no shortage of shots of the African dictator, whose battle-battered face was hard to judge. Neither of them looked anywhere near as old as Millie's materials claimed. Was the kind of life extension that medical quackery and fringe science were always touting as just around the corner already a reality?

Clinton made two quick decisions. He was going to stop being Clinton Rodrigues for the time being, and he was going to pay a visit to the Biontolics lab.

Chapter 8

Bright sun and a warming fall day had already inspired Clinton to drive with the windows down as he turned left out of the driveway of the Country Garden Inn in Rowley. Growing up in the area, Clinton had thought of the tiny town as essentially a geographic placeholder between Newburyport to the north and Ipswich, the next well-known colonial seaport to the south. Rowley had no real town center, and its one nominal claim to fame seemed to hinge on a weekly flea market of some renown along with the stretch of antique dealers that dotted the secondary road leading to Ipswich.

The About Us page on the company website for the North Shore Laboratories of Biontolics Research, LLC, placed it in Ipswich, near the end of Argilla Road, the street leading to duly-famed Crane Beach. Clinton knew of the beach and the adjacent Crane Estate by reputation, but he had never been there. Living up in Amesbury, his mother had always headed to the closer and cheaper Salisbury Beach for relief from midsummer heatwaves.

Trees speckled with the first colors of autumn crowded Argilla Road, and the pavement was slick with dew-wet leaves. Clinton knew he had missed the turnoff when he reached the entrance to the beach at the end of the road. He circled around outside the gatehouse and headed back toward the center of town, driving slowly and searching for a sign. He would have missed the unmarked driveway a second time had there not been a blue minivan just pulling out, a discreet Biontolics logo painted on its sliding door. Clinton waited until the van was out of sight before turning into the curving driveway. The low sea-blue sign that confirmed he was in the right place was halfway up the long approach, where it would have been invisible from the road. If you didn't know where you were going, you didn't belong here, it seemed to proclaim. It was another reminder to Clinton that he was back in New England, where signage had a reputation as often being confirmatory at best, mostly useful only if you already knew the way, and confusing to all others.

Clinton parked in a visitor space out front and walked up the broad front steps onto the porch of what had once been a large private residence. The façade was vintage New England, a gentleman's farmhouse fronting on a sprawling complex of converted old lap-sided buildings and newer board-and-batten construction, all painted in drab grays and muted greens to blend in with the surroundings. Except for the sign at the entrance and the two large parking lots, it could still be taken as a bucolic estate with its gabled main house, a barn, and a guesthouse linked by covered passageways.

"I saw an ad," he told the guard at the desk just inside the front entrance. "It said that you were hiring, looking for a statistical programmer. I know R and have worked with Matlab. Can I talk with someone?" It was blurted out, the rehearsed lines he had settled on after scouring for references to Biontolics on the Web. He stood there, suddenly feeling awkward, telling himself there was no point reciting his résumé to a guard.

"Yeah, sign in here, put the number of this badge next to your name, add the time of arrival, and initial. I'll buzz Dr. Kenilworth."

Clinton wrote "Neal Blake" in neat block letters on the bottom line of the register, scribbled initials and a wavy line in the signature box, and copied the three digits from the badge at the end. "What time do you have?"

The guard looked at his computer screen. "It says 8:33. Clock over there looks like 8:37. Take your pick. You can take a seat over there."

Clinton split the difference to fill in his arrival time, then sat down. He feigned interest in the copies of *Nature* and *Science* neatly arrayed on the coffee table in the reception area. For the next twenty minutes, he pretended to read as his anxiety kept rising.

The man who approached looked like a middle-aged Harvard humanities professor in shirtsleeves and bowtie. "Hi, I'm Rich Kenilworth. Sorry, but I was just settling into my morning routine, which involves responding to a deluge of overnight dispatches from overseas before it gets too late there. Bill here says you're a statistical programmer. Did you see our little ad in *New Scientist* or what?"

"I . . . yeah, I saw the ad and happened to be in the area for an interview with New England Biolabs. It seemed a shame not to check you out."

"Ah. So, they're also looking. Interesting. You know, we are nowhere near as big and not as well known, but we're doing interesting work in genomics and epigenetics. Of course, it all ultimately comes down to numbers, which is where our statistical programming team comes in. The stats team works hand-in-glove with our subject-matter experts from the get-go: experimental design, data processing and quality control, right through to data analysis and visualization. Did you file your résumé through our website?"

"No, but I will. As I said, this was a last minute decision to drop in. I mean, the job over at New England Biolabs is basically mine already, but I really wanted to check them out in person before committing. That's why I'm in the area. It's a big move from . . . UCLA."

"That's where you're working now?"

"Yeah, until recently. I've been doing R programming and teaching it to undergrads for five years." The only truth behind the claim was that he knew what the R language was, having once mistakenly signed up for an elective in statistics that was taught using the popular open-source programming language. He hoped he would not be called on to demonstrate any expertise. "I realized awhile back that this—the programming and statistics—is where my heart really is. And now it seems time for a jump, time for a West Coast native to check out New England. This sure isn't Los Angeles. I don't think I have ever seen so much green. Know what I mean?"

"Yeah, I imagine, what with the drought and all, Southern California must be pretty much all brown. Well, as long as you're here, let me show you around and see if I can convince you to consider Biontolics. We can worry about HR and the paperwork later. Just follow me."

"So what do you do here?"

"I'm head of the Statistical Programming Team. As I was saying before, we are trying to take some of the number-crunching heavy lifting off from the shoulders of our scientists and researchers, give them more time for the think work. This is a relatively new way of doing business for us, and we are still finding our way. It requires a particular kind of person, with a deep knowledge of statistics, experimental design, and fluency in statistical programming, especially in R, which is our go-to-ground language for most applications, but at the same time you need an ability to collaborate closely with research scientists, who are another species altogether. You gotta have your head wrapped around R code at the same time you're talking turkey with geneticists and biochemists and neuroscientists. You know what I mean?"

"Yeah, but I meant what does this lab really do? The stuff on the Web about Biontolics was not all that informative."

"Well, we're about basic research at the leading leading leading edge in human biology: genetics, epigenetics, genomics, cell energy economy, apoptosis mechanisms, gerontology, you name it. We're funded some by government grants but mostly by a few private sources, like the Berkowitz Biomedical Foundation. We pitch our ideas to them, they write a check. It's a lot more efficient than the whole drawn out drama with government grants and peer-review panels and funding cycles and stuff like that. But that's not my bailiwick. As I said, I'm a numbers nut, but I trained as a biochemist. Everyone here is a trained scientist in some area, some in more than one, even if they are crunching numbers or pounding out programs. What's your PhD in?"

"Ah, doctoral work . . . seems like a lifetime ago." Clinton was thinking fast. He needed something plausible but with little risk of being caught out on. "I started out—would you believe it?—in sociology, ended up doing a dissertation on the sociology of science, which got me interested in what real scientists do. It was a little too late to take a U-turn, but I found I had a real knack for stats and cutting code, started doing little things with Systat and MatLab as favors for other profs." He was grinning at his own BS. "You know how it goes. The rest is history. Not sure I could even tell you much about that other life."

"I understand. I'm not sure I could even make much out of the molecular structure of chiral cytokines anymore—my dissertation subject. Anyway, here we are in our Neuroscience Section. They're doing basic science but focused on the aging brain." The elongated room with a wall of windows along one side was occupied by half a dozen people in front of computer screens, most of them wearing headphones or earbuds. "Not much to see, unless you read their papers. The functional MRI and positron tomography pictures are stunning, but the actual imaging is farmed out or done at our Research Triangle Park facility, our headquarters down in North Carolina. Anyway, I hope you don't mind if I don't do introductions. I hate to interrupt when people are deep into it, you know."

Clinton followed Kenilworth down the aisle between the desks. Just past the open door into a conference room, someone called out. "Clint! Hey, Clint."

Clinton stiffened and tried not to show any reaction, but he could feel the spasm starting in his cheek. He kept walking and turned around only when he felt a gentle tap on his shoulder. "What?"

The woman, about his age, with sun-hued skin a shade darker than his, was dressed in jeans and a magenta silk blouse. A matching reddish smudge marked her forehead above black eyebrows and near-black eyes. She looked perplexed.

"Clint, don't you remember? Sahana, Sahana Patel. From high school."

Kenilworth was now watching both of them with narrowed eyes.

"I . . . I'm sorry," Clinton said, before Kenilworth could jump in with questions. "I think you have me mixed up with somebody else." He held out his hand. "But I'm glad to meet you, Sahana Patel. I'm Neal Blake. I'm applying for a job here. I take it you're a neuroscientist."

"I am. But OMG! You look so much like him, like this Portuguese guy I knew in high school. You sure you're not Portuguese, maybe with a long lost twin brother?"

"I'm sure not either of those. English on my father's side, some Cherokee way back on my mother's." It was the sort of quick thinking that had earned him a reputation as a master bullshit artist. "But I would definitely remember you if we went to high school together. I don't think we had many future scientists where I went to school in Oakland." His focus kept shifting between her dark eyes and the red dot on her forehead. He did remember her, and now he found himself hoping the mark did not mean she was married.

Her head pivoted slowly to one side as she kept her eyes on him. "It's uncanny. You look so much like this guy. A bit older, of course, but, like, still the same. Anyway, I'm sorry for interrupting. Good luck with the job app. Maybe I'll see you again."

"I hope."

As they left the room, Clinton could feel the aftereffects of the rush of adrenaline. It had been a close call. He had no intention of following through on any job application, but he now knew he had a potential inside contact at Biontolics, and he would follow up with Sahana. He was already thinking ahead to how he might do that.

He meticulously managed the rest of the interaction with Dr. Kenilworth to make it increasingly clear that Biontolics and Neal Blake were not a good fit. At the same time, he knew he had to make the mismatch seem natural and mutual without raising suspicions. He wrapped things up with a halfhearted promise to forward his résumé, a promise that they both knew would not be kept. As he left the main building, he was thinking that maybe he was not so bad as an investigative journalist as he had once thought. Or at least he was not too bad as an actor doing somewhat risky improv.

Chapter 9

Tracking down Sahana proved to be easier than expected. If she had been a Paula Smith or a Joan Brown, there would have been several hundred thousand hits on Google, but Clinton was able to locate the right Sahana Patel in only a few minutes of digging. She lived in Ipswich, and her name showed up among top finishers in local short-distance races, such as, the Thanksgiving Day "Run for the Pies" and the annual "Chase the Gorilla Down Argilla" sponsored by the Ipswich Y. A search for her name and first digits of the local telephone exchanges turned up two PDF documents that included her phone number. Clinton called.

"Sahana? Sahana Patel?""

"Yes?"

"You may not remember me, but this is Clinton Rodrigues. We went to Newburyport High together."

"Ohmagod, this is just too weird. You won't believe this, but I saw this guy today who looked like you. I mean, just like you."

"That's funny. I met someone today with the same name as you. How unlikely is that?"

"Wait a minute. Is this some kind of a prank? Are you trying to pull something?"

"No prank, but I am trying to pull something. I'm a journalist now, and I'm working on a story but couldn't take a chance on playing it straight under my own name at your laboratory. I had to play it cool when we met today."

"You have to tell me. I mean, you absolutely have to tell me. What is this about?"

"I'll tell you, but not over the phone. Can we meet somewhere that's nowhere? A quiet bar? Or maybe a really loud bar, out of town but not too far? Or better yet, I'll buy you dinner."

"This is sounding better and better. Do you like seafood?"

"My favorite."

"Then there are a lot of possibilities nearby. Of course, we might be spotted by people I know. How about heading down to Gloucester. Do you know Gloucester?"

"I know it. I was born there."

"Well, there's a place called Latitude 43."

"I don't remember it—it's been a few years since I was back—but I'll find it. Eight o'clock work for you?"

"Sure, I'll meet you there."

~ ~ ~

Latitude 43 turned out to be a classy bar-restaurant, all glass and exposed wooden beams, next to a craft brewery on Gloucester's renovated waterfront, itself a quirky blend of working fishing harbor and upscale tourist target. The online ratings of the venue and the food had been promising. After a little pleading and negotiation over the phone, Clinton was able to get an 8:30 reservation for an inside table overlooking the harbor. He was gambling that they might be able to be seated early, so he didn't text Sahana about the change in time. When she arrived, they ordered two glasses of sauvignon blanc and appetizers at the bar. While they waited for their table, Sahana broke the ice.

"I remember you—from AP calc—this mysterious brainiac who always hung back." She winked. "You had this knowing half smile most of the time, like you already knew all this stuff and found everyone else's struggles marginally amusing."

"That? Just cover for my paralyzing shyness. And I remember you from AP calc, too: this brainy girl with the exotic looks who was always in the center of a circle of friends, talking nonstop."

"Was not." Their wine arrived, they raised their glasses in a toast, and she took a sip. "Mmm, nice. Mind if I ask you something, something personal I always wanted to ask?"

"No, I don't mind. Go ahead."

"Your name. I remember you getting teased over it. Was your mother a Hillary fan or something?"

"No. Clinton is actually a pretty popular boys name in Portugal—at least it was then. It was my father's choice. He made all the decisions when I was young. Then he disappeared, and my mother made all the decisions. That's how I ended up going to school in Newburyport. So now it's my turn. Personal question."

"Okay, fair is fair."

"The little dot on your forehead, which was magenta this morning and now has turned bright blue, like some kind of magical mood mark. What exactly is that all about?"

"You mean my *bindi*? It's decoration, a Hindu tradition. It actually has religious significance for some people—chakra stuff—but I just like the look. And I changed it to blue to match my blouse."

"So it doesn't mean you're married or something?"

"No, not that, definitely not that. And you? You're not married?"

"No, definitely not."

After their shrimp and scallop ceviche arrived, she sprang the big question on him. "So, now that we cleared up names and marital status, what is this really about? I mean, you pretending you don't know me, claiming to be somebody else. What is this story you say you're working on, and what does it have to do with the lab?"

"Wow, a lot of questions. You know, I probably shouldn't be having this conversation with you, but my instincts tell me to trust you. I hope my instincts are right."

"Ooo, you make this sound all cloak-and-dagger-y."

"It is. I'm investigating the death of someone, someone you knew, I think." She waited for him to continue. "You remember Mrs. Geller, the middle school science teacher? Did you have her?"

"Yes, I remember Mrs. Geller. Who can forget? I heard about what happened to her from Betsy Whitman. It was terrible. I was going to post a note on her tribute page."

"Well, I have good reason to believe what happened to her was not an accident. The police are looking into it, of course, but I'm doing some investigating on my own. Did you, by any chance, know her husband, Dr. Rosen David? He worked at Biontolics."

"He was her husband? I didn't know that. I didn't actually know him personally, except for what a friend told me. I mean, everyone knew about him after that story came out about his dying of Ebola or something. We all knew the story was bullshit. The hospital and reporters got it garbled up somehow. He couldn't possibly have been handling tissue samples. He didn't do that kind of work. No one up here does. The clinical stuff is all done down in North Carolina. Up here, we're mostly computer nerds with fancy titles."

"Can I ask what you are working on?"

"Well, you know all our work is very hush-hush."

"You mean, like military stuff?"

"No, not that kind of confidential, but the company is absolutely paranoid about tipping its hand. Maybe, like, half the requests to publish are turned down by corporate. We joke about them as the 'science censors.' I swear, it seems they only let the crap be submitted to journals; the really good papers mostly get filed away."

"What kind of papers? Any of your stuff?"

"Ah, I don't know. We're not supposed to talk about our work."

"Well, just talk about what you can, then. Anything." It was a reporter's ploy, an end run around the confidentiality excuse.

She stared at her food for several seconds. "You won't name names, will you? If you do the story, I mean."

"Look, I'm a journalist. We protect our sources. Or you can talk off the record, if you want." At that point, he figured he had her.

She leaned her head close to his and lowered her voice. "Well, I had this one paper. I was doing work on cognitive decline in normal aging, not field work or clinical studies, but theoretical work on the functioning of memory consolidation and retrieval and changes over time in the aging brain. I devised this systems model, very detailed, then collaborated with a guy down at Research Triangle—that's the other East Coast unit of Biontolics. It checked out. I mean, this was breakthrough work, maybe Nobel material eventually. Squelch. Then Rustum—that's my co-author at Research Triangle—says the funding source wanted some added runs in the clinic from another population using a convenience sample. That means people not really picked at random but who just happen to be available. Well, he does it, and all of them are outliers, off-scale for their recorded ages. It completely breaks the model."

"That must have hurt."

"No, don't you see? This is science. Whatever you find is good. So what if the model was wrong? Models can be fixed. Besides, the results on these five subjects were so far out of line that this was another must-publish result. Once again, no go. So, two-and-a-half years of work with no new papers.

"But—and get this—Biontolics doesn't care. Rustum and I got hefty bonuses and commendations for 'outstanding contributions to neuroscience.' What the fig was that all about? You tell me."

"I see. So you think your work is being suppressed?"

"No, I wouldn't say that, exactly." She paused to take another sip of her wine. "Oh, I don't know."

"Okay, we'll leave it at that. Back to Millicent Geller. You didn't know Dr. David personally and didn't know he was married to Mrs. Geller. What about this friend you mentioned? What was his name?"

"*Her* name. Jeannine Carston, one of my best friends here—actually got me my job at Biontolics. She was having an affair with him."

Clinton tried not to look too interested. "You don't happen to know how I might get in touch with her, do you? I'd like to get her story."

"That would be a little hard, unless you believe in communication with spirits."

"She's dead?"

"Yeah, cancer. She died in his arms, so they say. After she was diagnosed, they both dropped out for a while. Eventually he reappeared, promoted to a new position at the lab, but he was never the same. It must have hit him very hard. From what Jeannine told me, they were really in love. I really didn't know he was married. Of course, not long afterwards, he too was dead." She set her fork down and scowled in concentration. "That's three people, closely connected, all dead within a few short months. Wow! Is that why you started your investigation?"

"I started out because of Millicent Geller. She was one of the best teachers I ever knew, because she changed the course of my life and I owe her something. Now I may have more reasons." He held her gaze for several seconds before she suddenly found her drink interesting and looked down. "I need you to take me seriously. I don't think it would be safe to talk with anyone about this or even to mention that you know me."

"I am taking you seriously. I'm expecting the same from you." She stared out across the dining area toward the windows with the lights of the harbor beyond. "I just thought of something. Jeannine had two sisters living in the area. I don't remember their married names—the family was Catholic, so they probably didn't keep their maiden names—but you might be able to track them down."

"I already have an idea how to do that."

"I bet you do. You might have been a pretty good scientist if you had stuck with biology."

"I might have been a pretty good journalist if I had stuck with journalism."

"What do you mean? I thought you said you were a journalist."

"Well, I teach journalism. You know what they say: those who can do, those who can't . . ."

"I don't buy that for a minute. The best teachers teach from what they know and what they do." She suddenly looked up. "Ah, here comes our bouillabaisse. I think they are finally going to seat us."

~ ~ ~

Dinner lasted longer than either of them expected, and a stretched-out stroll along the harbor boardwalk extended the evening even further. On the way back to Sahana's car, Clinton made a detour into the still-open Walgreen's on Main Street and bought a prepaid phone with cash. He turned off location tracking, deleted several junkware apps, and disabled text and call logging, then entered his cell number into the contact list before handing it to her. "This is what they call a burner phone. It's only for messages between us and only in an emergency. After one use, we dump it or replace the SIM card." She took it and slipped into the pocket of her jacket.

"One more thing," he said. "Do you know about public-key encryption? Do you know what PGP is?"

"I have a *pretty good* idea."

"Ha ha, right: Pretty Good Privacy. Well, set yourself up to exchange PGP email so we can be in touch without eaves-droppers. And don't ever use your computer or the phones at work to contact me, okay?"

"Wow, you really are looking out for me."

And for me, he thought, as he gave her a quick hug.

~ ~ ~

It was past midnight when Clinton got back to his motel. He immediately slipped his laptop computer from the backpack on the bed and booted it up. "Well, Jeannine Carston, whoever you are or whatever part you played in this story, I think it is time to see what we can learn from Google."

Clinton was in his element when online: digging, dodging and weaving from link to link, uncovering unexpected resources through sophisticated searches, and doggedly chasing down information. It did not take him long before he had unearthed citations to scientific papers linking a Jeannine Carston to Dr. Rosen David. An obituary in a newspaper archive provided further details, giving the cause of death as cancer and saying that Jeannine Carston was "survived by her loving husband, Dr. Rosen David of Essex." So, they might have been married. Were Rosen and Millicent divorced, was he a bigamist, or had it just been an affair? The obit also named the two married sisters, Elise Carston McDermott and Angela Carston Farini, along with the names of three nieces and a nephew. He had done his journalistic duty: he had his multiple sources of confirmation linking the three deaths.

Jeannine Carston had worked with Rosen David at Biontolics and been involved with him, yet Clinton didn't remember seeing the name in the packet from Millie Geller. He got the envelope from his suitcase and slipped out the documents. On the cover letter was a smudge near the bottom that he had not noticed before, a smear where something in pencil had been erased. He held it at an angle, trying to make out the faint traces of what had once been written there in firm block letters. With the light just right and his eyes squinted, it was just visible, one word: Carston—Carston with a question mark.

Millie Geller had made an annotation on his copy of the letter, then changed her mind. Or was it intended to be discovered, a tantalizing teaser or, in this case, a clear confirmation.

The deaths were linked. How? Biontolics, obviously. How else? What else did he know? The dictator in Africa who died the same way as Dr. David. Perhaps he could learn something in the Republic of Busanyu. It would be a logical step for a reporter. Not as logical as getting some interviews with the top dogs at Biontolics, but that route looked like it was probably strewn with landmines. Staying in the area much longer also had begun to feel risky. Ipswich was a small town, and it would be all too easy for determined parties to track him most anywhere around Boston's North Shore. The whole quest was beginning to seem quixotic, but maybe he needed to put some distance between himself and New England.

Before turning in for the night, he picked up email. There was another note from the girl in his journalism class.

*Your sub is so boring. She drones on like a UAV flying over
Iraq. (Nice simile, huh?) I want you back. She gives the
weirdest assignments and she doesn't even stick to the syllabus.
I don't think she likes me. Please come back soon. –Julia*

Chapter 10

Bertrand Lyon rechecked the transaction summary, then tapped the Enter key to complete the electronic transfer paying off the renegade commander for the attack on Nichevo. He was ahead of schedule, but he liked tying up loose ends as quickly as possible. It was one of the reasons he had come to trust and rely so much on Gus Holzinger. Gus finished the assigned job, whatever it might be, quickly, quietly, and without leaving tracks.

Bertrand retrieved the Express Mail package from his briefcase for one last check for tracks that might need erasing before it was digitized and destroyed. He scanned once more through the double-sided attachment to the cover letter that listed, in alphabetical order and conveniently numbered, all the recipients and their addresses. They were a mix of well-known journalists and news editors with others he had never heard of. He stared at the last entry on the flip side: Giles Underwood at the *Sydney Morning Herald*, number 32 in the list. Something bothered him.

He fished his smartphone out of his pocket and tapped a contact icon. "Gus. Lyon here. Sorry to bother you at this hour, but I wondered if you remember how many mail packets you intercepted. And remind me: what exactly happened to them?"

"I saved one for you and shredded and then incinerated the other thirty."

"So, thirty-one, you say. And you're sure of that?"

"Sure as I can be. I was rather surprised by the size of the stack that I slipped from the bag in the truck. I counted them on the spot and again when I disposed of all but that one. Why?"

"We have a problem. The packet itself lists thirty-two recipients."

"Shit."

"You should have cross-checked against the list. You missed one. Presumably it was delivered."

"I didn't ... I ..." He stopped protesting. "Yes, you're right, sir, I should have examined the contents and cross-checked."

"And you destroyed the others, so we have no idea which one is missing."

"I thought it was prudent."

"Prudent. Right." Bertrand considered his words. "Well, we have our work cut out for us, Gus. We can cross Sanger off the list because his packet is in front of me right now, but we have thirty others to eliminate—and one to sniff out, someone who did receive the material but hasn't acted on it, at least as far as we know. This could bring down the whole operation. Get on it, Gus. Now!"

"Yes, sir. That's not going to be easy. We can't just go up and ask everyone on the list. What do you propose?"

Lyon took the phone from his ear and looked at it in disbelief. "I don't propose anything." His voice had taken on a hard edge. "Figuring out how to do this is what we pay you for."

"Yes, sir. Send me an image of the list, and I'll start on it right away."

"And Gus, I don't need to remind you that we do not want to tip our hand to anyone—not those who didn't get their copy and certainly not the one who did."

"No, sir. You don't need to remind me."

～ ～ ～

Holzinger's mind raced through possibilities. There had to be a way to find out which packet had been delivered. The US Postal Service was hardly at the center of his area of expertise, but there would have to be some sort of audit trail at the post office where the packets had been posted. He looked at his watch. Another drive up to Maine would be the tedious but easy part; getting access to records would be far harder. And a third unfortunate accident in the same area, should it become necessary, would magnify the attention that was already being focused on just one small town.

It was time to slow down in order to speed up, get some background on how the packets were sent. Express Mail. He remembered the labels. He could go to the local post office and ask. Or he could just go online.

A few minutes later, he was calling back to the Sellian Atlantic offices in London. "Sir. Holzinger here again. There should be a number on the label of that packet. Would you please read it to me?"

"What good will that do? We already know what happened to this one."

"I have an idea, sir. That number might help."

"All right then. Ready?" He read off the letters and digits of the number.

Holzinger had guessed that the Express Labels at any given post office would be numbered sequentially, or at least be issued in blocks. He clicked through to the USPS tracking page and stated entering numbers, varying the last two digits, but every number he entered was rejected. He tediously checked all numbers within 100 to either side of the one he'd been given. No luck. Maybe the numbers printed on the labels were not used for tracking. He checked his watch. The post office would be closed; he would have to find another way.

Clinton, who had told no one about returning to Sacramento State or about his immediate plans, hiked across the river on the elegant Guy West footbridge and slipped onto campus without announcement. He was sorting through the file drawer of his desk, when he heard a voice from the doorway, high and melodious, with the laid-back rhythm of California's Central Valley.

"Hey, professor. Welcome back. How long you staying this time?" It was Julia Sousa. When he swiveled his chair to face her, she flashed him a megawatt smile that dominated her round, milk-chocolate face.

"Not staying long. Just until I can arrange my next trip. I'm afraid you'll have to grit it out with Dr. Grist this semester. If you're really so sold on the superiority of my teaching style, maybe you can take my journalism ethics class next semester. If I'm back by then."

"When do you leave for Africa?"

Clinton's mouth hung open in astonishment. "What? What makes you think I would be going to Africa?"

"You make me think. Simple: trip, arrangements. Sounds like bigtime prep, maybe visa application, might not be back by next semester. You were out east, posted about a teacher who died recently, dateline was Falmouth, had to be this Millicent Geller, wife of Rosen David, worked with Jeannine Carston at Biontolics, she died, then he died of the same tropical shiz as that African dude, both tied to Biontolics. Four weird deaths within months, all tied to the same company. You already were out there, now you're back here. Simple deduction. Next stop: Mbutsu City, Busanyu, West Africa."

"Holy shit. You put all that together just now?"

"No, I did my Google research while you was away."

"Were. While you *were* away."

"Yeah, you were. When you said you were leaving again, it was just a good guess. If not Africa, one of the other places Biontolics operates. I got lucky." She crossed her arms across her chest, displaying the tattoo on her left forearm: "YOLO" encircled by barbed wire: You Only Live Once.

Clinton was shaking his head. "That's not luck, that's professional-caliber investigative work. I wish you were already through with the program and working for me."

"Your lucky day. Your wish is granted. I'm through with the program."

"What are you talking about. You have at least another year of coursework plus an internship."

"No way. I quit today. A whole fricking term of Dr. Bonnie Grist grinding away like some millstone—you like my plays on words?—that's not in my plans."

"But you didn't know until just now that I wasn't teaching any more this semester."

"That's when I quit."

"Just like that?"

"Just like that. How long do I have to get my visa and that shiz?"

"Hold on there." He held up both hands in protest. "What are you talking about? You're not going with me to Busanyu. No way."

"Click." Her index finger tapped an imaginary touchscreen in the air. "Confirmation. Destination: Busanyu. Thanks, professor. I better start packin'."

"Now you're talking crazy." For no reason that Clinton could figure, the girl started humming the chorus of "Beware the Dog" by The Griswalds. "No, I said no. I am not taking a student with me to Africa. Absolutely no. Look, I don't have time for this. I have a lot of things to do over the next three days."

"Click. Departure date confirmed. See how good I am at getting people to tell me details? You need me."

"Why? Why do I need you?"

"Portuguese."

"What about Portuguese?"

"You, you're Portuguese?"

"Well, yes, I am part Portuguese, on my father's side, and Moroccan Jew on my mother's side. But what has that got to do with—"

"*O senhor fala Portugues?*"

"No, I don't speak Portuguese, but I do know a few phrases. Like that one. And I remember how to curse in Portuguese, thanks to my father, who had a talent for it. That and chemistry, the kitchen variety. *Merde!* That's pretty much the extent of my Portuguese shit."

"Exactly. I'm fluent. Both my parents are from Cabo Verde. I was born here, but at home we spoke nothing but Portuguese. You'll need a translator."

"But I'm not going to Cabo Verde or Angola or Mozambique. I'm going to Busanyu." He zipped his backpack closed and stood.

"Without doing your homework, Professor?" She wagged her index finger like a metronome, then straightened and stood with her hands to her side as if reciting. "Owing to its historic roots, the two official languages of the Republic of Busanyu are Lusanyu, the dialect of the dominant tribal group, and Portuguese. Do you speak Lusanyu?"

"No, I—"

"Didn't think so. Neither do I, but I can sing the national anthem in Lusanyu. It's on YouTube." She sang out in a dramatic soprano voice. *"Basanya kyahm ngala, ga'atni o mkam a'ana."*

Clinton waited patiently until she finished the first verse. He clapped. "Very impressive, but you are still not going with me. It would be against the rules for me to take a student with me on a trip, certainly not on an international trip."

"Exactly. But I'm not your student, not even a student anymore."

Clinton dropped his backpack into the chair in exasperation. "Look, you're underage, you—"

"Am not. I'm twenty-three. I know, I look young for my age. It's the Cabo Verde genes, I think."

Clinton turned back to shuffling through files and tried to ignore her.

"Okay, then," she said, turning to leave. "I'll meet you in Mbutsu City. Try the Hotel Palácio Real. It's cheaper than the name suggests, and the bar is a favored hangout for journalists."

"How the hell would you know something like that?"

"By doing my homework. See, you need me."

"NO!"

"Then I'll meet you there. I'll be staying at the Palácio Real. Later, professor." She pivoted and started strolling away.

"No, wait. You realize, the country is on a State Department caution list. I can't have you flying to West Africa alone."

"That's chill. Then I can ride with you to the airport." She returned to his desk.

"Wait. How are you going to get the right tickets? How can you afford this? How—"

"I'll get the right tickets because we'll both be on the only connecting flight that leaves in three days. Like, there's only a couple of flights a week unless you do something weird like fly through Japan or something. And I can afford this because I have a travel grant built into my stipend from the Strathmere-Lewin Foundation."

"Strathmere-Lewin? Never heard of it. Wait a minute. I thought you quit."

"I did. Or will. I'll do the paperwork at the end of the semester. Right now, I have to go see the bursar to get the travel funds for a study trip abroad. You will be listed as my sponsor, of course, but you don't have to tag along. I can forge your signature."

Clinton didn't know which part of her whole improbable story to confront first. "You . . . you are . . ."

"Awesome. Yes, I know it. So are you." She hugged him and danced away. "Later, professor," she said, without looking back.

He was still sorting papers into his backpack when she returned a few minutes later.

"I just wanted to thank you, professor." She hugged him once more. "We're going to make such a team in Africa. I am so there." She skipped out of the room again.

Clinton put his hands over his eyes and bowed his head. "What am I in for? This is nuts to the nth."

Chapter 12

Clinton picked up his email one last time before leaving his apartment. There was an encrypted message from Sahana. He drummed his fingers on the table as he waited for the plaintext to appear.

> *I've been doing a little digging on my own, covering my tracks so as not to set off alarm bells. I've found evidence that the archives at the lab have been sanitized. There are occasional citations of internal working papers that ought to be in the system but seem to have been deleted. Almost everything by our friend Dr. David is "unavailable." I'm now using my own system and Internet resources to keep poking around. In my experience, if you dig long enough, you find that somebody somewhere has an unauthorized PDF copy saved on some server. I'll keep you posted. And thanks again for dinner.*
> *–Warmly, Sahana*

Clinton tapped out a quick reply.

> *Be careful. I'm traveling and may be out of touch for a while, so don't panic if there is a delay in responding to emails. Check out the attachment and let me know what you think of it, but don't discuss it or show it to anyone. –Yours, Clint*

He attached an encrypted digital copy of the two unpublished papers that had been included in the packet from Millicent Geller.

~ ~ ~

When he arrived to pick up Julia at her mother's place, she insisted on introductions all around at the curb. "Hey all, this here is my professor who I'm working for."

"Whom," he corrected in an aside, "for whom I'm working."

"Right. I'm working for him. This is my mother, Anabella Sousa. And that's my kid brothers, Denzil and Daniel. They're twins, but you wouldn't know it. And standing in the doorway is my stepfather, António, but he won't talk to you. Or me."

Clinton waved in the man's direction. "So, your parents are all right with this trip?"

Julia gave him a surreptitious scowl just as her mother took a step toward them and reached to take Clinton's hands. "It is so wonderful you to do this. And I am so surprise that the University pay to study abroad for students. America! Amazing! You take care of daughter. And all students on trip."

It was Clinton's turn to frown at Julia. "Pay? Study abroad? All students?"

Before anyone could say anything else, Julia started hugging her mother, with air kisses to the left and right. "We really need to leave. It's a long drive to the airport. I'll send email through Denzil or Daniel. Okay?"

"Okay. *Adeus.* Go with God."

Clinton concentrated on his driving through the heavy traffic getting out of town, which spared him from making conversation until they were speeding down the 180 freeway. "Uh, your mother's English is pretty good. I thought you spoke only Portuguese at home."

Julia pulled out her earbuds. "What did you say?"

"I said your mother speaks English better than I would have expected, considering you spoke nothing but Portuguese at home."

"Well, yes. But mother is smart, and she has learned a lot. I also tutor her. She . . . ah . . . practiced before you arrived."

"She practiced, huh? And you? Did you practice?"

"What do you mean?"

"Nothing. Look, we have a long drive and a couple of even longer flights ahead of us. On the way to the airport, why don't you tell me a little about yourself so I have a better idea who it is who manipulated me into this trip."

"Who me? Manipulated? You asked for my help. That's the only reason I'm doing this. I figure you'll owe me big time and give me good grades in the class."

"You're not in my class anymore. Don't you remember? You quit school."

"Oh, yeah. Right. But I'll probably have other classes with you, so, like, it's an insurance policy, sort of, for when I'm back in school."

"Back? Isn't it time you came clean and told me what this is really about? I checked. You're not enrolled as a regular student at the university, and you're not on any stipend or scholarship that the administration knows about. You are taking one class—mine—and you are behind on the tuition payment for that class. What gives?"

"Must be some kinda records screw-up. You know how the California universities are at messing up records and stuff."

"Cut the crap. You are trying to bullshit a BS champion. What is your story? You tell it to me straight, or you don't get on that plane."

"Then you'll be the one who gets stuck for my plane ticket."

"How do you figure that? You bought the ticket."

"On your credit card."

"What the fuck? You're a thief, some kind of hustler. How did you manage that?"

"I boosted your wallet when you were getting ready to leave. Took down your Visa card number and the little code on the back. That's all they need through the website. Slipped it back to you when I returned."

"You little . . . how the hell am I going to pay for two tickets to Mbutsu City via London. I should pull over at the next rest area and have you arrested."

"No you shouldn't. You really do need me. My Portuguese is actually pretty good; I didn't lie about that."

"What else didn't you lie about?"

"That you're a great teacher, that I'm really learning lots from you, and that I really want to someday be a journalist like you."

"Oh, no. You may want to be a journalist, but you really don't want to be a journalist like me. You—"

"Yes, I do."

"No, I don't think you understand. I . . . oh, never mind."

"No, tell me." She reached over and placed her hand on his forearm. "I really want to know."

He glanced down at her hand. It felt warm against his bare arm. "It's just that . . . well . . . the work can be a little scary at times."

"Well, yeah, which is what makes it exciting. Hell, you packed up for darkest Africa on a whim. Flying half way around the world to chase down some bad guys: that sounds pretty brave to me."

"It may sound like it, but, believe me, it's a lot harder tapping a state senator on the shoulder and asking him questions."

"Yeah, I suppose. Never tried that, but I did lift a radio from a state trooper once."

"No shit! How in . . . ?"

"Roadblock, he's running a field sobriety check, I stumble into him. He says, 'You flunked, young lady.' I insist on a breathalyzer, and it comes out clean. He walks back to his car perplexed. Got into trouble, I would guess, when he showed up at the end of the shift without his radio. I tossed it in a dumpster on my way back to my boyfriend's place. It was his car, and he would've been royal pissed to have to get it out of impound."

"I don't get it. You have a nice home, a family, you're studying journalism. What's with being a scofflaw or a pickpocket."

"Scofflaw? Now there's a real vocab word. But I don't live there, you know, at my mother's place. I just stopped by in time for you to pick me up. I've been living on my own since I was sixteen—hustling, boosting, whatever pays for groceries—ever since they kicked me out."

Clinton changed lanes to pass a slow truck train. "What happened? I mean, why did you get kicked out?"

"My stepfather was trying to hit on me, but when my mother caught him, he said I was coming on to him. She believed him. Hey, I don't blame her. He was the one paying for groceries; I was the one eating them. Simple economics."

"And why are you coming with me to Africa?"

"Why not? I'm between gigs. Besides, I was about to get kicked out of school for not paying my fees, but I wanted to keep learning from you. You're a good teacher. And I like you. The way I figure it, just give us some time on the road, and maybe you'll like me, too. Anyway, now we're stuck with each other." She loosened her seatbelt enough to slide down and stretch out. "I'm gonna catch some dreamtime. You drive careful."

"Carefully. I'll drive carefully."

"Right, like I said." She closed her eyes.

He looked over at her, so lovely in repose, and shook his head. "Danger in denim," he whispered to himself.

Chapter 13

Holzinger's hands hovered above the white-lit letters of his laptop keyboard. He was running out of trick ponies to call into the ring. His own hacking skills, once first rate, had not kept up with the rush of advances in cyber-security and the malicious tools that exploit their vulnerabilities. In recent times, he had become too much a jack-of-all-trades, too much a hands-on enforcer. Not long ago, he could have hacked into any number of facilities on his own, as he once did with the arXive servers at Cornell University to make an unpublished paper vanish. That was then, this was now, and the US Postal Service was proving beyond his flagging skills.

His hands, still poised an inch above the keys, were beginning to cramp with tension from the struggle with an inner self that had long ago been paved over. It was a self that wanted to form his hands into fists and pound the laptop in helpless fury, a self that had erupted in rage when he was offered no explanation of why his security clearance for a promotion in Germany's BND had not been approved. It was the self that turned red in the face when a target recovered from the poison Holzinger had carefully painted on the inside of a coffee mug. It was the self that Gustav Holzinger had vowed to defeat, to keep sedated in a straightjacket in a well-guarded mental prison at the back of his brain. Training, discipline, perpetual practice: these had enabled him to maintain his calm and controlled exterior for all the years he had worked with Sellian Atlantic and Biontolics and Pan-Africa Pharmacometrics.

The responses from his extended network of hackers in China and Russia were not placating that dark inner self. They all had different ways of expressing it, but the answers were, at the heart, the same. It would take too long and cost him too much to hack into either the USPS databases or, alternatively, the systems of more than two dozen separate organizations to which the packets had been sent. Money itself was not the issue—it never was with Biontolics—but too much money chasing one job could attract unwanted attention. In any case, just putting such a job out for bid could be a bad idea because it had too high a risk of exposure.

Holzinger looked up from his tense hands to focus on a spot in space just above his laptop screen and a half meter beyond. He watched as his smoky visualization of his breath jetted out and then was drawn back in, an unseen but not unreal cloud, pure thought, pure vapor. He followed his thoughts and his feelings without judgement, without response, letting his mind stray from the breath that ebbed and flowed, allowing its return to that living vapor that sustained him, letting go of everything wanted or needed. With this meditative practice, the tension gradually drained from his fingers, which floated upward as if buoyant. Somewhere, beneath the waves of nothingness that spread over his being, a desperate and angry inner voice muted, grew silent, and once more slept inside his head.

"More than one way," he said in the whisper of a slow exhale. "What do I know? What are my assets?"

He imagined his problem floating above and beyond the laptop screen in the void wiped clean by his breath. He pictured a glowing list of names on the left and a bright single name on the right. He visualized a line slowly materializing in the space between, jumping around erratically like the artificial lightning from an electrostatic generator, finally establishing a bright connection from the name on the right to one of those on the left. That was it. He did not need hacking skills that he no longer had; he only needed to do some clever online research. Thirty-two names against one. What were the matchups?

He shifted his focus back to his laptop screen and let his fingers tap away at the keyboard. He first established a secure connection through the Sellian Atlantic VPN tunnel, then launched a browser inside a software sandbox that would isolate it from the rest of his system and make everything he did disappear when he shut it down. The queries were straightforward, variations on "Frieda Abinger" AND "Millicent Geller" or "Johnathan Beltram" AND "Millicent Geller"; "Washington Post" AND "Millicent Geller" or "Times-Picayune" AND "Millicent Geller." He created a simple text file, then wrote a script to crawl through the file, posting all the combinations against both Millicent and Millie Geller. He launched the script. In a few minutes, he had the consolidated results from Google, Bing, and Yahoo.

Among scattered pairings that were easily dismissed as spurious, one stood out: Clinton Rodrigues at the *Sacramento Bee*, tied to Millicent Geller by a blog post. He popped it up in a new window and skimmed through the blog lauding the late teacher. He was about to close the window when he noticed the dateline: Falmouth, Maine. "Son-of-a-bitch!" He had been right there. What the hell was a reporter from California doing in a suburb of Portland, Maine, if not responding to a packet sent to him from there?

Holzinger checked his watch. Three hours earlier on the West Coast. It was worth a try. He Googled to get to the contact page of the newspaper website, then dialed the main number. He got a voice menu and selected the option for a dial-by-name directory. Entering the first letters of the first name got him a voice mail for someone in the finance department. He decided to try for a live operator by holding down the zero-key. After a seemingly unending series of rings, an operator finally answered.

"I'm looking for Clinton Rodrigues. Can you connect me?"

"Just a moment." He was put on hold. "I'm sorry, there is no one by that name in our directory. What department are you looking for?"

"News?"

"I'll connect you."

The news room was no help except to say that Rodrigues didn't work there and they could not help locate him. The secretary who answered the phone suggested he try searching on the internet. Holzinger was already launching a new search as the woman on the other end droned on about what he might do. He disconnected.

And there it was, on the first page of results for "Clinton Rodrigues"—a half dozen publications, a blog, and an entry in the faculty listing for the Department of Communication Studies, Journalism, and Film at California State University Sacramento. He dialed the number in the entry but got shuttled to a voice-mail message. "Hi, you've reached the robo-domo for Clinton Rodrigues, lecturer in Communication Studies, Journalism, and Film. If you are a student, please use your SacLink account to contact me. Anyone else, send me email. Don't bother to leave a voice message; it will only get swallowed by digital demons."

"All right, Mr. Rodrigues. Now that we know who you are, I think it is time we make your acquaintance in person."

Chapter 14

On their tickets it had looked so straightforward: SFO to LHR to MBI. The reality was two brutal days of flying. Clinton had never been good at sleeping on airplanes. He spent much of the ten-hour-plus overnight flight from San Francisco to London's Heathrow reviewing the pages from the packet that he had photographed and stored in an encrypted file on his laptop. He wearily plowed through a second reading of the two unpublished scientific papers that he had passed on to Sahana. Most of the first, "Cancer expression, cell longevity, and mosaicism in *Rattus norvegicus*," made little sense to him, but the accompanying material suggested it was behind the anti-aging strategy that scientists at Biontolics had devised. Of the four authors listed on the typed cover page, he recognized only Atchison Dougherty, former head of Biontolics. The other paper, by Dr. David Rosen, "Role of selected oncogenes in regulation of telomere activity in genetic chimeras: a multi-factor meta-analysis," made even less sense to him in detail, but the overall conclusion was clear enough.

Julia, with the resilience of youth augmented by a couple of little white pills, had slept through the whole flight and awakened, refreshed, in time for breakfast before landing. As she fairly bounced through the day of enforced tourism in London, Clinton shuffled along like one of the living dead until their return to the airport. Finally overcome by exhaustion, Clinton slept on the overnight flight to Mbutsu International.

~ ~ ~

"Hey, my sleepy professor, wake up. We're in Busanyu. Can you believe it? We have to get off before this plane takes off for Cape Town."

Clinton opened his eyes to see a smiling, wide-eyed face hovering inches from his. He managed a sleepy smile in return and struggled to orient himself. "What?"

"We're in freakin' Africa, professor. Awesome. Grab your stuff and let's get to work."

Perched on the shaved-off top of the once-majestic Mount Durban, the airport, small but surprisingly modern, overlooked Mbutsu City and the valley beyond. Passengers were efficiently escorted across the tarmac toward the multi-colored glass face of a graceful terminal. The building, an architectural monument to the excesses of the previous regime, seemed to float amidst jets of water spraying into early morning air that smelled of a recent rainstorm. Black-draped portraits of the late Dr. Edgar Jabari Mbutsu greeted new arrivals as they entered the building. The country, still in official mourning, was under the guidance of a caretaker government trying to fill a power void until the elections promised for early in the next year.

Edgar Mbutsu had been a brutal despot, but his violent and heavy-handed regime of more than four decades had brought prosperity to the country—at least to those in his favor—and had helped stabilize the region. The latter had made Busanyu's President-for-Life the darling of the West even as its leaders condemned his undemocratic regime. His sudden but not entirely unanticipated death had made many in Busanyu uneasy about the future. The rebel group, *O Exército de Unidade Nacional*, the self-styled Army of National Unity, had taken advantage of the unease and the power vacuum to up its game and stage increasingly bold incursions into the nation's heartland from the remote regions where it exercised its own brand of repression.

Despite the abundant presence of soldiers patrolling the airport armed with AK-47s, the customs and immigration clearance was perfunctory. Almost before they knew it, Clinton and Julia were standing outside in the still morning air looking for a taxi into town.

Clinton turned toward a queue near a covered kiosk painted in the ubiquitous national colors of blue and orange, but Julia tugged at his arm. "The taxis, when they get around to showing up, will charge you big time. That's for ignorant tourists or business travelers who can afford to throw money away. See that guy over on the other side of the parking lot, the one with the red jacket? We tell him where we are going and get there much cheaper and faster."

"How do you know that?"

"Got it from the PlanetStudentwise travel site."

"You sure it's okay? Is it legit?"

"No, it's not legit, but it'll be okay. Those guys are the ones taking the chances. They park here at the airport and stay out of sight until the flag—as they call the guy in the jacket—signals them by texting their cell phones. Then they pop up from under a blanket in the back seat of some old Peugeot, and, ba-bing, you have your own private driver, half-price."

"Don't the airport police or whatever know about this?"

"Of course, and the driver will slip some cash to the guy at the gate, who will then spread it around. Don't you know anything? Haven't you ever been to Africa?"

Clinton thought about lying, but just shook his head. "And you?"

"Once before, when I was little. Back to Cabo Verde to meet my grandparents. I was maybe six. I remember the way my grandmother smelled of sour sweat and wood smoke and the way this sand beach we visited seemed to stretch forever. Not much else. Anyway, let's talk to the man in red and get to our hotel."

~ ~ ~

The newly paved road from the airport zigzagged down the mountainside, past tin shacks and tiny terraced vegetable gardens interspersed with elegant mountain-side retreats protected by high concrete walls. The driver kept up a running commentary in a mix of Portuguese, English, and a language that seemed constructed of gutturals, grunts, and tongue clicks. Clinton thought it might be Lusanyu, but Julia said it was another dialect. "You can tell," she whispered, "by the nose that he's not a Basanya. Didn't you check out the photos on Flikr?"

Commuter traffic into the city slowed them to a walking pace once they were off the mountain. Sprawling suburban slums slowly gave way to blocks of businesses in buildings that kept getting higher as they approached the city center. There, office buildings sheathed in bronze-tinted glass towered over squat pocket malls with open stalls in their parking lots. Black Mercedes limos with darkened windows competed for the right-of-way against bicycles piled high with goods and produce. The cacophony of horns and curses and shouted conversations pummeled them from every direction.

The Hotel Palácio Real was a four-story yellow-brick building on a quiet cul-de-sac a few blocks from the central business district. It displayed three stars on a painted plaque beside the entrance, but Clinton had his doubts. Maybe Busanyu had its own rating system.

The lobby was dark and austere. A gray-haired housekeeper marched a whining upright vacuum cleaner back and forth over worn carpeting. At the unmanned front desk, Clinton tapped the nickel-plated bell and waited. The housekeeper turned off her noisy cleaner and said something to them in heavily accented

Portuguese as she walked around and took up her spot behind the desk.

"She says her brother is at the market, but she can help us," Julia said. "It's a family that runs this place. Don't worry, I'll take care of this." She turned to the woman and started talking in Portuguese. The maid-turned-clerk responded in a sing-song variant punctuated by smiles and pulses of laughter. The registration process dragged out for many minutes as Julia and the woman talked amiably. "She was telling me about her boys, Alejandro and Filipe. Oh, she needs our passports. She will photocopy the identification page and return them to us later. It's the law here. She also needs your credit card for the deposit. It's also the law. She promises the deposit will be credited once the bill is settled."

Clinton fished out his passport and Visa card from his travel wallet and handed them to Julia, who delivered them with her own passport. The woman took an imprint of the card on an ancient hand machine that jammed twice before finally passing over both card and slip. She then studied each of their passport photos and glanced up at their faces. She laughed and said something in Portuguese before turning to fetch two keys from a cubbyhole behind the desk. Julia took them and handed one to Clinton. "*Obrigada, muito obrigada*," she said to the woman.

Clinton nodded and said, "Yes, thank you."

"Your wife speaks very good Portuguese," the woman said, switching to English as she turned toward Clinton. "I hope you both enjoy your visit to Busanyu. It is a poor country, but is beautiful."

"She's not m—"

He was cut off by Julia's elbow in his ribs. "Let's go check out our room," she said to him, as she shouldered her backpack and started dragging her duffle bag toward the stairs.

The room on the third floor was clean but spartan in its furnishings, with two narrow beds pushed together on one side and an open armoire against the opposite wall. Straight ahead, French doors opened onto a balcony deep enough only for standing.

Clinton slid his luggage into the space beside the nearest bed. "So what happened to the two rooms I reserved?"

"I changed the reservation. This way we get a 'deluxe room with balcony' for less than the two rooms."

"And we just got married, did we?"

"Well, just for our cover purposes. And to save money."

"Cover? You do realize we are journalists, not spies. Or at least I'm a journalist. But I am grateful that you are looking out for my financial wellbeing, especially after you had me pay for your airfare."

"Chill. I'll pay you back."

"What century will that be?"

"This one, right after we win the Pulitzer." She noticed him studying the beds. "Hey, don't worry. There are two beds. We can pull them apart. I get the one closest to the window."

"Fine, as long as you keep to yours, and I'll keep to mine."

"Duh. What else?"

Clinton sat down on the bed and leaned back against the headboard. "I suppose we better start to work. We only have four days and three nights to decipher the connection between Biontolics and Busanyu and figure out what that has to do with Millicent's death. But first, I need to pick up email, which might not be easy in Mbutsu City. We have to figure out where we can get Wi-Fi service."

"There's an Internet café two blocks away." She slipped a map from the outer pocket of her backpack and unfolded it. "See? I already marked it. PlanetStudentwise again."

~ ~ ~

The Internet café was no Starbucks. Rows of young people, mostly male, sat at simple wooden tables outfitted with old-style small-screen glass monitors and grimy keyboards. Julia asked if there was Internet *"sem fios"*—without wires—and the tall man at the table nearest the door shook his head, but he reached under the table and pulled out a coiled cable with Ethernet connectors at either end. He gestured toward the back of the room where barstools were lined up in front of a deep shelf running along the wall. A power strip was taped to the wall alongside a network router with flickering green lights. It took a few seconds for Clinton to realize why all the stools were empty. Since it required owning a computer, it was probably beyond the reach of most of the other patrons.

Clinton plugged in, connected the network cable, and booted up his laptop while Julia tried to talk the man at the front into providing another cable. She returned with a pout on her face. "He says no more cables. Besides, only the far left port on the router is working. We'll have to take turns."

When at last he worked his way past a string of connection problems, Clinton found an encrypted email waiting for him.

Not sure if I should keep emailing you. The head of the lab has been finding excuses to drop into our section, and the section lead has been watching all of us like a lioness over her cubs. I've been trying to be careful and clever, but espionage is not in my job description. I think they may have smart monitors on "selected papers" that raise a flag whenever these "land mines" are accessed or even referenced. Where are you? I tried to call you at the university and got your stupid voicemail. I copied your telephone number from the burner phone (didn't think this qualified as an emergency) but kept getting an "out-of-service-

*or-out-of-area" message when I called. Are you okay? Should I
be worried? Well, I am worried. Find a way to get in touch with
me. Oh, there was nothing in the system about either the
Dougherty file or Rosen David's paper. Very suspicious. Should
have known. –Warmly, Sahana*

Clinton swore under his breath and quickly tapped out a reply.

*I'm all right, just out of reach for a while. Better not do
anything connected with me or this story at work. Nothing. Sit
tight, and don't worry. –Clint*

"My turn," Julia said. "You can chat with your girlfriend some
other time."

"I wasn't chatting, and she's not my girlfriend. She's . . . she's
an old acquaintance. We went to high school together."

"Sure you did, now scooch over and let me log on."

"I've got several more emails. Just hold on." He opened the
next one. "All right. This is the one that counts. We have a 9:30
interview tomorrow morning with the Deputy Minister of
Tourism."

"I didn't know Busanyu had any tourism."

"It doesn't, really, but that doesn't stop them from having a
full cabinet post. Another opportunity to spread the wealth from
blood diamonds, yellowcake, small arms, and everything else
that gets skimmed as it enters or leaves the country."

"So why are we talking with Tourism?"

"Because we have to start someplace, get a foot in the door.
So, here's the deal. We are doing a feature story on the state of
Portuguese-speaking Africa, working our way from Angola,
Busanyu, and Cabo Verde to Guinea-Bissau, Mozambique, and
São Tomé and Príncipe. Who in the government would feel the
most need to spin such a story their way? Who is a small enough

player that he would care? That's why tourism is our entry point. As we discussed in class: find a door, then go through it."

"What do we do between now and our interview?"

"We do some poking around, man-on-the-street, study the lay of the land and get some background that we can use going into the interview tomorrow. What I am hoping is that after meeting with the deputy minister, we'll draw the interest of someone more important than our Mr. Rúben Magellan. So, watch what I do, take notes, and learn from the master."

"I will, after the master gives me the damn network cable."

Chapter 15

Gus Holzinger did not act precipitously, but he also did not hesitate to move quickly when needed. Before booking a flight to California, he had called the main number of the Department of Communications Studies to verify that Rodrigues was still with the university, obtained the location of his office, and attempted to get his home address. When that request was denied, he went online to track down where Rodrigues lived, then turned to the university site to verify that the man had a class scheduled for the term. The seminar was being taught Tuesdays and Thursdays in a Mendocino Hall classroom. That would probably be the best starting point to intercept and follow Rodrigues. There was even a convenient picture of Rodrigues on the man's LinkedIn profile.

The Core were having a late meeting at the clinic outside London when Holzinger made his Skype call. He was put on speakerphone. "Gus, this is Ferguson here. Can you hear me all right?"

"Yes, just fine, sir."

"Good. Sorry I missed you in Boston. Bertrand, Xander, and Ysabel are also here with me. Bring us up-to-date on the situation."

"Dr. Lyon, Mr. Quarry, Dr. Mandelova, you must know already that one set of the documents was actually delivered. I tracked it down to one Clinton Jorge Rodrigues, presumed to have been a reporter at the *Sacramento Bee*. He is now on the adjunct faculty at Sacramento State University. I am about to leave for California. I have a plan, subject to revision as needed, to deal with the problem. It will be resolved within twenty-four hours."

"Ysabel here. What about the other problem?"

Holzinger, caught off guard and unsure how to respond, probed. "What about it? What is your specific concern?"

"The woman at the North Shore lab, the one who has been making inquiries on Norwegian rats and other sensitive matters. Have you followed up on that?"

"That's next on my list." He was already scrolling through his recent messages. There it was, a text message from Bertrand that he had somehow overlooked: "Check on possible mole at NSL." He was slipping; he had seen it but not understood the urgency. "I'll take care of her, too."

"Wouldn't it make more sense, since you are already on the East Coast, to deal with her first."

"I considered that," he lied to buy time. "I believe Rodrigues is the priority, since he has the material and is almost certainly the instigator. We need to stop him before this spreads further. Besides, she's inside where we can keep tabs on her; he's not."

"Good enough. Under the circumstances." It was a typical response from Ysabel Mandelova, who never expressed unqualified approval or outright disapproval. Of The Core, she had always been the most difficult for Holzinger to read and to work with.

"This is Bertrand speaking. We'll up internal surveillance at the North Shore lab. You deal with Rodrigues and check in before moving in at North Shore."

"Of course."

"Hey, Gus, this is Xander Quarry speaking. While you're out on the Left Coast, stop in at the Ranch for a dip and a recharge. You're always welcome, whether I'm there or not. Tell Nadia I sent you. I'll be back at the end of the week, but I imagine you'll have moved on by then."

"Thank you, Mr. Quarry, I'll consider it if I have time."

"You know what you have to do, Gus." It was Bertrand Lyon's unmistakable voice again, the voice of command. Whatever the official definitions might say, there was never any question who led The Core.

"Yes, sir." The call was terminated from the other end. Holzinger lifted his palms from the wrist rest of his keyboard, where two sweaty imprints now glistened.

The West African morning, still cool from the rains, had been spent exploring the city, a city of deep contrasts, where lighter-skinned descendants of the colonial Portuguese jostled natives with blue-black faces and where a checkerboard of buildings advertising wealth abutted crumbling proof of permanent poverty. White faces were rare and mostly seen entering or leaving the tall buildings of the central business district. In the *Jardim dos Exploradores*, the city's botanical gardens, Clinton and Julia encountered their first genuine tourists: pasty-faced elderly Brits and bored German youth ambling through the maze of plants from around the tropical world.

The former responded eagerly to their questions with complaints about the tour company that had disappointed them with second rate accommodations and a charter flight that had left two days late from London's Gatwick airport. The German young people, part of a joint Portugal-Germany initiative to raise awareness of Sub-Saharan Africa, found Clint's name and his stumbling German riotously funny. "A day here and a day there," said a slim blond girl with a boyfriend's arm permanently dangling around her neck, "it raises the awareness so much. You can learn more on Wikipedia. But, this is also free. And we get away from classes."

By the afternoon, Clinton and Julia had swapped places. She was the journalist taking the lead with spontaneous interviews, and he was the photographer tagging along to document everything. Clinton was surprised to find his anxiety abated as long as

Julia was fronting for them, and her easy bravado escalated with every encounter.

Striding in the lead late in the day, she suddenly pivoted and pushed through the revolving door of a glass-and-stainless fronted office building. Quickly scanning a short building directory posted on a stand in the lobby, she approached the sleepy, bleached-hair receptionist with the announcement that they had an appointment at Berman and Gillmere, Limited. "Can you tell me what floor they are on?"

"Third floor." The woman reached for a telephone handset. "And who is your appointment with?"

Clinton swallowed his impulse to correct her grammar and waited to hear what Julia would say.

"We are meeting with Mr. Gillmere," she said.

"I'll have to call ahead."

"Oh, please don't. We're late for this meeting already, and you know how those types can be. Calling will only make us look bad, worse than already." She held her hands prayerfully in front of her.

The receptionist pursed her lips and hesitated, then broke into a smile. "Okay. Go ahead. Lifts are on your right."

In the elevator, Clinton admitted he was impressed with Julia's quick thinking. "But what are you going to do when we get there?"

"Watch. And learn from the master." She winked.

The elevator doors slid open to a reception area paneled in Bubinga wood with the blue-and-orange Busanyu flag draped behind an expansive desk. A grim-faced young man in a short-sleeved white shirt and patriotic blue-and-orange tie stared and waited as they approached.

With her warmest smile radiating, Julia started in Portuguese. "We are from the Sacramento Bee, and we are doing a story on companies doing business in Mbutsu City. We under-stand that Mr. Gillmere would help us with this story."

"Sacramento Bee? What is that?"

"The newspaper. We're reporters."

"You have identification?"

"Of course. Rodrigues!" She gave Clinton an impatient flick of her chin and switched to English. "The man wants to see some identification." Playing his part as lackey, Clinton dutifully ex-tracted his expired press pass and a business card from his wallet. He fanned and turned them to face the receptionist, then promptly put them away again. The man looked dissatisfied but said nothing.

Julia filled the gap. "Would you please let Mr. Gillmere know we are here. He should be expecting us. My editor said it was all arranged."

The man, clearly operating well outside his comfort zone, reached reluctantly for the desk phone. "Your names again?" He held out his hand expecting them to supply business cards.

"Julia Sousa. And Clinton Rodrigues."

The man smiled briefly at their Portuguese names before tapping out an extension on the telephone keypad. "Yes, I have Senhorita Sousa and Senhor Rodrigues here from the news-paper, the Sacramento, uh . . ."

"Bee, the Sacramento Bee."

"From the Sacramento Bee. They said it was already ar-ranged with you." He listened for several seconds. "Yes, of course." He replaced the handset. "Mr. Gillmere asked that you have a seat and make yourself comfortable. He'll be with you in a few minutes."

They took seats on the padded black-leather chairs lined up on one side of the room. Julia inclined her head toward Clinton's and spoke in a low voice. "See, that's how it's done."

"You're good at thinking on your feet, but we're not out of here yet."

Clive Gillmere, a red-cheeked dumpling in suspenders with fly-away hair that might have crowned a mad scientist, emerged from the far door a few minutes later. "Welcome to Busanyu. I am not sure what this is about, but please come along to my chambers." His British accent was as crisp as the conditioned air in the suite.

A short corridor led them to an airy office with an entire wall of windows overlooking the terraced plantings of the Garden of the Explorers. The rest of the office was paneled in pale box-wood. "Imported from good old Mother England," Gillmere said, when he noticed Julia admiring the surroundings. "A bright reminder that not everything is dark in Africa. Now, what is this all about?"

Julia continued to take the lead. "We're working on a feature series about Portuguese-speaking Africa for the business section of our paper. My editor was supposed to have okayed this with you and your firm."

"And are you from Portuguese Africa yourself?"

"My parents emigrated from Cabo Verde; I was born in the US. And you?"

"Manchester by way of Cambridge. But I've been here twenty odd years. Closer to twenty-five, but definitely odd. So, what is it you want to know about Berman and Gillmere, Limited?"

"We would rather hear it from you, in your own words. Tell us about your business. What brought you to Busanyu? What is it like working here in Mbutsu City? How do you think the business climate might change with the elections next year?"

"What brought me to Busanyu was the pound sterling. The money was the draw for Otto Berman and me, certainly not the culture or climate. Rising into the moneyed ranks was far swifter here. Better sweating through hazy tropical nights than clawing up some London law-firm ladder. My wife—ex-wife, I should say—was from Angola, originally. It was easy to switch sides when Busanyu gained independence and Mbutsu started rewarding his closest and most loyal supporters. He needed import-export help, and Otto Berman and I were ready to supply it. That's what we do, handle the paperwork side of moving goods internationally. It's more exacting than exciting, but it covers expenses and buys much more here than it would in London."

"I would say so, judging from your offices."

"Oh, you should see the laddies down the street. We are small and spare by comparison."

"Laddies down the street?"

"Mbutsu's own crew of expert exporters and . . ." His voice trailed out and his lips pursed as he considered whether to continue.

"Please, go on."

"This is Busanyu. It is a country peopled by fact-fakers and nimble-fingered skimmers. Import-export here is a business based on playing with labels and taking liberties with bills-of-lading. At least, though, we do not all make our millions on outright fraud."

"Now that is interesting. Could you elaborate?"

"No. I thought you wanted to know about our business. People who talk out of turn around here do not stay in business for long. The country is classified as a democracy, but that mostly means we can vote to keep our dictators in office. Mbutsu was elected President-for-Life by a landslide, as will his hand-picked successor, that toady Raul Gomes. People will vote for him because he appears to be benign, and because nobody dares vote against *O Partido da Revolução*. The Revolutionary

Party is everywhere." He paused. "Even here. And, of course, they are also a force within certain interests back in Britain."

"Can you say more?"

"Oh, I could say a lot more, but that does not mean that I will. As I said before . . ."

"These interests, more financial than political, I assume. And British?"

"Is the Queen English? It's no accident that regular air service from London was among the first on the scene after UN recognition. I can tell you that an awful lot of money flows from here to London."

"And how is it that you know this?"

"You forget how small this slice of a continent is. Little happens in Mbutsu City that is not known to nearly everyone. You did not hear it from me, but nearly anyone can tell you how much is lost to graft and corruption in the government. Gomes, our former Minister of the Interior, may not prove to be as brutal as his predecessor, but he is no more trustworthy. Those bloody bastards in the Ministry of Industry and Trade get their percent of every deal handled by this office, and we are nothing special. Not that I would complain. We all get our nibble of the pie, all except the poor bastards on the street and in the countryside who get the crumbs left on the plate."

Julia pretended to be checking her notes before continuing. "We're meeting tomorrow with the Deputy Minister of Tourism. What should we ask him about?"

"His salary. And how, on his salary, he can afford a second home and second family in South Africa. No, I jest. And I said nothing, remember that."

"Of course, off the record, all of it, not for attribution."

"Good, we understand each other. I wish you luck tomorrow —and after." He stood and came out from behind his desk. "You are a lovely and clever young woman." He took her hand in both of his. "You just might get what you are after, whatever that may be. Rúben Magellan is a fool for pretty young women and an easy mark for anyone with intelligence, something he has no abundance of."

He turned to Clinton and held out his hand. "And you, good sir, do keep watch over the young lady."

~ ~ ~

It was the cocktail hour, but the hotel bar at the bottom of the stairs off the lobby was nearly empty. A middle-aged German couple had barricaded themselves in one corner behind schooners of warm beer and a rampart of guidebooks and maps. A man in shirtsleeves and wrinkled khakis sat half-on, half-off a barstool; a leather-trimmed canvas courier pack was stowed at his feet. All three patrons and the bartender eyed Clinton and Julia as they entered.

The man slid off the barstool and walked toward them holding a near-empty martini glass in his left hand while extending his right. "Olá! You must be the American journalists that Suzana mentioned. I am Hidalgo. I work for the Valley Free Press, which is an absurdist name for our sorry excuse of a newspaper. 'Why?' you ask, as you are journalists yourself and naturally curious about the curiosities of life. 'Because.' I answer, 'our office is on the road halfway up Mount Durbin and in Busanyu the press is decidedly not free.' But the press part of our name is valid. And you?"

"Sacramento Bee. I'm Julia Sousa. This is my photographer, Clinton Rodrigues."

Hidalgo shook hands with each of them and gestured toward the bar. "Come, please join me. I'll buy you a drink. Sacramento, you say. Central Valley. You are a long way from home."

"You know California?" she said.

"Oh, yes. I have visited there. I have cousins who live in Oakland. I would like to live in Oakland, too, but it is hard to get away. And hard to get in. Under Mbutsu, curse his memory, some sought asylum and were admitted to the US, but not many. Most who were in actual danger were simply eliminated by Mbutsu. Who was left to flee? Not me. They ignore me because I am nothing, and the Valley Free Press is published in English. Who reads English in Busanyu? A few tourists and no one else who is not already part of the Mbutsu machine, that is who."

Julia climbed onto a stool, leaving one between her and Hidalgo. "But there is now a caretaker government and elections coming after the first of the year. Don't you expect things to change?"

"Yes, I expect things will change. There will be new faces to fear, new pockets to fill, and new rules to memorize—and circumvent. What will not change is that the few will live well off the backs of the many. But that is hardly unique to Busanyu; it is the way of things nearly everywhere, and your much lauded land of opportunity is no longer an exception. But please pardon any offense."

Julia shrugged. 'No pardon is necessary for the simple truth. The US is now a nation of haves and have nots, with no road forward other than toward more of the same."

"Ah, I see you are a cynic. How does one so young and so beautiful succumb to such a disease of the soul? That malady is understandable in the old and disillusioned, like your jaded photographer here, but you and I, we have no excuse for catching the contagion of lost hope."

"I for one haven't lost hope," she responded, "but neither have I lost my eyesight. What's happening back home is plain enough to see. But tell me, what is happening here?"

Clinton, content to hang back, smiled his approval of her tactics.

Hidalgo leaned across the intervening seat and arched his eyebrows. "What is happening here is that we have somehow suddenly been blessed by an influx of reporters, including a clever young journalist who no doubt writes as well as she speaks and who brightens our dark city with her lovely face."

"Oh. My. God." Julia spread her hands in mock surprise. "Do all Busanyu males slather it on so thick? Or is it just lonely journalists."

"I am a journalist, true, but I am no longer lonely since you arrived. What would you like? I promised you a drink."

"*Caipirinha.*"

"And you, sir?"

"*Cerveja.*"

"The beer will be warm, you know. One of the few British influences, warm beer, an unfortunate legacy at that."

"Then I'll have what you're having."

"I'm having the vapors above a vanished dry martini, shaken not stirred."

"Then make it two James Bond martinis. Are you a spy in reporter's clothing?"

"No, just a lifelong Ian Fleming fanatic. Marmdu,"—he raised his empty glass toward the bartender—"two more of these, please."

"Are you staying here at the hotel?" Clinton asked him.

"Hell no. On the earnings of a reporter in Busanyu? No, I came here when I heard that there were foreign journalists in town. They always stay here and hang out in the bar because all the online crap says this is where journalists hang out. I don't know how that particular urban myth ever started, but it is self-fulfilling and self-sustaining. I suspect Suzana and her husband first planted the story to bring more business travelers to the hotel. A clever invention."

"Like the plaque out front with three stars?"

"No, that's legitimate, like the wall at the entry hall of your CIA. It means three people have been killed here. No, no, just a jest. Many more than three have been killed here. The stars are the official rating by our own Ministry of Tourism. One star if you have a bar, two if you have private toilets, three if you pay the substantial fee for the 'special review' by the Tourism Board."

"Four and five stars I suppose cost extra."

"No, they are reserved for hotels run by members of the royal family, that is, the brothers and sisters and cousins and children of our late President's many wives. Well, not so much his children, who are mostly still quite young, since he had rather a preference for young women, some of them very young themselves, some of them not quite women."

"I see."

"It is even said that one of the young women who he picked for special attention tried to kill him, but nothing came of it. He lived, and she disappeared. There were reprisals against her relatives, yes, but these were justified by the regime as attacks on rebel strongholds, strongholds that had always been remarkably well disguised as peaceful villages, if you understand what I am telling you."

Clinton smiled grimly. "Mbutsu was the Energizer Bunny of despots, wasn't he? He seemed able to survive every attack and to outwit every enemy, even old age."

Hidalgo finished his drink and signaled for another. "Yes, and in the end our survivor succumbs to some mysterious disease, despite being under the personal care of an entire company of physicians and specialists from England. One wonders."

Clinton set his drink down. "Tell me more about these doctors from England."

"What can I tell you? Nothing is known, but everyone knew. The Presidential Palace had its own fully-equipped hospital, and doctors would fly in regularly to give Mbutsu some kind of special treatments. I once interviewed an old man named Fallu who said he had been taken to that private clinic to be used as some kind of guinea pig for the treatments Mbutsu was getting, but some English doctor talked Mbutsu out of the idea. The man was let go, perhaps because no one knew he understood English. Shortly after I interviewed him, he was found dead outside his village, supposedly the victim of a random attack by rebel forces. Supposedly."

"Can anyone confirm any of this? Do you have evidence?"

"You need to understand about this country. We do not have confirmation or corroboration. There are no witnesses, no evidence, not even facts. Ours is a country of rumors and supposition, of stories unproven but universally known. The bankers in the central business district could tell you the exact number of millions that flow every day from here into numbered accounts and private investment arrangements. They could tell you, but they won't. Hell, the bartender here could tell you about secret deals and undocumented transactions. This is how the country works. And it does work. Why would anyone want to replace a proven regime, a stable system that works, with the uncertainty of genuine democracy and transparency. Who would favor a government that might distribute wealth away from those who have it, those who sustain the current system on behalf of wealthy patrons here and elsewhere?"

"But . . ." Clinton left the word hanging in the air.

"But. Yes, but what about principles, justice, equity, fairness, freedom? Empty words, like my martini glass again." He ran his finger around the rim, filling the bar with a sweet ringing. The bartender started making another martini as he talked with Hidalgo in Lusanyu. Hidalgo leaned toward Julia. "He says you should ask the Minister tomorrow about his garden."

"He's been listening? He understands English?"

"He's a bartender. Listening is his profession. He understands everything and everyone and betrays no one. I have been trying to tell you, this is the way Busanyu works. Everyone listens, everyone knows; no one speaks, no one does anything about what they hear. Even the rebels, the self-styled Army of National Unity, are also part of the system. They have no chance of victory, and they cannot be defeated. They need the government as the source of the plunder that sustains them and to seed the discontent that supplies recruits to their cause. The government needs the rebels to divert attention away from real problems and as a scapegoat on which to blame those problems. Everyone knows this is how it works, but no one ever says so."

"Except you, you are telling us."

"But who am I? I am no one. And who are you? In a few days you will be gone, with nothing but stories and suppositions in your notebooks, the ravings of a drunken reporter in a shitty little bar."

"Are we in danger?"

"What danger could you be in? If anything happened to you, American visitors, then there could be real problems. But if you return home, knowing everything but with nothing you can tell, you are harmless. Besides, who cares what happens in this tiny African country that no one can even place on a map? You have enough problems back home." He chug-a-lugged his last martini and slid off his stool, swaying as he bent over to retrieve his courier pack. "Do ask the Minister about his garden. That should be amusing."

Chapter 17

It was mid-morning in California, and Holzinger was pacing the empty corridor outside a classroom in Mendocino Hall, waiting for his target to emerge. The door opened and a gaggle of chattering students burst out and spread in all directions like water from an open hydrant. He watched attentively while trying to act uninterested. No one who came out matched the mental snapshot he had of Clinton Rodrigues. He decided to risk a quick glance inside the room.

At the front stood a Kathy Bates look-alike with close-cropped gray hair and large eyeglasses, two blue-outlined perfect circles covering half her face. She glanced up at him with a questioning look magnified by her glasses. "Yes?"

"I was looking for Professor Rodrigues."

"Well, he's not a professor, and I am not him."

"Do you know where I might find him?"

"No, do you? No one knows, except he is not here teaching his class. I am." Annoyance flashed in her eyes. "And I am none too happy to be doing his job for him. I should right now be writing, working on a textbook, the final draft, that is, and that's what I should be doing. I have better things to do with my time than to be holding the hands of third-year students who think they already know something. It was unprofessional and irresponsible of Rodrigues to pull out at the very last minute."

Not expecting the rant or the disappointing news, Holzinger took a moment to gather his thoughts. "And do you know what he is doing if he is not teaching?"

"I don't even know where he is, much less what he might be doing there. Of course, there are rumors, but journalists don't traffic in rumors."

"But these rumors—what do they say? It really is rather important that we find him."

"And who, exactly, is this 'we' who must find him?"

"Jackson, Polan, and Lieberman. We're attorneys." It was one of Holzinger's favored instant covers because it carried a certain implied threat and lent an aura of legitimacy and power.

"Is he in legal trouble of some kind?"

"No, not trouble, but our client is eager to locate him. I'm not at liberty to discuss details, but the stakes are rather high. Anything that you could tell me that might be of help would be most appreciated. What sort of rumors are making the rounds?"

"Well, this is an interesting story. A student from this class said he thought that Rodrigues had taken off with one of the other students."

"Another student?" He leaned in to encourage the talkative professor to keep talking.

"Well, I don't know, but there is a student, female, who has also stopped showing up for class, an African-American girl, rather attractive, I would say, who kept asking after him when I started teaching his class. It could be just a coincidence. I didn't know Mr. Rodrigues that well, but he always seemed to be very responsible in his teaching—at least until dropping his course load—and much liked by his students. Of course, one can be too well liked. It's not our job to be liked by students but to teach them what they will need to know to become journalists."

"Of course. Did any of these rumors hint at where Mr. Rodrigues might be headed?"

"Well, the girl was from Africa—Angola or something like that."

Holzinger was suddenly more interested. "The student who dropped out. You know her name?"

"Yes," she looked down at a class list. "But I couldn't just tell you."

Holzinger followed her eyes. One inverted name drew his attention; it looked like Sousa. "Of course, I understand. Student privacy. Still, thanks for your time." And thanks for pointing the way to Portuguese Africa, he said to himself. He was beginning to get a clearer picture of just how messy the scenario he was facing might be.

~ ~ ~

AfrikAire was yet another of the Biontolics companies. It had been started specifically to service the newly recognized Republic of Busanyu and to serve as a captive conduit to Mbutsu City and on to Cape Town, where the vital facilities of PanAfrica Pharmacometrics were located. Like most of the Biontolics operations, AfrikAire was no mere front; it had exclusive rights to the routes, ran a robust operation, and traded with other parts of the financial hydra that was The Club, helping to channel earnings back to the coffers of the parent company.

Except for Bertrand Lyon, even the four in The Core did not know the exact extent of the many companies and organizations they controlled. Gus was not privy to the financial details, but his job required him to know which companies were theirs and which were not and who to contact and who to leave alone.

He checked his watch, retrieved the number for the Atlanta reservations service center that handled the AfrikAire account, and wracked his brain for the name of the woman who worked at the extension he was calling. He was never sure of it. That was the mnemonic.

"Shirley, it's Gus Holzinger here. I need you to check into passengers on recent flights to Busanyu."

"How are you, Gus? We never see you around here anymore."

"I've been busy. Traveling. Can you do a search for me? See if a Julia Sousa or a Clinton Rodrigues has recently flown into MBI."

"Sure thing. Do you have an authorization code?"

"Give me a break, Shirley. If you want to put me on hold while you call corporate, that's just fine with me, but you'd only be making more work for yourself."

"Okay, okay. Your caller ID is right, and I'd know your voice anywhere, but you gotta promise you'll find a way to swing through Atlanta on your way somewhere. I know a great little Jamaican place here."

The great little Jamaican place was actually Shirley's apartment, which had been an occasional stopover when Gus was working his way up in the organization. Now, though, he had no use for the Shirleys of the world and no interest in overnight delays. "Sure thing. I'll let you know. Can you do that search?"

"Already did. They traveled together, LHR to MBI, arriving Thursday. They have a return booking next week. They should be there right now. Do you want me to link over to the hotel system and see if I can find where they are staying? It might take a few minutes to get through the layers."

"Yes, do it. Send me a text message when you find them. And I'll catch you at that Jamaican place sometime soon." He disconnected before she could press him for a more specific commitment.

He checked his watch again, did the math, and decided to call London. He got the administrative assistant at Sellian Atlantic who told him that Lyon and Ferguson were having dinner at "the Table." Holzinger knew exactly where she meant. It was a touristy beef-and-ale place called Nights of the Round Table where private dining was available and no one who really was anybody in London would ever be seen. Holzinger called Lyon's cell phone, but there was no answer; he got an answer on the second ring when he called Ferguson's cell.

"Holzinger here. I found Rodrigues. He's in Mbutsu City with one of his students."

"Bloody hell. Well, at least he's isolated. Do what you need to do."

"What about the mole at the North Shore lab?"

Ferguson hesitated. "I . . . Look, it's practically on your way. Make a stopover in Boston en route to London and Busanyu. In the meantime, we can be sure our pair are tied up until your arrival in Mbutsu City. I'll see to it. You better get moving. Take care of that woman."

"I'm on my way. I'll catch the red-eye to Boston."

Chapter 18

Clinton opened his eyes, suddenly aware that he did not know where he was. It was not his apartment in California, not the motel in Massachusetts. The night sounds of a city drifted in on muggy breezes stirred by a slow-turning ceiling fan that buzzed with each rotation. He stared up at the turning blades, barely discernable in the darkness. Mbutsu City. It was a sound in his head more than words or letters.

He lifted his left arm and strained to make out the faint glow of the hands and the cardinal points on his watch. The hands were an italic L: a few minutes after three, so predictable. Whenever he crossed too many time zones, in either direction, he would awaken the first night right around three, suddenly alert to some internal alarm that did not actually keep time but merely reliably complained that something was off kilter.

He stared at the ceiling, letting his eyes adjust until he could make out the swirls and swipes in the sand-finish plaster. He started thinking ahead, as he often did when awake in the middle of the night. In the morning, they would be making their first open move into Busanyu officialdom. A meeting with a second-tier appointee was only the beginning. If they could parlay it into connections closer to the real seats of power, perhaps they could learn something. If need be, they could extend their stay.

But. There was always that word in Clinton's head. But what if they were going about it backwards, what if the real sources they needed were not the faces at the front, but the ones at the back, the ones in the crowd or the backrooms? Perhaps they needed an unconnected but knowing informant. Hidalgo had said that was how Busanyu worked. What if they were wasting their time with the Deputy Minister for Tourism?

Clinton tried to smooth over the anxiety that was rapidly rising, taking over his breathing, squeezing his throat. He rolled restlessly onto his side, and there she was, not even an arm's length away, eyes closed, her face turned toward him, sweetened in sleep into an innocence that was such a contrast to the tough, streetwise exterior of her daytime self. In the heat, she had shrugged the thin sheet down off her shoulder almost to her breasts.

As he studied her face in the dim light and watched the steady rise and fall of the sheet, his thoughts danced around the obvious. She was smart, pretty, inventive, and her affection seemed genuine. And she is your student, he reminded himself, and you her teacher. It would be a tough few days, but just that: a few days, only that. He could resist.

He closed his eyes, rolled onto his back, and lay there, willing himself to sleep.

Julia tentatively opened her eyes, watching as his breathing slowed and grew more even. She studied his profile until he was asleep and sleep finally came again to her.

~ ~ ~

There was a message at the front desk when Clinton dropped off their keys in the morning. Their meeting with Rúben Magellan had been moved from the downtown office of the Tourists' Bureau to the ministry's main office on the grounds of the Presidential Palace. When they asked the young man at the desk how to get to the Palace, he raised his eyebrows and whistled. "Taxi. But it is many miles out, very expensive."

"Are there buses?"

"Buses? Why would there be buses to the Presidential Palace?"

"How expensive?"

"Maybe fifty American dollars. It might be cheaper if you have euros."

"We have Busanyu *cruzeiros*. How much would that be?"

"Oh, a taxi would not accept *cruzeiros* from you. They would want hard currency. But . . ."

"Yes?"

"My brother has a car. I think he would take you for maybe thirty dollars. Do you want me to call him?"

Clinton shook his head in amusement. "Everybody here is a hustler. How long before he could be here?"

"Not five minutes. He is parked in a lot just near here."

"Will there be enough time to get us to the Presidential Palace for a 9:30 meeting with the Deputy Minister of Tourism?"

"Oh, I am sure Filipe can do that. Yes."

"Alright, then, call your brother."

~ ~ ~

The ride out of town to the Presidential compound was harrowing. First, there was the traffic getting out of the city, then there was the road without traffic, a deserted stretch of paved but narrow highway that snaked alongside meandering streams and made sudden hairpin turns for no apparent reason. Filipe attacked these switchbacks like a Formula One driver gunning for position.

They finally approached the gray fortress-like walls and gate of the compound at twenty past the hour. Guards on either side of the open gate stepped out of their booths and watched warily as Filipe sped toward them. Clinton cringed and involuntarily slunk down in his seat. At the last second, Filipe slammed on his brakes and skidded to a stop. The guard to the left lowered his rifle and grinned. Apparently this was not the first time Filipe had hurriedly delivered visitors to the Presidential Palace.

Filipe and the guard laughed as they chatted in a mix of Portuguese and Lusanyu. "My brother-in-law," Filipe said, as they were waved through the gate. "He is married to my youngest sister. I do not envy him. She is a princess born into a poor family, and her fantasies for him are as rich as the palace here." He drove them through the gate and down a wide avenue between stately eucalypt trees. Ahead, framed by the rows of trees, was a white marble building with broad steps mounted by massive marble columns. They pulled beside closely spaced concrete bollards that prevented vehicles from getting closer than fifty feet. "It is a security measure. You will have to walk from here. I am sorry."

"And we owe you how much? Thirty American dollars?"

"Oh, my little brother, he always does this. He knows it is forty dollars, but he always tells people less. I do not know what I am to do with him. I am sorry."

Clinton stood with his wallet in his hand, not moving, not sure whether to argue or surrender to the scam. "I am also sorry. We changed most of our money into *cruzeiros*, and I only have thirty American dollars left. Ah, but I can give you *cruzeiros*. At the official one-for-one exchange rate, that would be forty *cruzeiros*. Whichever you prefer is fine with me. *Quarenta cruzeiros ou trinta dólares?*"

"I will take the thirty dollars and get the rest from my stupid little brother." He reached for the bills that Clinton held out to him. "Call the hotel when you want to come back. Maybe my little brother can come and pick you up on his Vespa."

~ ~ ~

The rush to arrive on time had been for nothing. Deputy Minister of Tourism Rúben Magellan was still in a meeting with the Acting President. It was nearly an hour before they were ushered into an empty office decorated with antique maps and paintings of fifteenth- and sixteenth-century sailing vessels. A gentle breeze drifted through tall open windows.

Magellan arrived to find them studying one of the paintings. "It's an oil, not a print, but it's only a copy. The map over there, however, is authentic sixteenth century."

"Are you related to the original, to Fernão de Magalhães, the explorer?" Julia asked. Clinton stood and started snapping pictures.

"Naturally, not directly—his two sons died young—but to the family, I think. My father anglicized the name to Magellan after studying at Oxford." He pretended to be oblivious to Clinton clicking away. "Now, what is this interview about. Suddenly, out of a cloudless sky, a fax arrives saying you are on your way and doing a story on us. Most amusing."

"Well, to be honest, it's only a small part of a bigger feature series about the countries of Portuguese Africa."

"Why all of a sudden?"

"Mbutsu. When he died, it put your country on the map with the media. The American public started thinking about this young country and its future. We wanted to do something to counter the Fox News sensationalism over Mbutsu, and, in the process, introduce our readers to some of the diversity of the former Portuguese colonies."

"We were never a colony. We were born a democratic republic."

"Yes, of course. Well, then, let's begin there, with the early days. Were there tourists right after independence from your neighbors? Fill us in on some of the history."

"That you can get from the national website. Or Wikipedia. Let me start instead with the last few years, since I was appointed by the late President-for-Life Dr. Edgar Jabari Mbutsu o Busanya."

Once started, there was no stopping Magellan, who droned on about numbers of endemic bird species and hectares of national parks and thousands of passenger arrivals at the airport as well as plans for expanded tourist attractions in the country's only real city.

Julia took advantage of a brief pause in his narration to jump in. "Speaking of tourist attractions, what exactly is the story of your garden?"

The man's face reddened noticeably. "Who told you to ask that? I want to know who."

"No one. I think it came from an Internet search. What is the story. Apparently, it is quite an interesting one."

"The *jardins botânicos* were under-budgeted, the contractors dishonest, the market in exotic plants volatile, and the accountants incompetent. That is the story. I personally benefited in no way except for the satisfaction of seeing the city gain a valuable and successful attraction for visitors. If anyone tells you otherwise, they are traitors. Or jealous of my . . . our success."

"I see. But of course. Charges of fraud and corruption fly like bats at dusk around here. None of it is to be taken too seriously."

"Oh, it is to be taken most seriously. I could tell you many things to be taken seriously. My garden pales by comparison to what I know has been paid into accounts administered by Revic Investments and other firms in Switzerland. I . . ."

"No, don't stop."

"I forgot myself. But you are interested in tourism, business not politics."

"Financial stability or impropriety is certainly of interest to visitors. In any case, we are broadly exploring the state of business in the countries of Portuguese-speaking Africa. Busanyu is the youngest sibling in this diverse family. It will interest our readers to compare and contrast. Cabo Verde, for instance, is widely regarded as one of the most democratic countries in Africa, Busanyu as one of the most—"

The Minister held up a hand in warning. "I would be careful. We have rather strict slander laws here, and you are in the Presidential Palace."

"We are, and we are your guests. As journalists, we do sometimes forget our manners in the course of trying to do our jobs. So, why don't you lead the way and tell us as much as you can about tourism here and your role in the business."

He opened his mouth to speak, but was interrupted by the ringing of the telephone on his desk, a brass and ivory model made to resemble an antique. "*Baya,*" he answered in Lusanyu. There followed a rapid exchange during which he kept glancing at the two of them. Just as he was hanging up, two armed men in camoflage uniforms entered.

"I am afraid you will have to go with these . . . gentleman."

Clinton started clicking away, documenting the scene. "What is this about?" he asked between shots. "We're journalists. You have no right—"

One of the two soldiers crossed the room in two strides and took hold of Clinton's Nikon. "*Fotos são proibidas.* No pictures. Forbidden."

"But, we're journalists." Julia came to his defense just as the other soldier took her arm, turned her toward the door and pushed against her back with the side of his rifle. "Where are you taking us? You have no right." Her voice was demanding, but it cracked with the last words.

Clinton was fighting to retain his camera, but the soldier heaved and spun, breaking the strap and leaving a friction burn on the side of Clinton's neck. They were pushed out of the room and were met by more soldiers, who escourted them to an office several doors down. They were shoved roughly through the door, which was slammed behind them and then locked.

Chapter 19

Julia kicked at the door after it closed. "What the hell is this all about? At least now I understand why they don't get that many tourists. These people have a warped sense of hospitality."

"Ha ha. Easy for you to joke. You didn't just lose several thousand dollars worth of camera and lens. And remember their reputation here. People they don't like tend to disappear. We are in a deep cesspool, swirling in shit." Clinton slumped down in an upholsterd chair.

Julia paced impatiently. "Not for long."

"But we're locked in."

"Der. Does this look like some kind of dungeon to you? We're in a frikken office wing. Like, they're improvising; they must be winging it on short notice. Hey, turn around. Check out the windows behind you. They're wide open, and it's only six or eight feet to the ground. Let's go while they're busy extracting their thumbs from their asses and trying to figure out what to do about us."

Before Clinton could argue, Julia climbed onto the broad window ledge, swung her legs out, and lowered herself from the window. He looked out in time to see her dusting herself off. She looked up and beckoned him to follow suit.

As soon as he was beside her, she led the way around the corner of the building, down an alley, and into the shadow of the private hospital positioned back from the main gate and to its left. They stood there for several minutes, waiting to see if there was any sign their absence had been discovered. There were no sounds of running feet, no shouts, no alarms. "We don't know how long we have," she said. "They might come back to the room in two minutes or leave us to cool our heels for hours. Let's get out of here."

"How?"

"Same way as we arrived. Just don't panic, don't run. Whatever happens, act normal. It's just like walking away from a department store that you just relieved of some merchandise."

She stepped out of the shadow and started walking casually but briskly down the avenue leading to the main gate, keeping to the edge in the broken shadows of the eucalypts. Clinton caught up and got in step with her. "What are we going to do?"

"You are going to shut up unless it's to use one of the nine words of Portuguese you know. Let me do the talking."

They reached the front gate and Julia walked up to the guard who had spoken with their driver on the way in. She greeted him warmly in Portuguese, and he responded with a smile. "And tell your brother-in-law to get his sorry butt in gear," she said. "He was supposed to be here to pick us up after the interview."

"Ah, that is just like Filipe. He thinks he is such a businessman, but he is always screwing up. I will call him." He pulled a cellphone out of his fatigues and punched in a number. "Filipe, you desert donkey, your riders are here at the gate, waiting for you. They are finished and want to return to the city. Where are you?"

He covered the phone with his hand. "He is in Rio Frio. It is in the hills. He says he can be here in fifteen minutes, but he lies. It will be twenty." He took his hand off the phone and put it to his ear again. There was a rapid exchange in Lusanyu before the soldier returned the phone to his pocket.

"Thank you so much." Julia held out a fistful of *cruzeiros* for him.

"Oh, no, that is not necessary. I am glad to help a visitor. And my brother-in-law is a stupid donkey." He took the money despite the protests.

Julia and Clinton sat down on the sloping grass a few feet from the guardhouse. Twenty minutes passed with no sign of Filipe. Suddenly there was a commotion inside the gate and loud cries: *"Fechar o portão! Fechar o portão!"*

Clinton turned to Julia. "What are they shouting?"

"Close the gate. I think they have discovered we are no longer where they left us."

The two guards looked at each other and shrugged. They had been given an order, a simple, direct order. Reentering the guardhouse, one of them flipped a switch, and the armor-plated gate rolled ponderously closed. It banged shut just as Filipe's dusty Peugot came into view. He skidded to a stop as he had done earlier and waited for his passengers to climb in.

"Okay," Clinton said, "let's go."

"First, I have to say hello to my cousin, then we have to agree on the price."

"Your cousin is busy, and the price is forty *cruzeiros*."

"One hundred."

"Fifty."

"Eighty, no less."

"For that, we'll wait and call a taxi."

"Sixty, then. But that hardly covers the petrol and oil."

"Okay, sixty. Let's go."

Filipe threw the car in reverse, spun the wheel, and braked in time not to slam backwards into the closed gate. His spinning tires left rubber on the pavement as he raced forward again.

"Filipe, is there any other way back to the city?"

"No, only the Presidential Highway."

"No back roads or turnoffs?"

"Only the road to Rio Frio, but it is just a tiny village in the hills. There is nothing there."

"Isn't that where you just came from? There must be something there."

"Well, there is my pretty Ovita, but . . . Do not say anything of this to my brother. Alejandro has a mouth that never closes. He will tell my wife."

"Don't worry, we will not tell him. And you will not tell anyone you took us first to Rio Frio." Clinton reached around and dropped an extra stack of *cruzeiros* onto the passenger seat.

Filipe smiled at them in the rearview mirror. "Unlike Alejandro, I know when to close my mouth. We will take the turnoff just around the next curve and spend the afternoon visiting the village and exploring the trail along the river."

"Most excellent. And when you make the turn for the village, try not to leave any skid marks."

"Ah, but yes, I do understand. I do."

They made the turn toward Rio Frio without squealing tires. As the Peugot climbed the steep unpaved road toward the village, they could just hear the sound of distant sirens fading as a caravan of vehicles from the Presidential compound rushed toward the city.

~ ~ ~

Clinton counseled against returning to the hotel, but Julia insisted. All their clothes and Clinton's laptop were there, and she was convinced that if they waited long enough, they could get back in without being spotted.

Filipe finally drove them back into town well after dark. "This way, we can see lights on the road if they have any patrols out," he said.

Julia had Filipe swing by the hotel and run in to retreive their room key from behind the front desk, then drop them off a block away. She led Clinton around to the back of the hotel, where she used the room key to open the after-hours entrance. The hallway on the third floor was deserted. She slowly turned the key in the lock and opened the door a crack. When there was no sound, she opened it the rest of the way. The beds were made, the armoire was open and empty, and their things were gone.

Chapter 20

Clinton, standing just outside the door to their room, lowered his voice to a whisper. "What are we going to do?"

"Not stay here, that's for sure." She left the room without closing the door, grabbed his hand, and pulled him back toward the rear stairway. At the sound of hurried footsteps coming up the stairs, she spun around. "Quick, out the front." She led the way down into the darkened lobby and toward the front door. They froze at the sound of steps behind them.

"Wait, it is me, Alejandro, Filipe's brother. Filipe called me while you were visiting Rio Frio. Your things are in the storage room, the door behind the front desk. It is not locked, and I will be asleep when your things are taken. I will not know what happened to them or who took them. *Entenda, Senhora?*"

"Yes, I understand. Thank you."

"Here." He slipped a piece of paper into her hand. "It is Hidalgo's telephone. He said to call him if you need help. I think you should call."

"Yes, I will. *Muito obrigada.*" She hugged him and kissed both his cheeks.

They were startled by a flash of blue light through the front windows. "Quick, before they get here," he said, "take your things and go that way. At the end of the corridor is the door for the help to take the *lixo* to the back, to the rubbish bin. I will delay them."

As they fetched their bags from the storage room, Alejandro positioned himself in a drunken sprawl across a sofa in the lobby. When the pounding at the entrance began, he stood and staggered slowly to the door.

~ ~ ~

Three blocks from the hotel, Clinton stopped to catch his breath. He flattened himself against a building, set his suitcase down, and slid the strap of Julia's duffel off his aching shoulder. "Whew. We'd better call Hidalgo, although I can't imagine why he would help us. I got the impression he was a failed reporter, resigned to the regime and to shuffling his disillusioned way through the rest of life. Of course, he seemed enthusiastic about hitting on you."

"Well, maybe your impressions were wrong. I saw him as a pragmatist with deep but disguised ideals. And he wasn't hitting on me. It was just a game we were playing."

"Well, let's call him. Maybe he can settle our disagreement. I think the only reason he would help us is to see you again."

Hidalgo answered on the first ring but asked for Julia to be put on the phone. Clinton raised his eyebrows and squinted in a smug look as he handed the phone over to Julia. "He wants to talk with you."

"Obviously, because he is more comfortable speaking Portuguese. That is why he wants to speak with me." She talked with Hidalgo in rapid Portuguese punctuated by quiet laughs. She disconnected and handed the phone back to Clinton. "He said we should be waiting in the alley behind a tobacconist several blocks away. I think I can find it, but we must hurry there."

When they reached the specified rendezvous, Hidalgo was already waiting. He threw their luggage in the front passenger seat of his car and hurried them into the back. "We must move quickly without attracting attention. And tell me what you did to bring the army and the police down on you. No, don't tell me. What I don't know I can't betray under torture." He smirked at them over the seat back. "Now, duck down and try to think small until we get to my cousin's place."

Clionton laughed. "It's always cousins: a cousin's car or a cousin's apartment. Is everyone a cousin here?"

"Yes, mostly. Family is what people turn to when they can't trust institutions. I learned that at the University of Porto, but it's true."

The cousin turned out to be an old woman, Safima, who spoke neither Portuguese nor English and had an unused room at the back of her cottage where they could hide out for a few days. "Until you leave to return to America. She will bring you food, and I will bring you news."

"Will they stop us from leaving at the airport?"

"They might, and they might not. It depends on what offense they think you are guilty of. But the caretaker government is indecisive, and they might be more than a bit wary of angering the Americans, who supply nearly half of their arms, either directly or through Israel. Unless you are spies or have committed treason—in that case, you could be shot on sight—otherwise, I think it will be in their best interest to let you go and be done with it."

Julia put her arms around Hidalgo's neck and kissed him. "Thank you, so much. Return with news soon."

"I will. Oh, I will."

Chapter 21

Dr. Silvio DiGiorno had the best publication record in the Neuroscience Section at the Ipswich labs, which, to Sahana, meant he churned out a steady stream of mediocre papers, none of them good enough to warrant sequester by the "science censors." She surmised that he had been elevated to Section Lead precisely because he had learned to play the game reliably according to its hidden rules, which meant he required no special attention from the management above him. It also meant that his own output was largely superfluous, hence the time he spent on administrative duties was no real loss to the organization.

He was as incompetent as a manager as he was as a researcher, but his limited ability seemed to match some need of the organization to keep a certain number of unproductive people on payroll. This at first had bothered Sahana, who had been raised by her Indian immigrant parents to excel at everything and never to settle for her own second best. DiGiorno, on the other hand, seemed to settle for second or third place in everything. As it became clear that his muddle-through methods were no barrier to her and no real drain on the section, she accepted the state of things. She herself did not aspire to move into management; it was the intellectual thrill of the science that drove her.

Of late, DiGiorno had been spending more time actually in the section than in his second-floor office. It was as if he had become a sudden convert after reading some popular book on the philosophy of management-by-walking-around. His version of the approach was to begin each day with a ritual stroll through the section, pausing at each workstation to peer over the shoulder of a researcher, studying intently what was on the screen, and nodding for several minutes until the researcher became sufficiently uncomfortable to take out her earbuds or turn around and ask if there was anything he wanted.

"No," he would say, "nothing special, just interested in what my people are doing." It was always "my people." He would give a flick of his long fingers in the general direction of the screen and continue. "Tell me about this. What exactly are you working on?"

This morning was different. DiGiorno strode in with purpose, accompanied by a taller man with an expressionless face and gray eyes that constantly darted and scanned his surroundings. The two of them walked down the corridor between workstations directly toward Sahana, stopping at her desk. Her heart sped up as she tried to concentrate on the paper she was reading on-screen.

"No, next one," DiGiorno said. He turned to Sahana. "Where is Nina Bracken today?"

"I don't know. She didn't say anything to me. Maybe she's tied up in traffic. She lives in New Hampshire, you know."

"Well, when she comes in, tell her I'm looking for her. She should see me in my office right away." He flicked his fingers. "Carry on."

"Yes, of course. And I'll tell Nina you are looking for her."

Nina Bracken, the youngest member of the section, showed up only a few minutes later wearing a too-tight tee-shirt and a short skirt over leggings with the sparkle of metallic thread. "There was a bad accident at the Whittier Bridge," she said. "95 was backed up for miles."

"Anyone hurt?"

"Well, there were ambulances, so I guess so. I don't like to think about that stuff. It was such a drag being stuck in traffic so close. I probably should have taken Route 1, but by the time I got stuck it was too late. I thought—"

"Silvio is looking for you, wants you to see him in his office as soon as you come in."

"Well, he won't see me until I get my coffee. He'll just have to chill for a bit."

Nina took her time filling her mug and adding soy milk from her private stash in the refrigerator. She smiled back at Sahana and then started up the back stairs with her coffee. She returned an hour later with a grim look on her face.

"What was that about, Nina?"

"That's what I'm wondering. They asked me a lot of questions about stuff I have nothing to do with, papers I never heard of, research that's not in my specialty. They seem to think I've been doing stuff on the side or extracurricular work using lab facilities."

Sahana turned toward the scientific abstract displayed on her screen, hiding her expression. "Were you?"

"No way. I told them that. I don't have time for everything that is already on my plate. Why would I take on anything else?"

"You told them that?"

"Yeah."

"And they believed you?" Sahana was hoping for reassurance.

"I guess so. Although they said they would be watching me closely, whatever that means."

"Are you . . . well . . . worried?"

"Shit no. I can walk into half a dozen places on the North Shore and have a job within fifteen minutes. I know I'm good, and if they don't recognize that, screw them."

"That's the attitude, girl." Sahana swiveled around to give her a high five.

~ ~ ~

Gus Holzinger suggested that Silvio DiGiorno should find somewhere else to work for a while and to close the door on his way out of the office. Gus used Silvio's computer to access the secure link to London. He slipped his Bluetooth headset out of his belt pack, paired it with the computer while he waited for the connection, then asked to be put through to Bertrand Lyon."

"Sir, it's Holzinger here."

"What's up, Gus?"

"I interviewed the girl."

"And?"

"Not sure, but she seemed genuinely perplexed by the questions. We know that the queries came from her workstation—the IP addresses matched—but she might not be our mole. If somebody else used her computer or fudged the IP address, it could be anyone."

"Or she could be lying."

"Yes, well we'll be tailing her, and we're now tracking all traffic in the entire section. We'll find whoever it is."

~ ~ ~

Sahana waited until she was back in her apartment before using the burner phone. She finally got Clinton to answer after many rings.

"I'm sorry it took so long to answer. What's up?"

"They may be onto me. A guy showed up today with my boss. They interrogated one of the researchers, apparently about the archive searches I did from her workstation. I knew she had the habit of not logging out when she quit for the day, so before the connection timed out, I would launch a program on her system to keep it logged in until everybody else was gone."

"Clever. But if you haven't already stopped doing that, stop now. They'll catch you. I told you not to do anything at work."

"Yeah, but you told me that after I had already done it."

"Hey, it's bridge water."

"What?"

"Water under the bridge, whatever. Look, it's the middle of the night here. Despite the adrenaline you started coursing through my veins, I'm not fully awake."

"Where are you?"

"Somewhere else. Better you don't know."

"Who is that talking in the background?"

"Uh, another reporter, my . . . my interpreter."

"A female reporter, from the sound of it."

"Well, yeah, we're working together on this story."

"And sharing a room." It sounded catty and insecure at the same time.

"No, it's . . . we're in a . . . a conference room, working late, planning our strategy for interviews tomorrow." He covered the phone with his free hand. "Cut it out, Julia. Just wait until I'm off the phone."

Over the phone came a tinny voice. "Are you still there, Clint?"

"Yeah, I'm here. Look, pick up a clean SIM card tomorrow. Pay cash. And destroy this one. Call me once and hang up right away so I have the new number in my phone. Sit tight at work, and don't worry. You'll be all right."

Chapter 22

Holzinger was becoming weary of living at 35,000 feet sharing a long, narrow room with hundreds of strangers, but he needed to conference in person with his employers, and he needed to pass through London on his way to Busanyu. After the stopover in Boston, he caught an overnight flight to Heathrow. He always found that flight to be too long to stay awake and too short to sleep. He popped a couple of uppers on arrival at Heathrow, rented a car, and drove out to the clinic, where he amused himself with Sudoku puzzles until Lyon and Ferguson arrived.

"Good morning, gentlemen." He stood and shook hands with each of them. "I will not take much of your time today, but I thought we should agree on what to do with the two we are holding in Mbutsu City."

Bertrand took the lead as usual. "We are not holding anyone in Mbutsu City. While you were winging across the Atlantic, we learned that they escaped from custody."

"How the hell did that happened."

"It doesn't matter how; it happened. The alert is out for them. It would not be easy for them to slip out of the country unnoticed, particularly without help, which it does not seem they had, at least according to the local police."

"But they are there, still?" Holzinger said. "All we have to do is ferret them out. I can leave on the next flight."

"Let us not act too precipitously. So far, you seem to manage to be always in the wrong city or on the wrong continent when it comes to dealing with Mr. Rodrigues and his friend."

"But, I . . . Yes, of course, but now we know where they are, and they are, effectively, trapped. Busanyu is a small country."

"And mostly jungle, peppered with tiny villages connected only by footpaths and rutted tracks. They could be anywhere."

"They could be, but they are not. I am certain of that, sir. I—"

Fergusson interrupted. "Wouldn't it be far simpler if we let them come to us."

Holzinger pondered this for a moment. "What exactly do you have in mind?"

"They have return tickets, with the return booking in two days: San Francisco via London. They are amateurs. It would be far easier just to let them come to us. We can intercept them at Heathrow instead of chasing after them through a million square kilometers of back country."

"That's if they do use the return. What if they don't."

"Then you can chase them on horseback or by Land Rover if you wish, but we have little or nothing to lose by waiting."

"Little is not nothing, sir. What if they approach the news media, as the Geller woman tried."

"Tried. That is the operative verb. Forewarned is forearmed. We now have our own people planted at every media outlet on her list. No, if they try to go to the press, they will get nowhere, and we will get them. Besides, there is no press as such in Busanyu. It is all controlled by the government or too small to be of consequence."

"Really, sir, I should—"

"Two days, Gus." Lyon was back calling the shots. "That's all. You know, I think you are becoming a little impulsive and impatient with the years."

Holzinger nodded and let the blinds fall over his expression. "Perhaps. I'll go ahead and book my flight to Mbutsu City and be ready should that be needed."

~ ~ ~

Holzinger was finishing a bowl of soup in his hotel room when the text message came in.

Our intrepid reporters, ready to call it quits and head home, telephoned AfrikAire for required 24hr advance reconfirmation of return flight K0-12, MBI to LHR, leaving tomorrow at 21:00 GMT+1, arriving LHR 05:25 GMT. Be there.

Chapter 23

Clinton had dozed off again. There was little else to do in the hot, dark confines of the fly-filled room, their temporary prison that might soon be bartered for a more permanent one. The sound of muffled laughter came from the high-fenced garden behind the house, a plot that was too small and too shaded to grow more than a handful of scraggly tomato plants with yellowed leaves and shrunken fruit.

Clinton pushed through the rear door that would not close completely and into midday sun that made his eyes water. Hidalgo and Julia were squeezed onto the single stone bench shaded by overhanging branches from a tree on the other side of the fence, talking quietly, as much with their hands as with their words, gesturing and touching, crinkling their eyes with the pleasure of the secret language building between them.

Clinton nervously cleared his throat. "What news, Hidalgo?"

"The soldiers seem to have given up. The official newspaper, *A Gazeta*, says only that two people were reported to have been on the grounds of the Presidential Palace without permission."

"And you still think it will be all right for us to leave tomorrow."

"I think the dogs have been officially called off for whatever reasons. As you requested, your return flight has been reconfirmed, and there has been no sudden manhunt, no massed militia in the streets. All is quiet."

Clinton half closed his eyes in an expression of deep skepticism. "Do you know any of the old American westerns, the classics? No? The soldiers in the fort always say when all is quiet that it's too quiet out there. What do you think is going on?"

"Perhaps they want you to come out in the open, to try to make a run for it. Perhaps they no longer care. Whoever 'they' are."

"Did you find out anything more about the doctors, the ones who took care of Mbutsu?"

"Only that they stopped coming after his death, and yet the money still flows out to the same accounts. So, perhaps you were wrong that the money was for medicine."

"Perhaps."

Julia stood and stretched. "I think it is time for a siesta myself. I'm going in, out of the sun. If you talk, talk quietly. Okay?" She bent and kissed Hidalgo on his sweaty forehead. To Clinton she gave a wink.

When the door had creaked nearly closed, Clinton walked over to Hidalgo. "Is there a back way out of here?"

"Over the wall, if you can manage. A footpath runs behind the houses and to a spring-fed stream that once supplied water to the residents but no longer can be trusted to be safe. Can you manage?"

"I can manage. Let's go for a walk."

Once they were away from the back garden, Clinton inched up close behind as Hidalgo led the way along the narrow path. "I don't even know your last name," he said.

"Laredo. Spinoza e Laredo. I should have properly introduced myself."

"Spinoza? Really? Are you also . . ."

"Yes, I am also. I am both a heretic and a Jew, like Benedito de Espinosa. And, in case you were wondering, there are no Jews in Busanyu—none that I know of—but no shortage of heretics. And you?"

"Both, you could say. My mother was Jewish, from a wealthy Mizrachi family, Moroccans originally, but when they disowned her, she disowned them and the entire tribe in turn. I was raised chameleon."

"Chameleon? I do not know that religion."

"I meant that she raised me to blend in, to disappear into whatever religious crowd I might find myself in. It proved to be useful training for doing journalism."

"I would imagine. I was raised *Catolica*, but like most Portuguese men, I outgrew it not long after my confirmation. My sisters, on the other hand, still live it, the religion, as do most Portuguese women. I only learned of my Jewish ancestry at university in England, where my classmates told me that a Jew is a Jew is a Jew, and a Jew by any other name would still smell. This I was told, repeatedly. And so, in response, I now call myself a Jew, although I have no real knowledge of what it means. It is a declaration that, though I may live here, I do not belong."

"Then you are. Then we are both Jews. As long as we are talking personally, can I ask whether you are married?"

"Ha. I know what this one is about and why you are asking. Yes, I am married, and no, I am not chasing your Julia. It is just a game, a most fun game that we Portuguese play. She and I both understand that."

"Are you sure?"

"I am sure. All she talks about is you. It is what gets us both to laughing so much. She has become my new little sister, the smartest and most interesting of the lot."

Clinton fought to keep from smiling too broadly. "Well, if we are to get Julia safely out of here, we had better do some planning. I don't like the idea of going to the airport right out in the open. Is there any other way down from the mountain in the event we need to change plans at the last minute?"

"Yes, there is a disused construction road from the other side, dating back to the mining that stripped the top of the mountain. It might still be passable in an off-road vehicle."

"Tell me, Hidalgo, what do you really think are the chances that we can board that plane and get away?"

"Those may be two different things."

"What do you mean?"

"They might not be letting you get away. They might be reeling you in."

"And then what?"

"What happens to fish that get reeled in? Still, you should get on the plane."

"Why?"

"Because you are not fish; you are smarter. And I will help you."

"Why?"

"It is your favorite word: why. Do not forget the other words that every reporter learns are the keys to a story: who, what, where, when, and how. But why do I help you? Because,"—he put his hand on Clinton's shoulder and squeezed—"we are both members of the same tribe."

"Jews?"

"No, heretics. Now, let us figure out the what and how of your story. Then we will return before your Julia misses us."

~ ~ ~

Clinton and Julia had showed up at the airport at the last possible minute and were inching forward at the very back of the check-in line at the gate. Julia was clearly perplexed and trying not to show it. "Why are they letting us do this? Why would they let us get away?"

"Maybe they are not letting us get away. Maybe they are reeling us in like fish?"

"Then why are we getting onboard."

"Because we are not fish. We are smarter than fish. Hidalgo said that."

They reached the front of the line and handed their boarding passes to the ground staff at the gate. While the woman examined their passports yet again, the man checked them off on the passenger list on a laptop computer, then they were ushered outside, the last to board the shuttle bus that would take them out to the aircraft.

At the door to the plane, they showed their boarding pass stubs to the purser, who ticked off their names on her copy of the passenger manifest. The aisles were crowded with people stowing bags and negotiating seat changes. It took them a few minutes to reach their seats in row twelve.

≈ ≈ ≈

From his spot against the windows on the observation deck of the terminal building, Hidalgo watched as the shuttle carrying the last load of passengers arrived at the bottom of the steps. He saw Julia and Clinton climbing the mobile stairs. At the top, Clinton paused and looked around nervously before entering the cabin. Hidalgo waited patiently until the cabin door was closed, the steps were rolled back, and the catering truck servicing the plane backed away to return to the building. Through the layers of glass he could hear the engines revving up as the plane inched forward and turned to roll toward the end of the runway. Hidalgo could sense the others watching the same scene. He shifted his gaze to focus on the reflection in the tinted window. A man in a business suit was just putting his cellphone away as the plane started its takeoff run. He was immediately escorted out by a uniformed guard.

As the plane gained speed, lifted from the runway, and began its steep climb to avoid the next peak in the chain of mountains, Hidalgo pressed his face to the glass and spoke quietly. "Godspeed on your journey, my friends."

Chapter 24

Heathrow Airport's Terminal 5 was especially busy, and, owing to a security alert, extra patrols and security personnel were everywhere. Holzinger edged toward the front of the milling crowd at the meeting point outside International Arrivals. An overnight connection meant his quarry would have to retrieve their luggage and clear customs and immigration in London. Gus was dressed in black slacks and a white shirt with epaulets and a shoulder patch that identified him as a member of airport security. A Glock 17 was holstered at his hip. He preferred a Kimber Custom or a Beretta, but the Glock, a favorite of United Kingdom law enforcement, was part of the disguise.

The rest of his people were stationed throughout the terminal, ready for any contingency. He watched as passengers on an Iberia flight from South Africa emerged through the swinging doors from the secure area, then the first arriving passengers gradually slowed to a trickle. At last, the AfrikAire crew came through the doors.

Holzinger stepped forward. "Excuse me, can you tell me if everyone is off the AfrikAire flight Ko-12 from Cape Town and Mbutsu City?"

"Everyone is off. We're the last of the flight crew. There's only ground personnel aboard now."

"Are you certain?"

"Yes, of course. I'm the Captain."

Holzinger walked away. He pulled a compact radio from his pocket and pressed the Page All button. "Everybody, heads up.

They slipped past us somehow. Fan out, cover the exits. We can't let them get away."

~ ~ ~

As they stood waiting beside the fat sculptured trunk of a baobab tree, Clinton turned toward Filipe. "You know, we almost didn't make it. Our little princess-of-all-she-surveys is so used to being in charge of everything." Julia bared her teeth at him and imitated a low growl before smiling sweetly.

"So, there I am," Clinton continued, "sitting on the aisle, row twelve, watching, checking my watch and eyeing the front of the cabin where the ground crew were finishing up. I wait until the maintenance guy steps out and the flight attendants close and secure the forward cabin door. The purser ducks into the cockpit with the flight crew as the other flight attendant starts down the aisle taking the passenger tally, clicking away at a little hand-held counter. I wait until she is past us before unbuckling my seatbelt. I tell Julia, 'We're both heading for the toilets. Now.' and she says, 'Not yet. Wait a minute.' Well, I don't want to wait a minute or even another second, so—"

"He says 'Move it!' and then practically drags me to the front where one of the catering guys closes the cockpit door in order to open the forward lavatory door, kind of blocking off the flight deck."

"Right. So, I push Julia ahead and reach behind me to open the door of the coat closet just aft of the galley, which blocks the view from the rear. A woman in a FoodForward Catering uniform nods to us."

"And he practically throws me toward this, like, platform extended from the food service truck. Two guys grab us and pull us inside—somebody's cousins, I guess."

"Yeah, and right behind us, the last two ground crew nimbly stepped across the widening gap as the catering truck backed away from the plane with the platform already starting to lower. The truck swayed as it swung wide to clear the wing of the plane—"

"I thought we were going over."

"—and it speeds across the tarmac toward the terminal. We reach the terminal building, the catering truck backs up to the loading dock, and we get hustled out of it and into the back of the Range Rover that heads us down the back way off the mountain." He took a little bow. "Just call me Harry Houdini. We checked in, got on the plane, were counted aboard, and yet, when the plane lands in London, we have vanished in midflight. Hidalgo and his friends are absolutely brilliant. And their brilliance bought us an extra nine hours before the discrepancy could be discovered and maybe a few hours more before they figure out we weren't actually on the flight."

"What I wonder, Mr. Houdini," Julia said, "is what about our luggage? It was checked. It left for London."

"Not the contents, just the cases. Our stuff is in the bags in the back of the car. And now we pull another disappearing act. Right, Filipe?"

"Right. We are just waiting for the signal. The border here is very—what do you say?—porous."

Clinton nodded to confirm the word. "And we are going to just walk across, get escorted to a remote airstrip, then leave from a different city by a different route on a different airline. It may not be perfect, but it will certainly buy us more time."

Julia looked puzzled. "I still don't see how we are going to afford this. I thought you were close to broke."

"While you were getting to know Hidalgo, I was busy hustling with of some of Hidalgo's scruffier friends. I maxed out my credit cards—well, nearly—for down payments on three expensive cars from three shady dealers, then fenced them on the black market, pretending I had stolen them. Then I fenced the credit cards."

"You cheated the cheats."

"Pretty much."

"You know, you're not as dumb as you look." She crinkled her nose at him.

"Neither are you, but you're not the only one who can pull off a stunt. Anyway, I . . . look, there's a light flashing over there."

"Yes, that's the signal: three short, then two. Quickly, grab your bags and hike over to that spot on the rise. Your border escort is waiting."

They embraced and said goodbye to Filipe and Alejandro, before shouldering the simple military-style canvas bags. "And tell Hidalgo *muito obrigado* from both of us," Clinton said, "especially thanks for helping us get away."

"Wait," Alejandro said. "He told me to give this envelope to you, but you are not to open it until you are someplace safe."

"What is it?"

"I think it is a reporter's notebook."

Chapter 25

Bertrand Lyon, his usual self-control fleeing like crows before a hound, paced as he ticked off events. "They cleared passport control, that was verified by our contact in the Border Protection Service in Busanyu. They got on the plane. AfrikAire confirmed it from the gate records and the passenger manifest. The passenger count tallied with the manifest. They were on that plane at Mbutsu International, and they were not when it arrived at London Heathrow. The plane was searched after they were reported missing on arrival.

"Unless they parachuted out somewhere over Morocco with no one noticing an open cabin door, there are only two possibilities: they never left Busanyu or they somehow managed to disappear at Heathrow in the midst of a security alert—with you and your men watching."

Holzinger nodded. "I'm already booked to Mbutsu City, sir. I think they must still be there someplace."

"Then tell me how in God's name they could have gotten on the plane and gotten off again."

"I don't know, yet, sir, but simple logic says it's far more likely for them to be able pull the wool over the eyes of security down there than at Heathrow. Think about it."

"I am thinking about it. And I'm also thinking about whether we need another major restructuring of our entire security operations. From the top down."

"Yes, sir. Let me find and take care of them first. Then, if you want my resignation, I will tender it."

"I don't want anyone's goddamn resignation. I want those two found and taken care of. Have I made myself clear?"

"Yes, sir, perfectly clear."

As he left the building, Holzinger took a grim mental inventory of his future prospects. Failure was not an option. No one ever resigned from Biontolics, not anyone at his level at any rate. That is not to say no one ever left the organization, but leaving was rather permanent and absolute. That precedent had been set from the earliest of days when Bertrand Lyon was still Atchison Dougherty and had quietly offed the young woman who was the first person to dare step outside the clearly drawn limits. Holzinger had no illusions that any exception would be made in recognition of his long service and unquestioned loyalty. If anyone knew there was no escape, no hiding from The Club, it was he.

~ ~ ~

The light across the Busanyu border must have been farther away than it had seemed. Either that, or they had misjudged the direction. It flashed once more—three quick flashes, then two—as they crossed a gravel-strewn dry creek bed. "Over there," Clinton whispered, "to the left."

"No, I thought it came from over there, to the right a bit."

"Just keep walking. They won't wait for us forever."

They crested the rise but there was no one in sight. A rocky trail led along the ridge, then down into the shadows below. Clinton started following it. Suddenly there was the sound of pebbles kicked aside and a muffled cry from behind him. He spun around and faced a man with a machete held high. Two other men were holding Julia, one with his hand over her mouth. She writhed trying to free herself. A man put a revolver to her head and said something to her in a low whisper. She nodded several times and the hand was taken from her mouth.

Clinton was too worried to say anything. Suddenly they were surrounded by half a dozen men in camouflage fatigues armed with machetes and Kalashnikovs. A man with a bandolier over his shoulder came up to Clinton and smiled. "Americans. I am General Cabral. You have money?"

"We have your money, what you were promised: three hundred dollars."

"Six hundred. It will cost you six."

"The deal was three. That's all we have."

"Six. Six or we bury you here. First we have some fun with the girl. Even in the dark, I can see she is pretty. And she has spirit. I like that—more fun. Perhaps she will fight to the end." There was quiet laughter around the circle.

"Six it is. We pay when we reach the landing strip."

"Ah, American, so you do have more than three hundred dollars. Rich American, yes? Perhaps we just take the money, all of it, and leave you here to walk back where you came from. First, some fun, of course. The girl, is she fun?"

"I wouldn't know about that. She's my daughter, and you better not touch her."

"I better not touch her? Very funny." This time the laughter was deeper. "And so, the father has spirit, too. Well, I am a father, also, and my daughter is only a little younger, so we will take you to the airstrip where the plane waits. See, we are men of honor, but we are also in need of better arms, so the price for safe escort is six hundred. Now, pick up your things and stay close. The trail is hard to follow in the dark."

~ ~ ~

They walked nearly through the night. The sky was already beginning to lighten when they reached the grass airstrip where a single engine Cessna 206, a favorite among African bush pilots, was waiting. Two of the escorts walked ahead out to the plane, where they banged on the cockpit to awaken the pilot. The other four sat at the edge of the field talking and sharing rations.

Julia looked at Clinton. "What do you think?"

"I think we may be screwed," he said, keeping his voice barely audible. "I don't trust these guys to let us go. Why should they? Kill us and everything we have is theirs. Maybe they are working a deal to split with the pilot. What do you think we should do?"

"Throw money at the problem, like any good American." She looked to see if he understood. "And follow my lead."

He gave a tiny nod just as the two rebels who had been talking with the pilot sauntered back. "He says wait," the General announced as they approached. "He warms up the plane."

"While he's getting the plane ready,"—Clinton gestured— "you can put our bags aboard." The two men looked at each other, uncertain. "Just put the bags in the plane," he said. It was a voice with authority. The leader, asserting his own position, snapped his fingers to one of the men and pointed to the two bags, then to the plane. The man shrugged and started dragging the bags toward the open rear cargo door of the Cessna.

"Now, where is our money?" the General said, grabbing Clinton's collar.

"I have it." Clinton glanced toward the plane, as the bags were thrown aboard and the pilot signaled a thumbs up. "Julia, you go get in the plane and make sure the pilot is ready while I pay our most honorable guide here." She started walking toward the Cessna as the pilot gunned the engine and turned the plane away from them to face into the wind.

"General, let me pay you personally." Clinton half winked.

The leader took a few steps closer to the plane and away from the other men. Clinton withdrew a wad of twenties and started peeling off bills like a bank clerk counting cash for a customer. "Twenty, forty, sixty, . . ." As he counted, he rocked from foot to foot, slowly side-stepping around so the leader was turned away from the plane. He kept watching as Julia climbed aboard through the open cargo bay. The pitch of the engine picked up again. "... five hundred eighty, and six hundred." He thrust the stack of bills out as the breeze picked up, letting go of it just short of the man's hand. The gust took the bills and spread them in a flutter.

As the men dashed about trying to grab the bills, Clinton ducked and made a dash for the plane, yelling, "Go! Go! Go!" The plane turned slightly, presenting its tail to them as it started to accelerate. Clinton pushed for all he was worth and lunged for the open cargo door. He caught the lip of it and tried to roll himself in, but the plane was picking up speed. Suddenly, he felt a tug on his pants belt and was propelled in. He rolled over as he tucked his legs inside and looked up into Julia's grinning face. The pop of gunfire from behind them could be heard above the roar of the single engine as the Cessna bounced down the field, took off, and climbed steeply to avoid the trees.

"That's some wedgy you just delivered, girl."

"You deserved it, slowpoke."

"Are we good with the pilot?"

"Yes, but I had to promise him five hundred more. Are you all right?"

Clinton was squirming, trying to push his pants back down. He grimaced. "Oh god. I think I banged something getting in." He put his hand to his side. "Oh, that really hurts."

"You're bleeding."

He pulled up his blood-soaked shirt and looked down. "Yeah, looks like it. A chunk is ..." His eyes rolled and he fell back against their bags.

Chapter 26

Holzinger wasted no time after his early morning arrival in Mbutsu City. He took a cab directly from the airport to the Presidential Place, paid the driver in US dollars, and told the guard at the gatehouse that he wanted to see the Acting President—immediately. When he was informed that it was impossible, he handed his Biontolics business card to the guard. In a tone that bordered on a growl, he suggested that, if the man valued his neck, he should get in touch with his superior officer without delay.

Within minutes, a limousine arrived, flying miniature flags of the Republic of Busanyu and escorted by Jeeps fore and aft bristling with armed soldiers. The motorcade carried him all of a half kilometer to the front of the Presidential Palace. There he was met by a slightly disheveled and clearly sleepy Chief of Staff, who escorted him up the Palace steps and into an anteroom the size of a small ballroom.

"I regret that the President is not available at this moment, but he assures me he will be with you as soon as he can manage. In the meantime, he has asked that I see to your breakfast." He snapped his fingers and a small platoon of waiters with carts entered through double doors at the side.

Holzinger held up his hand with a commanding gesture. "No, please. I'll just wait for the Acting President to arrive." He audibly underscored the word *acting*.

"Are you sure? Not even a coffee? Okay, as you prefer. I will see to the President and be back in a moment."

The moment was nearly forty minutes long, which Holzinger judged as about twenty minutes longer than the time it actually took to awaken, dress, and ready Raul Gomes for the world. The discrepancy he chalked up to a mandatory cooling off period intended by Gomes to send a message to his visitor, the gist of which was that Raul Gomes was not Edgar Mbutsu, but he was still a man to be reckoned with. Holzinger considered all such games of social or political one-upmanship to be silly, but that did not stop him from playing them with his own mordant style.

When Acting President Gomes arrived, Holzinger was not in the anteroom. The French doors to the terrace were open, and Holzinger could be seen outside inspecting the potted palms and climbing passion fruit vines, apparently oblivious to the President's arrival.

"Touché, Mr. Holzinger, well played. Now, would you care to come back in and tell me what this unexpected visit is about? Surely not an agricultural inspection."

"No, not agricultural. You know perfectly well why I am here. We asked you to retain two Americans, and you let them get away. That is not the sort of thing that makes us happy. I am here to make sure no effort is spared in retrieving these errant Americans and that no similar incompetence occurs in the process."

"Now, just one minute. I remind you that you are a guest in our country and that I am head of state."

"And I will simply remind you that we know the numbers and balances of all your off-shore accounts. As the majority of these are managed by Revic Financial, it would be most unfortunate if you suddenly found your balances in these accounts reduced to zero."

The President's bulging eyes widened enough to show nearly full circles of white, but he said nothing.

"Now that we understand each other, I expect you to direct your generals and the head of your police to cooperate fully and to put their entire forces at my disposal. I intend to find those two if we have to shake every tree in the entire rain forest and overturn every rock on the savannah."

Chapter 27

Julia huddled against Clinton as she looked out over the sun-dotted seascape stirred into a stippled surface by a stiffening breeze. "Why are we here?"

"Because," Clinton said, keeping his voice low, "Madeira is where my father said to meet." The two of them were standing on a white and black stone-tiled sidewalk in front of the small airport terminal on the Island of Madeira. "And please don't squeeze so hard. My side is still sore as hell."

"Just be glad the bullet only grazed you. Of course, you had to go and pass out as if mortally wounded."

"Hey, can I help it if the sight of my own blood makes me faint. Hell, the mere thought of it . . ."

"Now don't you go trying to get more sympathy from me. And again, why are we meeting here?"

"As my father told me, security at the airport here is very lax. You may have noticed that we walked from the plane, picked up our bags, and walked out without so much as anyone looking askance. Officially, we are not here." They had arrived by a tortuous route that had taken them first to Luanda, from there to the Canary Islands, and finally on a turboprop flight to Madeira. Rising crosswinds had almost prevented their plane from landing on Madeira's famously challenging runway that perched partially on concrete stilts marching out over the sea. The pilot had managed a steep drop and sudden flattening on the second approach, garnering sustained applause from the relieved passengers.

"I thought your father was from the Azores," she said. "Didn't he go back there when he ditched you and your mother?"

"He did, but apparently he was not welcome for long, so he's moved around a lot over the years. He sends a postcard to my mother every year or two with nothing on it but a new phone number, which she has never called. Not that she uses the telephone anymore. It was a long shot, but I tried the number I had copied from the last card he sent, and it worked."

"Your mother doesn't use the phone? What's that about? I don't think you've ever said much about your mother."

"What's there to say? She's in a nursing home south of Sacramento. I moved her out there after she developed early onset Alzheimer's. I visit her several times a year, but she usually doesn't know who I am. Anyway, we're here to see my father."

"Are you sure about this? I mean, the man is wanted in . . . how many countries?"

"I only know about two: the US and Spain."

"Isn't that enough? What exactly is he wanted for?"

"Drugs. He's a chemist, brews designer drugs, constructs new molecules just beyond the reach of current law. Under his pseudonym, Chemo Sabé, he actually has quite a reputation for concocting safe legal highs."

"Not all of his creations must have been just beyond the law or he wouldn't be wanted in at least two countries."

"Well, he started modestly in the States with a synthetic cannabinoid analog, but his synthesis was a little rough and yielded a mix that was contaminated. Some of the residue species were actually already on the Feds' list. He was self-taught, learning by doing. And then, of course, there are the sorts of people he has to deal with—not always your most upstanding citizens. I don't know the details of the Spanish misadventure."

"You sound pretty casual about a father who abandoned you and your mother."

"It's bridge water."

"You know, you're the only person I ever heard use that expression that way."

"It's a reference to a prison in Massachusetts: Bridgewater State. I picked it up from my father when I was too young to know what it was about. My mother once told me he had picked it up from a buddy who had done time there but would never talk about it. He'd just say it was bridge water, obviously meaning water under the bridge."

A short man in a plaid hunting cap approached them from the end of the walkway. "You want a taxi into town?" He gestured back toward a lemon-yellow cab with sky-blue trim parked in a lot at the end of the terminal building.

"No, thanks," Clinton said. "We're meeting somebody."

"And you would recognize this somebody if you saw him?"

Clinton was a little taken aback by the question. "It's been many, many years, but I think so."

"So, many years have passed," the man said, "It's all bridge water."

"Dad?"

"Angelo Rodrigues, in the flesh, Clinton. Get in the taxi before they come over and cite me for an unlawful passenger pickup." He reached for Julia's duffel. "I'll get that for you." He stepped up his pace to reach the cab ahead of them and open the trunk. "Oh, you two will be staying with me while you're here. It'll be a little cozy, just one extra bedroom, but I assume you two are . . . well . . ."

Clinton cleared his throat. "I can sleep in the living room."

Angelo looked from Julia to Clinton and back, shrugged, and said, "Whatever." With a hand placed loosely in front of his mouth, he turned to Clinton and spoke in a half-whisper. "You're not gay, are you?"

"Would it make a difference?"

"Not really."

"Then I'm not."

"You mean you would have told your old man that you were queer if I had said it mattered?"

"Probably."

"Now I see what kind of boy my Sarah raised."

The twenty-minute trip into town was a rush of tunnels and bridges and interspersed vistas over the sea, with Angelo constantly turning in his seat to explain what they were seeing. "That was more bananas we just passed, small bananas, not the super-sweet monsters you find in stores in the States. These *quintas*, little plantations, are all over the place. There's plantings of bananas and other produce even in the heart of the city. There's one right next to my apartment building, another behind the Modelo—that's the supermarket where I get my food and stuff." He turned back and slammed on his brakes to keep from rear-ending the car ahead that was slowing at the entrance to another tunnel.

"The whole island is gopher-holed with these things. People say there's more concrete in the roads and tunnels of Madeira than there is rock in the whole damn volcanic island. It's political currency. The politicians buy votes with promises of a new road and tunnel to someplace."

In fifteen minutes, they were emerging from a tunnel and looking out over Funchal, a city of stucco houses with terra cotta tile roofs all stacked up the steep hillsides. Within minutes, they were through yet another tunnel and into the Western districts. "That was Funchal. I'll show you around the waterfront and the Old City later after we get you settled in."

Angelo's building—"I own it, outright, thirty apartments"—was on a narrow street that looked too steep to drive. Angelo gunned the engine and shot up the road, just missing a scrawny feral dog stretched out by a boarded up building.

"Funchal's like that: classy next to crappy." He slowed and pressed a button on his key fob. A sheet-steel entry gate slid slowly aside, followed by an overhead door opening to an underground garage. "Perks of owning the place: indoor parking spot and an apartment with the best views. What's the point of having a place in Funchal if you don't have a view of the harbor, right? Wait until you step out onto *a minha veranda*, uh, I mean my balcony. I talk more in Portuguese than English these days. After I started the cab company, I made myself the relief driver—mostly because it meant I could chat with British tourists. A lot of Brits come to Madeira. Also Germans and Russians, but I don't speak German. Or Russian."

Inside, they took an elevator to the fifth floor, where Angelo escorted them into an airy apartment with windows on two sides facing the sea and the city. After he showed Julia to the spare bedroom, he asked Clinton if he really wanted to sleep on the sofa in the living room. Clinton nodded emphatically.

Julia returned from stashing her things in the bedroom. "I thought you said you had only the one extra room. What are those other doors to?"

"This is my home office."

Clinton sighed. "What he means is that he has to have someplace to cook."

Julia raised her eyebrows and pointed through a doorway. "I thought that was the kitchen."

Angelo smirked. "Not that kind of cooking."

"Right. Should have known," she said." So, like, I'll be sleeping next to a meth lab?"

"Oh, I don't do that kind of shit," Angelo said. "In fact, my newer work involves GMO yeast. You know, even high school kids can now do genetic engineering. I don't do much with anything that could explode. Not much, anyway."

"Not much? That's reassuring, Dad."

"I'm not trying to reassure you. I'm just giving my son and his ... friend a place to stay. Hey, let me show you the view." He reached for the handle of a sliding door.

Julia started back down the hall. "You two go ahead. I'm going to freshen up."

Standing on the wrap-around balcony looking back over the tiled roofs of central Funchal, Angelo lit a cigarette and turned to Clinton. "So, why did you suddenly contact me? I don't imagine it's about recreational drugs."

"No, it isn't. We need paper, and I figured you would know somebody you could refer us to."

His father studied Clinton's face and took several slow breaths. "Yeah, I know somebody, more than one somebody. I assume you need the best, something that can get you through airports and the CBP."

"Yeah, the best. We need to get back home without people knowing."

"These days, that can really cost. You know it's all electronic now, embedded chips, biometrics, RFID, and stuff. The blanks have to be stolen, real thing. Lots of people to pay." He was shaking his head slowly.

"How much?"

Angelo held up his thumb and index finger in a circle. "For you, nothing. It's on me. And I won't even ask what this is about. You're my son, and I was no father to you. This is the least I can do." He closed one eye and scratched at an eyebrow. "Of course, I might have to sell one of my yachts."

It took Clinton a second to react. Then he laughed and reached out to slap his father on the back. Angelo grabbed Clinton's arm and in a split second had his wrist in a lock and twisted behind his back. "Sorry," he said, releasing his grip. "I don't let anyone touch my back. Just a thing. You two must be hungry. Let me fix dinner for you. I'm a pretty good cook, and I do mean the food kind."

~ ~ ~

Dinner was spicy chicken with black-beans, a dish that Angelo called *frango piri-piri*, accompanied by mashed white sweet po-tatoes with slivers of red onion. Julia raved about the chicken. "This is fabulous. I haven't had piri-piri from Africa in years. The Asian and Mexican chiles are just not the same."

"I know what you mean. I love that touch of smoky-sweet that real piri-piri has. You should take a few jars of it back with you. Here in Madeira you can pick it up at any supermarket."

After dinner, the three of them sat out on the balcony sip-ping a fifteen-year old tawny Madeira. Angelo broke the silence. "You don't have to, but if you want to tell me what this is about, it might be useful in picking who we go to for your new papers. No sense approaching the mafia if that's who's after you."

Clinton held up his glass and studied the amber liquid lit by the late sun. "Not the mafia. Actually, we're not exactly sure who is after us. We assume it's some part of this corporate medusa." He gave his father a quick summary of what they knew and a run-through of their adventures in Africa.

"Wow, cool! You know, you could join my business—both of you. You guys are pretty resourceful. Let me tell you, life here is pretty damn good, and being rich makes it even better. I don't have to drive a cab, you know, but it makes for better appear-ances. Gives me a way to pay taxes and be a good citizen above suspicion."

Clinton looked at Julia before turning back to his father. "I don't think so, but thanks anyway. This is a problem we have to deal with. But there is something else besides getting the passports that you could do for us. I know you are not a biochemist by training—"

"But I am, just not with the degree. I can design and cook circles around the best psychopharmacologists in the world. So what do you want?"

"I want you to take a look at a couple of old papers I have stashed on my laptop, and tell me what you think of them."

Chapter 28

Clinton looked on as his father closed the second file. "So, what do you make of them?" he asked.

"I'm not going to pretend I understood every word—especially the second paper, the meta-analysis of all that research—but here's what I think. These people found a way to essentially stop aging at the cellular level by tricking oncogenes into replenishing the protective telomeres at the end of the DNA strands. At least that's part of the trick. It involves mosaicism, where a person's cells become a mix of multiple genetic lines creating a chimeric individual with more genetic resources for warding off pathogens and biological degradation. This happens naturally to a small degree whenever a woman has a baby. Fetal cells enter her system, are incorporated into her tissues, and improve her biological fitness."

"But this isn't about pregnant women, I mean . . ."

"No, this new treatment revolves around creating a more robust organism through an elaborately orchestrated balancing act between competing cell lines on the one hand and triggering cancer on the other. It depends, in part, on what is called hormesis, that longevity and stress tolerance can be enhanced by calibrated cellular challenges—kinda what doesn't kill the cell can make it stronger. Something like that. The summary of the second paper, the more recent one, suggests this could actually be put into practice with human subjects—or already has been."

"Thanks, Dad. That's pretty much what I thought. If we are right, the people who are after us have actually been doing this—

secretly—and they're willing to do almost anything to keep it to themselves and to prevent anyone else from finding out. They even killed my old biology teacher for trying to expose them. She's the one who tipped me off and passed on these papers—papers she had retrieved from her husband's laptop."

"Wow, I'm beginning to see what you're up against."

~ ~ ~

The next week was a mix of spy games and idyllic excursions. After a day of hiking along the gentle footpath of one of the island's myriad *levadas*, the narrow water canals that zigzagged the mountains, they returned to the apartment to work on small changes in their appearances in anticipation of getting fresh passport photos. "Nothing makes more difference than a change in facial hair," Angelo told them.

"Maybe I should grow a mustache?" Julia teased.

"No, but he should. He should ditch the half-shaved look for smooth cheeks and a hairy upper lip. And you, you should maybe shorten and straighten your hair. We're not talking about plastic surgery here, I hope, just enough so you are not too easily spotted in a crowd. Like maybe a pixie cut for you, little lady."

They did as Angelo suggested, then got new photos made at a little second-floor, second-rate studio near the *Lojas da Cidade* in the city. As they waited for their new documents to arrive, Julia started using evenings to study the notebook from Hidalgo. "There's a lot of good stuff in here, including interviews with people who once worked at the private hospital in the Presidential compound. It's pretty clear on the connection between Biontolics and Edgar Mbutsu. And there's a member of the presidential staff who verifies that large, regular payments were made to a South African company. According to a correspondent of Hidalgo's, that company is owned by Biontolics. And you know what else?"

Clinton looked up from his laptop. "No, what?"

"Our Hidalgo was a poet. Interspersed among his interview notes are a number of poems, most in Portuguese but a few in English."

"Any good?"

"Judge for yourself. This one is called 'Dark Forest, Bright Tutor.'" She started to read aloud.

> Dark forest, bright tutor, show me a path,
>> the secret math
>> of counting stones and steps unknown
>> until the turning point is reached.
> With leafy fingers point me down the road,
>> the rock-hard trail
>> where once I failed to learn what others failed to teach.
> Teach me to listen with uncovered heart
>> to the silenced part within the noise:
>> the whisper of the rising sun,
>> the soundless ticking of impending death,
>> the echoes unending of my own doubt.
> Let me learn to see by darkened beams
>> to find hidden routes out,
>> the unspoken dreams in shadowed uncertainty.
> Spread above me your canopy of indifferent caring,
>> that I may be sheltered
>> as I stand staring into emptiness,
>> from darkness still learning,
>> always learning,
>> still.

~ ~ ~

Most days were spent touring the island with Angelo in one of his cabs.

"Don't you ever have to work?" Clinton asked him one mid-morning, as they headed for the western tip of the island.

"No. Never have to, not anymore. But I love what I do. I design happiness for people who can't get it from friends or lovers or work."

"What a noble and bullshit reframe. You're a drug pusher."

"I don't push, and I don't get people hooked. I know how to dial down the addictive liability of my compounds."

"Are you a user yourself?" Julia asked.

"Nope. I always test them on myself, but I get my kicks out of molecular biology and biochemistry and tweaking the shape of a new molecule that neither nature nor man has ever seen before. I'm working on one right now that induces a deep calm without drowsiness. It's like being completely mellow and excitedly alive at the same time. So, maybe I am an addict; I'm addicted to playing god, making things possible that never were before. I—"

"Watch out for that truck!"

Angelo turned back to face the road and an oncoming delivery truck. He hugged the jagged cliff face on the right as the truck edged toward the unguarded drop-off on the ocean side of the road. It sped on as if the near miss were all routine. "Well, that was a little close," Angelo announced over his shoulder. There was a sharp crack as a protruding rock took off the passenger-side mirror. "Shit!" He leaned over and back to assess the damage as they approached the next hairpin turn.

"Better keep your eyes on the road, Dad."

"Look, son. I have a hundred thousand kilometers on this piece of shit, and I've replaced more mirrors than you could count. Cost of doing business, that's all. You don't have to worry about me. I'm fine." He braked suddenly for an unmarked turnoff, then accelerated up another steep road.

~ ~ ~

It was a rare stormy fall day with afternoon rain coming down in sheets when Angelo trudged up the hill from the waterfront with a hand-couriered package tucked under his rain jacket. "Okay, so here you are." He handed each of them a passport and driver's license. Clinton looked down at his. "Sean Collin Metzger? I see you shaved a year off my life."

"Yeah, and I added a couple to hers. Makes it look better with you traveling together, not so much like you were robbing the cradle or anything."

A look of horror spread over Julia's face as she opened her passport. "You made me Shandrise Barrows? You gave me one of those trendy made-up first names. Sounds oh so very 'black'. I hate it."

"Hate it, love it, who gives a shit? You look the part. Anyway, in the envelope is the rest of the paperwork, birth certificates, the works. This is almost as good as witness protection. These guys charge an arm and a leg, but they do good work, the best. The courier brought it in from New York just yesterday. You can go through airports, whatever. Hell, you can even buy a house with these. What you won't be able to do is buy a cup of coffee, so you'll need a little walking-around money." He handed each of them a fat business envelope. "There's $9,000 each. That's so you stay under the $10,000 reporting limit when you reenter the country."

"This is too much. We can't take this from you, Dad."

Julia punched his arm. "What do you mean we can't take this. Your father is trying to be generous, and you are being an ungrateful son."

"She's right, son. And there's more. This is a key to a safe deposit box, Progress Cooperative Bank of Sausalito. There's enough there for a down payment on a house. Well, not in San Francisco, but . . ."

"I don't know what to say."

"Well, son, at least I know what to say. Thank you. Thank you, Clinton, for giving me a chance to do some small thing to make up for skipping out on you."

"Why didn't you ever help while I was growing up? Do you have any idea how hard Mom worked just to keep it together and get me through school?"

"Yes, I do know—and I tried. Your mother would never accept a penny from me. It was drug money, tainted, she said. But that doesn't mean I didn't keep trying and waiting. Weren't you relieved when you learned that she somehow magically had long-term care coverage?"

"You?"

"I'm just grateful for the chances to try and set things right."

Clinton threw his arms around his father. Angelo winced. "I'm sorry," Clinton said. "I forgot."

"It's all right. It's . . . Here, I'll show you." He lifted his shirt up to his armpits. His left side and much of his back was angry scar tissue and what looked almost like exposed muscle.

"What happened?"

"Necrotizing fasciitis, flesh-eating bacteria. These bastards cut me bad, swabbed me with the superbug, and left me to die a slow death. I knew what to do, though, so I got myself to London for treatment with piperacillin/tazobactam combination therapy and debridement, but, well . . . Anyway, I lived. And now I've lived to see my son again. I wish I could go back to the States, but . . ."

"Why couldn't you pull the same thing as we're doing, start with a new identity?"

"Because the people who did your papers are the people who would never let me. We have a détente, a division of responsibilities and distribution of the spoils. They need me on the design and production side, and I need them on the sales and marketing side: a perfect symbiosis."

"And they helped you help us."

"Right. Put enough zeroes after the first digit and miracles can happen—like living to a couple hundred years." He winked. "Look, I have some errands to run. You two figure out your itinerary from here, then we'll get you off the island."

He slapped on his hunting cap, grabbed his keys and wallet, and left.

Julia studied the passport with her new look and new name. "How many zeroes do you think it took to give us new lives?"

"I don't know. Four, maybe? Maybe more."

"We owe him a lot."

"True. And I am in the funny position of going from thinking I had the worst father on the planet to ... now, I don't know. Maybe I owe him my life, yours, too. Becoming Sean Metzger will be hard enough; being Angelo's son is even tougher to wrap my head around."

"You have it easy. I have to be Shandrise Barrows."

"What's your middle name?"

"Jana. What kind of a mother would name her daughter Shandrise Jana?"

"Well, you could go by your middle name and be Jana to your friends. And we should get used to calling each other by our new names. What do you say, Jana?"

"What's your middle name?"

"Collin. I'll do the same. S. Collin Metzger. And C. Jana Barrows. Hi, Jana."

"Pleased to meet you, Collin."

Chapter 29

The connection was not very good. The voice on the phone was distorted and drowning in waves of static. Bertrand Lyon almost shouted into the handset. "What? What the fuck did you say, Holzinger?"

"I said we tracked them to a second-rate hotel in Mbutsu City, but they had already skipped out without paying—right after they escaped from the Presidential compound. We enlisted the help of the local military to apply a little persuasion to the family that runs the hotel. It seems that the late President trained his army interrogators better at administering pain than obtaining information. They learned very little before the two sons were 'taken ill'—the exact euphemism used. All we know is that our targets disappeared over the border. We . . . lost them again."

"You lost them again, Holzinger, not 'we'. You. Lost. Them. Again."

"Yes, sir."

"Don't bother to call or text me again until you have taken care of the matter." He hung up before there could be a response. He looked up to see Ferguson watching from the doorway. "What?"

"I heard you yelling. I think you need to get out to the clinic for a psych eval. Hell, we should run the whole battery on you. I think you may be at the edge of the cliff."

"I'm not at the edge of anything. I'm just goddamn fed up with dealing with idiots like Holzinger."

"Since when did your German golden boy become an idiot? I thought you were about ready to canonize him for entry into The Club."

"I was, but I was mistaken about him. And maybe you."

Ferguson recoiled visibly. "That sort of talk can be an early sign of cellular cascade. If it starts with the brain—"

"Fuck you, Charles or Andras or whoever you are now. I'll check myself in tomorrow for the full battery of tests just to prove you wrong."

"I hope you do. I do want to be wrong about this. We've never been able to pull anybody back once the cascade gets past stage one. And it's not a pretty way to go, with all your cell lines attacking each other." He turned to the sound of someone approaching. It was Prudence Tanner, latest in the very long line of Bertrand's personal assistants. She would have been vaguely attractive were it not for the look of constipation that continually camped on her face.

"Gentlemen, I am sorry to interrupt, but there is a man down at reception who is quite adamant that I hand deliver his calling card." She stepped into the office. "He says he has something to tell you and that you would know him."

"He gave his name?"

"He declined, but gave me his card to pass on to you, Dr. Lyon. He said you would understand." She handed him a small envelope such as might contain a gift tag. Inside was an embossed plain white business card printed in black ink with a classic typeface: Toto Brancaccio, Palermo, Import/Export Consultant. There was no address or telephone number.

Bertrand held the card out toward Fergusson, who took it. "Well?" he said with impatience as his partner studied the card. "Should we . . . ? I mean we do know who this is even if we don't know the man by name."

"Quite. And that's why we make it a policy never to deal with them."

"Would it do any harm to hear him out? We don't know what he wants to tell us."

Prudence cleared her throat. "He mentioned that he understood you were looking for some people."

"In that case, show him in, and then leave us undisturbed."

'Of course, Dr. Lyon," she said, then left.

Fergusson was clearly bothered by developments. "We do not deal with the mafia. Once we start, there will be no stopping them."

"You're being an alarmist, Chas. We are not dealing with the mafia; we are talking with one man, a businessman from Sicily. Here he is now."

Prudence ushered in a stout man wearing a charcoal gray Savile Row suit tailored to make him seem slimmer. She paused before closing the door behind her and glanced toward Bertrand with a carefully modulated look of disapproval.

Bertrand stood and offered his hand. "Mr. Brancaccio, I'm Bertrand Lyon, CEO of Biontolics Holdings, and this is our Chief Medical Officer, Dr. Charles Fergusson. Please take a seat and tell us about the nature of your visit."

"I'm here as an exporter. I have overseas information to sell."

"Yes? What information?"

"Are you buying?"

Bertrand steepled his hands, fingertips to fingertips, in front of him on the desk. "That depends on the cost and the content."

"I know about a couple of journalists. The price is entry into your country club."

"Out of the question." Bertrand stood, rounded the corner of the desk, and walked to the door. "I'll have my assistant show you out."

"You're making a big mistake. I have connections. I could be very useful to you."

"Connections? We're not in the market. We have an abundance of connections, and you can keep your information."

"Wait, okay. Fifty big ones, then."

"We're not in the market for overpriced imports, either. Ah, here's Prudence now." He smiled in the direction of the doorway. "Prudence, please see Mr. Brancaccio out."

The man stood, clearly agitated. "No, wait. Really, I know where they are. Twenty big ones and I'll tell you."

Bertrand raised his hand partway, palm in the direction of his assistant. "Perhaps Mr. Brancaccio will be staying for the moment. If we need you, Prudence, I'll buzz."

"Of course, Dr. Lyon." She slipped out again and closed the door.

"So, Mr. Brancaccio, first tell us how you know."

"A package was couriered to them."

"Where? Where was the package delivered?"

"Oh, no. Money first."

"I'll see that you are cut a check for twenty thousand as soon as you tell us what you know. So, what was in the package?"

"That, I don't know, but it was for this Rodrigues chap."

"From your firm, you're saying."

"Well, sort of, in New York. But look, that's it. You got all the freebie tasting you're gonna get. Twenty, and no check. Hard currency only."

"Regrettably, we don't keep that much petty cash on hand, Mr. Brancaccio. I'm afraid ten thousand is the best we can do on short notice. Take it or leave it."

"Show me the color of your money first."

"Well, we are talking about British pounds, so the color varies with the denomination."

"I meant, show me the ... Wait a minute, you're joking, right?"

"Right. So just tell us where they are, and I'll have my assistant arrange for the money to be waiting at the guard desk in the lobby for collection on your way out of the building. It'll only take ten minutes or so."

The man licked his lips in concentration. "Okay. But if you fuck with me you will know who you fucked with."

"Of course, Mr. Toto Brancaccio. Now, where are they?"

"Madeira, the island, you know, in, ah, Funkle." He mispronounced the name of the city. "You know, the capital."

"Right, okay. Please wait here with Dr. Fergusson while I arrange for the payment." He smiled broadly at Charles as he left the room.

~ ~ ~

Ferguson watched with amusement as the Sicilian was finally ushered out of Bertrand's office. "You played our Italian visitor rather well."

"I knew the moment he walked into the room in his brand new suit that he was no mafia don, probably just a courier himself. And he bargained like a foot soldier, first overplaying his hand and then letting himself be talked down to a price tag that won't even give him bragging rights. Even before he told us where Rodrigues is, he told me plenty, including that the Sicilian mafia knows what business we're in and they somehow knew we were looking for the journalists."

"Obviously, there are leaks in the pipelines. My guess would be either in Busanyu or Russia."

"You see the Russians more often than I do. Do you think the Russian mafia would deal with the Sicilians?"

"Somebody somewhere did. It only takes one overly ambitious or overly talkative person. Perhaps we should arrange an accident for our Sicilian businessman. He strikes me as the type who would tell all for just a beer or two."

"It's already arranged, but not here. Back in New York."

"Holzinger?"

"No, he's about to be on his way to Madeira in a G6, courtesy of the Acting President of Busanyu, who is temporarily rather in our debt after failing to get either the people or the information we needed. Even if he wins the upcoming elections, I don't see Senhor Gomes getting into The Club like his predecessor. Added to his ineptitude, we would have to factor in that he is not nearly as corrupt or brutal as Edgar was, which translates into a much lower net worth."

"Does it always come back to that? Wealth?"

"As you were lecturing me not so long ago, Chas, operations are becoming ever more expensive, and it is harder and harder to keep the lid on things. By my projection, we will need at least another decade, maybe two, before we have cornered enough wealth to really be in charge. Then we can step out into the sunlight because there will be no one and nothing to stop us."

"You really think in terms of world domination?"

"No, not really. For me, power is merely a means to an end, and the end is living at least a few hundred years."

"Well then, my French-Canadian colleague, you had better keep your appointment at the clinic."

Clinton's cheek finally stopped twitching after he and Julia exited Terminal E at Boston's Logan airport. He took a deep breath of air heavy with exhaust from the idling taxis, limos, and buses. "Well, it worked. We made it through US Customs and Border Protection."

"I was more worried about dropping off the package from your father at the stopover in the Azores."

"I guess it comes with the tickets. If you fly SATA, you stop in Ponta Delgada. Hey, at least it gave us a chance to see a bit of the island and sample some of the local cheeses."

"Do you know what was in the package?"

"I assume it was chemical, but I didn't ask." He looked down the line of cars waiting to pick up passengers. A state trooper was walking up along the queue, telling drivers of cars that had overstayed their welcome to move on. "I should have thought more about what we would do when we got here. I can't use my old credit cards without risking tipping off our pursuers that we're back. We have a bundle of cash, but it won't last long if we're staying in hotels, renting cars, and taking taxis all the time."

"What about the safe deposit box in Sausalito?"

"Oh, yeah. I forgot about that. Problem is I have work to do here: research and people to see. I want to find out what happened with Dr. David's laptop that Millie Geller had. Did it get destroyed in the fire? Was it stashed someplace before? Or what?"

"I could fly back to California to collect the contents of the box while you stay here and keep digging. If you trust me, that is."

"That's a good idea, and I do trust you. But before you fly off again, let's take care of a few things. We need to figure out a place to park ourselves. For now, let's get a taxi and head up to one of the cheaper motels, preferably near a shopping center. We need to set up fresh email accounts, get new burner phones, buy a couple of pre-paid debit cards, get new clothes. And I need a camera. I'm going to miss my Nikon, but I suppose I can make do with one of those new compact superzooms that go for a few hundred—not very professional, though."

"My poor, poor professor, having to make do with a slick new camera." She put on a pout and patted him. "Let's get in line for a cab."

~ ~ ~

Returning from his daily shopping trip at Modelo, Angelo hip-checked the apartment door closed behind him and looped his keychain over the deadbolt latch so he wouldn't forget it on his way out again. He flipped on the lights, walked into the kitchen, and set the bag of groceries down on the counter. When he turned back to hang up his jacket and cap, there was a man with a drawn handgun standing in the entryway.

"Hello. You must be Rodrigues," he said. "I understand you took delivery of a package not so long ago."

"And who are you?"

"You could call me a talent scout. I'm looking for a couple of creative young people. One of them happens to have the same last name as you, so I am guessing from the look of you that he's related somehow, maybe your son. And he's traveling with a young girl, African-American, very pretty, I'm told. Does this jog your memory?"

"Nope. I do have a son, but I haven't seen him since I left Boston more than twenty years ago. Didn't know he had a girl-friend. Good for him."

"What was in the package?"

"Package? Oh, you must mean the DHL shipment from New York. Wait here. I'll get it for you, but I don't think—"

"No, thank you. Just tell me where it is. I'll get it."

"Sure, suit yourself. It's on the bench, second door on the left down the hall, box about so big marked DHL."

"I do hope you don't mind if I make sure you don't go any-place while I check it out." He spun Angelo around, grabbed his left wrist, and handcuffed it to the handle of the refrigerator, all in a single unbroken movement. "I'll be right back." He paused in the doorway and looked back. "Do understand, I'm just doing a job. Your son and you got in the way. Nothing personal." There was the weariness of a veteran in his voice, and his shoulders slumped as he left.

He returned with a sealed carton and set it on the kitchen counter along with his 9 millimeter Beretta. "You haven't opened it yet?"

"Didn't need it yet. Already know what's in it."

"Which is?"

"Laboratory glassware, ultra-high-temperature."

"Sure, right." Holzinger slipped a paring knife from the wooden block on the counter, slit the sealing tape, and pried open the carton flaps. The box was filled with green packing peanuts. He pushed some aside, spilling them onto the counter and floor and exposing an inner liner of heat-sealed plastic. He cut through the heavy film revealing the top of a large glass flask. He freed it from the liner, and lifted it from the box to hold it by the neck at eyelevel. "Smooth, almost slippery." He placed his other hand beneath to keep from dropping it.

"Must be residue of the manufacturing process," Angelo said. "Maybe a film from the final oil quenching."

"Looks rather ordinary to me."

"Looks can be deceiving; take a closer look."

Holzinger stared at the empty flask as if studying some work of art. "What? What the fuck . . . ? How in hell do they do that? The colors, swirling . . ."

Holzinger slumped slowly to the floor and rested with his back to the under-sink cabinet. "How did you . . . ? What did you do to me?" His head lolled slowly from side to side.

"I'm a chemist. It's a small molecule, a sulfone that easily penetrates the skin, quickly enters the bloodstream, and passes the blood-brain barrier. The visual hallucinations should be rather entrancing. I wouldn't know myself, as this particular compound is rather toxic. By now you should have absorbed a lethal dose. Nothing personal."

Holzinger dropped the heavy flask, which shattered on impact with the tile floor.

Angelo clucked his tongue. "Now, look at the mess you've made. I should make you clean it up, but I don't think you're quite up for much in the way of housework right now."

Holzinger's eyes widened, and his mouth started opening and closing as if he were a fish gulping water. He struggled to reach up for the handgun on the counter behind him, but only succeeded in knocking the box and the gun to the floor. His chin dropped to his chest and his arms started to spasm. When he stopped moving, Angelo kicked the man's legs to one side. He used his free right hand to roll the body over and retrieve the handcuff key.

He stood over the body as he rubbed his left shoulder that had been wrenched behind him. "You should have checked the date on the DHL package, you dumbass. And you should learn what the terms 'customer loyalty' and 'customer service' mean. My New York people warned me you might be coming by. Now, for some more chemical magic—a little smelly and not as colorful, but very effective. Let me go fill the tub for your bath." He stepped carefully around the shards of glass and started toward his supply closet.

He felt the sharp pain in his back at the same instant he heard the sound. The second shot went wild, and the bullet ricocheted off the metal door of the circuit breaker box in the entryway before lodging in the wall next to the doorframe. There was no third shot. Angelo realized what had happened and cursed himself for not kicking the gun away and not making sure the man was dead. He tried to stand but found that his legs didn't work. He dragged himself over to the straight-back chair in the entryway and pulled himself partially erect. At his waist, his shirt was already dark and soaking, and he wondered how long he had before he bled out from the wound in his back. There was not much he could do himself, and by the time an ambulance arrived, it would likely be too late. It was coming down to what he might do with his last minutes.

Chapter 31

Julia gave Clinton a big hug before going through security for her early morning flight to San Francisco. He watched as she put her new backpack on the conveyor into the x-ray machine, then held her arms above her head in the scanner. On the other side, she looked back to see him still standing there. She blew him a kiss. Poor girl, he thought, as he walked slowly out of the terminal to wait for the shuttle back to their hotel.

In the room again, he booted up his laptop and scanned his notes. He reminded himself that, even as S. Collin Metzger, he would have to be careful. He did not know how extensive or efficient the Biontolics espionage network might be. Too many contacts or inquiries by him might set off alarm bells, and his new cover would be blown.

He started by working with what was available. Luckily, before losing his camera, he had swapped out the SD card with the photos of the burned out mobile home and had uploaded the pictures to his laptop. He spent several hours studying them at full magnification and eventually spotted what he was convinced were the melted and charred remains of a cellphone, but nothing that looked like it might have once been a laptop. What could have happened to it? Was it now a carefully labeled bag of charred wreckage in some evidence locker? Had Millicent earlier given it to someone for safekeeping or stashed it somewhere?

He started by making notes about what he knew and what he could guess about. Three people had died in succession. When people die, they usually leave wills bequeathing their estates to other people. Jeannine Carston died first. Might she have left everything to Rosen David? Or maybe her sisters or nieces and nephews? With Rosen's death, his estate would have passed to his wife, Millicent Geller.

He decided it was time to start acting like a reporter again. Through online records, he was able to track down Carston's younger sister, Elise Carston McDermott, at an address in Manchester-by-the-Sea. Clinton had never been to Manchester, but he remembered hearing of it as a child, a place his mother had described as full of rich people, "most of whom are full of themselves." He remembered the mix of envy and resentment in his mother's voice, but it wasn't until many years later that he learned there was a personal story behind it, a well-to-do boy-friend who had unceremoniously dumped her not long before she had met Clinton's father.

Clinton could feel the twitch in his cheek start as he slipped the strap of the new Canon PowerShot around his neck and put the keys to his rental car in his pocket. He knew there was no alternative; it would require talking in person to get what he needed from the sister. He would have to knock on the door of a stranger.

~ ~ ~

The door to the house on the way to Singing Beach in Manchester was dark walnut, deeply carved, massive, and flanked by leaded-glass sidelights with an art nouveau floral theme. Clinton climbed the wide pink marble steps and rang the doorbell. A young woman in a white-ruffled maid's uniform opened the door and asked him in Spanish-inflected English if she could help him.

"Is Mrs. McDermott home? I'm looking for Elise Carston McDermott."

"And who should I say is calling?"

"My name is . . . Collin Metzger." He handed her a business card he had printed at Staples the day before. "Tell her that I knew her sister Jeannine. I would like to talk with her for a few minutes, if she wouldn't mind."

"I'll see. Please wait here." She closed the door on him. It reopened after several minutes. "Mrs. McDermott asked me to show you in. Please follow me; she's out on the back patio."

He was led through a cathedral-ceilinged living room, past a stone fireplace with a hearth almost tall enough to stand in, and out onto a patio facing a teardrop-shaped swimming pool. At a glass-top table under an umbrella of blue sailcloth, a woman in velveteen sweats and matching plum hoodie sat with a drink in one hand and his card in the other.

"You'll forgive me if I don't stand, I hope." She set down her drink and held out her hand toward Clinton. "Have we met?"

"I don't believe so." Clinton took her hand lightly for a moment; it was cold from holding the drink. "I'm Collin Metzger."

"Elise McDermott." She brushed back her hood to expose diamond stud earrings and long hair dyed in a subtle ombré of brown ochre and spun gold. "You knew Jeannine?"

"Yes, and I do apologize for barging in this way and doubly so for bringing up your sister. I am sorry for your loss."

"Of course you are." She closed her eyes wearily. "Would you like a drink? I know it's really too late in the season for mint juleps, but I so dearly love them." The ice in her glass rattled as she took a sip. "Jimena!" The maid appeared quickly. "Please get Mister . . ."—she raised his card and squinted at it—"Metzger a drink. What are you having?" She raised her glass toward him.

"Nothing, thanks. Or just water, please. I don't drink before noon."

"Oh, come now. How are you going to be ready for the afternoon cocktails without a morning warmup?"

"I guess I'll just have to face that challenge when I get there."

"All right, then, a mineral water for Mr. Metzger, Jimena. Ice or no ice?"

"No ice, thank you," he said.

The maid returned with a glassful of ice and a small bottle of San Pellegrino on a tray. Elise stood and swayed. "Damn it, Jimena, he said no ice."

The woman backed away with the tray. "I am so sorry, madam. I'll not be a moment, sir."

"No, that's all right," he said. "Ice is fine." He reached for the glass and the bottle, leaving the woman holding an empty tray and looking unsure about what to do next.

"You may go, Jimena." Elise gave her a stern look, then shrugged as she turned back to her guest. "These Latina types. My husband picks them. Because they work for less, he says. He's a lawyer, but he doesn't bother about checking their documents. He says the younger ones learn faster, but, I'm the one who has to train them, and ..." She trailed off and stared into her glass. "My husband likes ..."

Clinton waited, but she didn't complete the thought. "If this is not a good time, Mrs. McDermott, I could come back."

"One time is as good—or bad—as another. The house is empty, the kids are in school, and my dear husband is, mercifully, in Hong Kong or some other God-forsaken place for the week. What is it that you wanted."

"I'm a journalist, working on a story about small-cell carcinoma. I understand that is what your sister died from."

"I thought you said you knew her."

"Uh, yes, I did. I worked for a while at the lab in Ipswich."

Elise stood again and steadied herself on the table, setting the umbrella to swaying. "I ought to ask you to leave. You're all bastards. It was the chemicals that killed her, that's what I think.

"And that doctor she fell in love with. You know, Jeannine left everything to him, including her share in our lakeside place up in Maine. Can you imagine that? The family compound, and she leaves it to this Hebe. How did she think that was going to work? I mean, sharing the house and cabin with one of . . . them? We were fighting that in court, but then the bugger goes and dies, too. What a mess."

"I can see how it must have all been a shock. So, was that it? I mean in her estate."

"Just her share of the place on the lake and her own land in northern Maine—wilderness, really. A modest retirement account, some personal things, a wine collection, stuff—you know. But I thought you were interested in this cancer thing."

"I am. It seems there have been an unexpected number of deaths recently from this very rare form of lung cancer. Your sister appears to have been part of a pattern. I wondered if you might have some information that would help me figure it out: papers, correspondence, medical records, anything."

"You think it might be, like, chemicals from your lab?"

"Not my lab, and I wouldn't know. I only worked there for a few months . . . as a technical writer."

"I see. Well, I don't think I have anything about Jeannine that might help, but I can give you the name of her doctor: the one who treated her, not the one she, well, fooled around with."

"That would be great. Just one more question: Is there any chance you might have a copy of her will?"

~ ~ ~

Clinton now had two places to look for the missing laptop. Both were longshots, but longshots were all he had. He called Julia to let her know he was heading back up to Maine to do some poking around, starting with the Carston summer compound. "The death certificate I got from public records shows that

Carston drowned at the lake. But a contributing cause was that she was weakened by lung cancer, a rare form called oat-cell carcinoma on the certificate but otherwise known as small-cell carcinoma."

"Does that mean anything?" she asked.

"I don't know yet. Before I head north tomorrow, I'm going to check in with Carston's doctor, Bradley Jervis, at a clinic in Peabody"

"Be careful, Clint."

"Collin. After all this time, Jana, I would think you could remember my name."

She laughed. "Right. Oh, say, I met your mother. I drove down to the nursing home. I hope you don't mind."

"Why did you do that?" There was annoyance in his question.

"Because I wanted to know her, too, not just you and your father. You're right, she's not all there, not hardly at all. She kept on talking about Angelo—my Angelo, she called him—about how he had called and they talked on the phone."

"See what I mean? And the sad irony is that she's still fairly young and healthy, at least her body. She could have decades left of advancing dementia until there's nothing left but a body, just a shell stubbornly holding onto life."

"I'm sorry."

"It's okay. Did you get over to Sausalito?"

"Not yet. Tomorrow, probably. Oh, guess what. I'm meeting with friends tonight, some of your students from the seminar. Isn't that way cool?"

"No, that is not way cool. You were never in my class. You have to remember who you are now: Jana Barrows. We just cannot take chances at this point."

"Hey, chill. I think you're worrying too much, but I'll play it cool. If you want, I can tell them I can't make it."

"It's not about what I want, it's about staying alive. I'd rather you play it smart than play it cool. Remember, we're investigative reporters working on a big story. Blow your cover, and the whole thing blows up in our faces. Anyway, I'll talk with you again later. Well, tomorrow. I'm seeing somebody tonight."

"Seeing somebody. As in . . . ?"

"As in a contact inside Biontolics, that's all. Anyway, bye for now."

"Yeah, later. I . . . whatever." She paused before disconnecting.

~ ~ ~

Since Clinton's motel was not far from Route 128, the beltway ringing Boston, Sahana suggested they head over to Woburn to eat at a South Indian restaurant. "It's the real deal," she had told him, "literally like my mother's cooking. I'll pick you up at your hotel. I insist."

Later, as she pulled out of the parking lot at the down-market all-suite hotel where he was staying, she chided Clinton about his taste in accommodations. "Not sure whether this is a step up or down from your last motel."

"Well, the Wi-Fi's faster and there's more room, but we're still kinda living on the cheap for now."

"We?"

"Well, my student intern has to sleep someplace. Don't worry. She has the bedroom, and I have the sofa-bed in the sitting area."

"I'm not worried, and I'm certainly not prying into your personal life."

"Maybe you should. I think the poor girl has a crush on me."

"Men always think that, especially male professors." She slowed at the top of the on-ramp and slipped into southbound traffic that was still fairly heavy. "I remember this prof I had for

Neurochemistry of Memory and Learning. I was a senior, and by that time I was really hooked on neuroscience. I kept pushing for extra readings and answers to tough questions, and he acted as if I were coming on to him. I finally had to tell him straight out that I was only interested in the subject matter, nothing more. He said, like, 'I understand,' but it became clear before long that he thought this was just another ploy in some game."

"What happened?"

"He finally took the hint when I left a copy of the student guide on his desk open to the page on sexual harassment with the number of the reporting hotline highlighted in yellow. The ultimate pisser is that he stopped answering questions and gave me a C on my term paper, which brought my grade down to a B. I appealed, of course, but he only raised the mark to a B-, which still left me with just a B+ in his class, so my straight A streak was broken. It was only the second B I ever got in twenty plus years of school."

"How very, very sad."

"Hey, don't mock me. This is serious. I deserved an A for that paper. It was a complete meta-analysis of dozens of studies on neurotransmitters in the hippocampus. In fact, I expanded and polished it up a bit over the summer before I started grad school, and it was accepted for publication in PLoS Biology. I sent my professor a link but never heard back from him, the jerk."

"I guess it's different at different times."

"Yeah, like different for guys."

"Maybe. I can't say I've ever had a female professor come on to me, but I've had crushes on teachers, women, that is."

"So have I. Actually both—men and women—but that's adolescent stuff. Well, or post-adolescent. I had this one course, Feminist Theory and Scientific Progress, with a lesbian lecturer I thought was gorgeous. She had a mind that could wrap around layers of inference and implications, and I loved the fact that she never wore a bra. Let's just say she had a way of inspiring the curious experimental side of more than one of the women in her seminar."

"I think I understand. I really had the hots for one of my teachers in middle school. She was ... oh, wait a minute, now I remember. You said you had Mrs. Geller, too."

"I did. I can see how you might go for her. She was cute and bouncy and non-threatening."

"Do you always put that kind of spin on things?"

"What kind of spin do you mean?"

"I mean like, gender politics, male-dominance sort of stuff."

"Hey, it's all gender politics if you're an aggressive, over-achieving female trying to make it in any field dominated by men, which is most of the really interesting ones. That's a big part of why I'm quitting Biontolics. The atmosphere there is heavy with rancid testosterone, and it oozes down from the top. I met The General once, the previous CEO. He was exactly the kind of domineering dick that unenlightened research assistants or grad students fall for if they haven't been clued into what goes wrong when he tires of them and moves on to the next younger one in line. Then it's dump city, girl."

"There's a new CEO, right?"

"Yeah, and frankly, from what I've gotten from his memos and seen on his all-hands pep-talk videos, he was cast from the same mold as his predecessor. I wouldn't trust him closer than ten meters."

"Is that why you're leaving Biontolics?"

"Hold on, this is our exit." She down-shifted as she took the off-ramp. "In a sense, yes, that's part of it, but I'm not so much leaving Biontolics as moving on to something better. I'm joining a startup in the Bay Area. I'll be out in your end of the country.

Isn't that cool? It's a woman-headed software house that's building some innovative new brain-training and cognitive enhancement apps."

"Is that stuff real? I mean, from what I've read, it's fairly solid pseudoscience."

"Most of it is, but this is different. That's why they're hiring me. Anyway, here we are; this is the place. Doesn't look like much from the outside, but get ready for some of the best Indian food you'll ever taste, that is until I invite you home to meet the family and you get to try my mother's cooking for real."

~ ~ ~

They were back in the parking lot of his motel, still talking after a long dinner, when Clinton suddenly interrupted her. "Sorry, but I just flashed on something you said earlier. How soon do you actually leave Biontolics? Or are you already gone?"

"No, I'm still there, finishing out the month. Why?"

"I wonder if you could get something for me, but only if you can do it without putting yourself at risk."

"What do you want?"

"I was wondering if there was any way you could get me copies of a couple of those videos: one from the current CEO and one from the previous guy, the one you called The General."

"I don't think so. There really is no way of getting digital copies out of the building, no open ports or USB slots or ... I certainly couldn't email them to you. No, I don't see how. Why?"

"I've just got a funny hunch. You said they were both cast from the same mold. That got me thinking. Oh, well."

"If I think of anything, I'll let you know. Okay?"

"Okay, but no heroics."

"Is this more macho posturing or are you simply being unnecessarily protective of me?"

"I just—"

"Shut up. I'm teasing." She leaned over as far as her seatbelt would allow and gave him a conciliatory look.

"I had a great time this evening," he said. "Thanks for a wonderful dinner." He hesitated, then gave her a quick kiss and started to reach for the door.

She took his hand and pulled him back for a longer kiss. "I wish it wasn't a week night. But it is, and I really have to go."

"Yeah, me, too. Both. All of it."

Chapter 32

It took persuading to get Jeannine Carston's doctor, Bradley Jervis, to agree to meet in his Peabody office, a suite in one of the string of medical facilities arrayed behind the North Shore Mall. Jervis insisted on waiting until the end of the day. When Clinton arrived, the doctor told his nurse that he would be using Examining Room B. "I know it's unscheduled, but Mr. Metzger is only in town this afternoon and needs to be seen right away."

In the room, Jervis closed the door, turned on the water in the sink, and sat down on his stool. "Now, tell me what this is really about."

"Jeannine Carston. Her sister told me you were her doctor. She died of a form of cancer she shouldn't have had. What's the real story?"

"I'm sorry, I can't help you. Medical records and patient information are confidential. Without a release or a court order, I'm afraid there is nothing I can tell you."

"Then let me tell you some things. I assume you know that Carston's lover, Dr. Rosen David, died not long after. Did you know that Dr. David's wife, Millicent Geller, also died recently?"

"You're talking about the teacher, from the Middle School up in Newburyport? I don't see—"

"The death was suspicious, a fire that shouldn't have happened. I was investigating it, and now people are trying to kill me. Informed sources cast doubt on the reported cause of death for Dr. David, supposedly the same rare tropical disease that killed that African dictator, Edgar Jabari Mbutsu. Except, I just returned from Busanyu, and that story doesn't hold water. What's clear is that some people are very determined not to have the real story come out, determined enough to eliminate anyone who threatens to expose them. I believe you know something about this, Dr. Jervis."

"If I did, why would I tell you . . . or anybody else?"

"Because it keeps getting worse. Your proximity to Carston puts you on the radar. Sooner or later the beam will swing around and shine on you. These people are relentless, and they have enormous resources."

"Then let somebody else put themselves in the radar beam. I know nothing about these mysterious and malevolent people you refer to, and there is nothing I can tell you about any of my patients without releases or court orders. Besides, even that would get you nothing. Do I make myself clear?"

"Perfectly."

Dr. Jervis escorted Clinton out, then slumped into a chair in the waiting room with his head in his hands.

~ ~ ~

Clinton left the office convinced that Jervis knew something important but would say nothing about it. It was time to try different channels. He headed back toward the Interstate but immediately whipped across traffic into a strip mall where a Starbucks beckoned him to refuel before hitting the highway. He ordered a latte and fired up his laptop while waiting for the barista to work her way through the queued orders. On impulse, he tried a new Google search, combining oat-cell carcinoma with Biontolics. Below a stack of misleading hits, the results page included references to two papers out of Biontolics Southland in North Carolina. A switch to Google Scholar netted him abstracts that reported development of a strain of exceptionally virulent oat-cell carcinoma that was actually communicable.

It was possible, then, that Jeannine Carston had been deliberately infected with lung cancer. Could that have been what had killed Rosen David and Edgar Mbutsu, too? It didn't make sense. Hidalgo's notebook had included interviews with staff from the Presidential Palace that claimed Mbutsu had died when the so-called rejuvenating treatments failed or were stopped.

Okay, Clinton told himself, time to head north. He looked at his watch. It would be after dark by the time he reached the lake. Good, he thought. He closed his laptop, retrieved his latte, and left.

~ ~ ~

The Carston family compound proved to be a small lake-front property with a two-story cedar-shingle house and a small outbuilding that looked as if it had long ago been a large storage shed. Both buildings were boarded up for the winter, and signs warned that they were protected by a central alarm system. Clinton wondered how long it would take for anyone to respond to an alarm. It was a mile of deeply rutted dirt road back to the turnoff, then nearly ten miles of country roads to the nearest town. How long would he need? He switched his flashlight to low and kept it pointed downward as he scouted out the property. At the back of the house he found the electric meter missing. The electricity had been disconnected. What were the odds that the alarm system had no power?

He decided to chance it. He retrieved the tire iron from the trunk of the car and slowly pried one of the plywood panels off the back porch. He used a pocket knife to slit the screen enough to crawl through. The door from the porch was locked, but one kick sent it swinging open.

Inside smelled dusty and dank. Sheets were draped over most of the furniture. It did not look promising as a place to stash a laptop, but he went through the house anyway, opening drawers and cupboards, looking under beds and along shelves. He was about to leave when he noticed a small door under the stairs to the second floor. It was secured with a padlock, but the hasp was easy to pry off. Inside were stashed a stereo, a small-screen television, and a DVD player. No laptop. He closed the door and pushed the screws of the hasp back into their holes. "Good as new," he said.

He left the way he had entered, doing his best to make it look like the place had not been broken into. He worked the same procedure on the outbuilding, which consisted of a single room with two sets of bunk beds. He felt bad about the breaking-and-entering but forgave himself. Nothing was missing, and the repairs would be trivial. He put the tire iron back with the spare before closing the trunk. He was about to start the car when he saw a light out over the water and heard a motorboat approaching. He hadn't thought of that. The lake was only a mile across.

Hide? Run for it on foot? No, tear-ass back up the dirt road, he concluded. He started the car but left the lights off. In turning around, he backed into a tree, then struck a boulder with his right front bumper before aligning with the road out. In the pale light of a waning moon, it was almost impossible to see the road ahead except as an absence of dark shapes. He twice struck rocks or tree roots before he reached the paved two-lane road again. He headed north, tromped on the accelerator, and turned on the headlights after rounding the first curve. Behind him he heard sirens, first approaching and then fading.

Carston's wilderness parcel was even less likely than the family compound, but the satellite view on Google had shown what looked to be two small buildings of some kind nestled in the woods. He had come this far; he might as well keep going.

Chapter 33

When Fergusson arrived at the office, Bertrand Lyon was pacing, wearing a figure-eight path into the carpeting. "What is it this time, Bertrand?"

"Well, it's bad enough getting test results that say I have to go back in for an early treatment,"—he waved a stapled sheath of A4 paper—"but now Holzinger seems to have dropped off the edge of the earth. Nothing from him in over two days."

"Gus Holzinger has been known to go incommunicado before. He'll phone home when he's ready. But what's this about the tests?"

"Borderline."

"Let me take a look at the results." He reached for the papers.

"And you think you'll see something I didn't? I invented this whole thing, remember."

"We invented it. Technically, it was Janella Kai who ought to be credited, since it was her discovery of the anomalies with the mosaic lab rats that was the basis of everything that came after."

"Janella was nothing but a pretty young lab assistant with a nose for trouble, nothing more. It's a dead issue."

"Appropriate choice of words."

"Fuck you, Charles. I protected our interests. From the very beginning, I protected our interests."

"My, we are touchy. When do you go back for the unscheduled treatment?"

"I'll admit myself tonight after I clear up this Holzinger business."

"Just send somebody else to go in after him."

"The problem is I only know what city he's in, not his exact whereabouts."

"Surely, there is somebody else on our security team who has the talent to track him down."

"There is, but I'm hesitant to send her in."

"Now I get it. Who is it? The Chinese girl, the one I told you to leave alone?"

"She broke it off anyway, once she learned she couldn't sleep her way into The Club. Of course, she didn't actually know what all the membership perks were, just that the members were all fit and fabulously wealthy."

"So, you don't trust her?"

"No, that's not it. Zhu Huang is trustworthy, I suppose, as most all true mercenaries are—so long as they're well paid. I just hate to send a girl on a man's mission."

"And right there, Bertrand, is the nub of the problem, why you can't keep administrative assistants for more than a year. You should hire a competent male secretary, preferably gay." While the open-mouthed Bertrand was pondering a retort, Fergusson left.

~ ~ ~

Before she landed in Madeira, Zhu Huang had checked the online editions of local newspapers, relying on Google Translate to give her the gist of stories that interested her. She had also already cultivated a contact among the *Bombeiros Municipais do Funchal*, the local firefighters. He was Han Chinese by descent but had been born on the island. Like Zhu, he preferred a physical to a cerebral life, which had been a profound disappointment to his parents, both professors at the University of Madeira. She guessed that Bohei had taken much teasing over his name when he was growing up in Funchal. She caught up with him after he finished his shift at the station on the steep thoroughfare of Avenido Calouste Gulbenkian.

"Yes," he told her, "there was only one body recovered from the burned building, an intruder, the police believe." He spoke to her in Mandarin, but so heavily accented that Zhu had difficulty understanding him. She asked if he spoke English, but he hung his head in shame and told her no.

"And the others all escaped unharmed?" she asked.

"No, four victims were hospitalized: burns and smoke in the lungs, one of them also had a gunshot wound. He was the one who sounded the fire alarm about the time of the explosion. They found him in the stairwell outside the apartment where the explosion set off the fire. He had dragged himself there."

"Was the body identified?"

"No, nor did anyone claim it. The matter is still under investigation. A pistol found in the wreckage near the body was not registered and could not be traced because it had been altered."

"This pistol, do you recall anything about it? What kind? What caliber?"

"I don't know. I am sorry Zhu Huang. I think it had an Italian sort of name."

"Beretta?"

"Yes," his face lit up. "That's what the papers said."

"What about the explosion? Has anything been figured out about that?"

"It seems some chemicals in the apartment were ignited when the gun was fired. That is the theory, but it is still being investigated."

"And these victims? Where are they now?"

"They were taken to the main hospital, at Cruz de Carvalho. I would not know if they are all still there, but I think the man who was shot might be."

"His name, would you happen to remember his name?"

"Yes, he was Portuguese. It was Rodrigues, but I do not recall his Christian name."

"Thank you, Bohei Wong." She bowed. "You have helped a great deal in this. Do not speak of this meeting. I trust you understand it is a matter of national security and very sensitive."

"I am honored to be of service to you, Zhu Huang." He bowed in return and respectfully did not ask her which nation's security was at stake. "I hope your long trip here has not proved to be a disappointment to you."

~ ~ ~

At the hospital, Zhu inquired at the reception desk whether anyone spoke English. "I speak a little," the woman said.

"Good, I am here to find out about a patient named Angelo Rodrigues."

"I am sorry, but we can answer questions about patients only to people in the family."

"We are investigating the fire." She showed the woman an Interpol identification that she used with people who would not know what the real thing looked like or what it meant. "I need to talk with Mr. Rodrigues."

"Oh, but that would not be possible."

"Why not?"

"Because he is not here. He was discharged yesterday, in the company of some of your colleagues."

"Colleagues?"

"Yes, from Interpol."

Chapter 34

It was bitter cold, nearly dark, and after almost two days of trudging the wilds of northern Maine, Clinton had found nothing. He turned away from the frozen lake to skirt a fallen tree. As he trudged uphill, there was a brief flare of white, then yellow, through the trees. He stopped and held his breath, but now there was nothing. He took a step back, and there it was again, in a narrow gap between tree trunks: a light. He walked slowly forward on the unmarked trail up from the water, gradually turning his head to keep his eyes fixed on the same spot some distance away. Finally, through another somewhat wider break between trees, he saw it once more: two lights, flickering, seeming to float in space about chest high. Candles.

The snap of a twig underfoot was followed almost instantly by the double-slap of a pump-action 12-gauge shotgun being cocked. Clinton froze, his foot in the air as if he were about to step into a bear trap.

"If you want to keep your balls," a voice said, "you better turn tail and head right back down the path. This is posted property, and you are trespassing."

Clinton tried to place the direction of the voice, but the trees and uneven snow cover played tricks with the sound. He glanced from side to side without turning his head, but darkness was advancing over the forest like a fog rolling in, and Clinton could see no one.

"I'm looking for someone," he called out, still frozen in place.

"Well, no one by that name is here. Better look somewhere,"

—there was an audible intake of breath and a sharp sneeze—"somewhere else." A triplet of sneezes followed.

Something was oddly, impossibly familiar about the staccato sneezes. "Who's there?" he said. "Do I know you?" There was no reply. "I'm,"—he hesitated for a moment before using his real name—"It's Clinton Rodrigues."

"Are you alone?"

"Yes. I mean no. Someone is waiting for me in my car, back on the fire road."

"Rather fond of that name: someone. How do I know whether to believe you or not."

"I received a package. One of thirty-two identical packages mailed at the same time. Who else would know that?"

"Anyone who intercepted any of them would."

"Okay, fair enough. Mine had a scribbled note, written and then erased."

"Clinton? Is it really you?"

"For real. Would you shoot a former student?" He turned toward the sound of boots breaking the crust on the snow to his left. A small woman, with short-cropped corn-silk hair peeking beneath her knitted ski hat, smiled at him. She was dressed in jeans, Bean boots, and a blue fleece under an open red-plaid outer shirt. Clinton grinned back at her. "My, Mrs. Geller, don't you look the part of the Maine woodsman."

"You'd think it were the dead of winter the way you're dressed, Clinton. That California sunshine must have softened you some. You look like the Michelin man in all that puffy down outerwear. Come on up to the cabin and get some of those layers off before you start sweating and catch cold." She tugged at his arm and steered him to the left. "And try to stay on the trail instead of trudging cross-country like you've been doing. Tramples down the underbrush and leaves tracks that are too easy to follow. Step over that creek and come up this way. And watch your step. Getting too dark."

She marched on ahead of him, deftly sidestepping deadfalls and skirting large rocks as if she were using night-vision goggles. They reached the cabin and Clinton could see that the light he had spotted came from two candles on a table near a small window.

She noticed him looking. "Friday night, Shabbat. I never miss lighting the Sabbath candles, although I don't always bake challah. You're in luck tonight; I had two eggs and decided to use them and some of the flour. Only one loaf, though."

"You need more? Isn't one loaf enough?"

"Jewish tradition, two loaves, proof of plenty. Plus, then you don't bake again during Saturday." She reached around the rough-hewn door jamb and tugged at a hidden pull cord that lifted the latch. "Hurry on in. Don't let the heat out."

It was surprisingly warm in the cabin, a twelve-by-sixteen slope-roofed structure that looked like it had started as a lean-to hiking shelter before being closed in and weatherized. A green painted spindle-leg table and two matching chairs stood by the only window. Split logs burned in a field-stone fireplace on the opposite wall where a ladder led to a sleeping loft under the sharply angled peak of the roof. Along the wall to the left of the door was a shelf that held stacked jars of food, books, a pair of binoculars, and a microscope under a dust cover.

"I see you haven't lost the bug for biology," he said.

"I'm researching changes in insect pest populations with changing climate. Another five years and I should have enough data to publish. I'll pass it on covertly to someone who still has a name and a career. So, do you really have someone waiting in a car?"

"No. That was just a bluff."

"Good. It gets pretty damn cold up here at night. You'll have to wait until morning to hike back out. I have a spare sleeping bag. It's a little drafty on the floor, but you can curl up close to the fireplace. Well, not too close. Fire screen has a tear in it I haven't gotten around to fixing." She twisted one of the chairs out from the table. "Here, sit. First take off some of those layers or you're going to be sweating like a pig that just ran the Boston Marathon." She paused and looked at him expectantly. "What? Don't you remember anything from eighth-grade science? We covered this. Pigs don't sweat to cool off; they wallow in mud."

"Right, I don't remember much about eighth-grade science, but I do remember my amazing teacher."

"Whom you and your friends called Sneezy behind her back."

"At least you weren't called Grumpy like the shrunken Mr. Duff."

"He wasn't all that grumpy, maybe a little dyspeptic."

"Great choice of words, but that makes me think you actually have read some of my writing, because that's exactly how I referred to him in one of my essays: the dyspeptic Mr. D."

"Of course, I was plagiarizing you, testing you. I read everything you wrote. Why do you think I put you on my special mailing list."

"You know, don't you, that your packages didn't get delivered —except for mine—and they think you're dead."

She punched the air. "Yes! It worked."

"Well, I can see that you're not dead, but they identified the body. They actually got a DNA and partial fingerprint match from . . ."

She was holding up her left hand. The tip of her fourth finger was missing.

"Oh, wow, you did that? You really, like cut off . . . ? How could . . . ?"

"I'm a biologist. Had to do something that no one would imagine I would have done. No big deal. Didn't even hurt all that much until the next day."

"This is some story. You have to tell me everything. How in hell did you pull this whole thing off?"

"I'll tell you, but first hang up your things on the pegs by the door and sit down while I make tea. This is a celebration."

~ ~ ~

Clinton wrapped his hands around the mug with the broken handle and sipped. "The tea is really good. Is it Lapsang souchong? I think I detect just a hint of smokiness in the blend." He winked and nodded toward the fire.

"Okay, so I mostly use the fireplace for my cooking. I do have a propane camp stove, but packing in spare cylinders is a nuisance and then there's the problem of disposal. And please excuse the mug. I've had exactly one visitor since my untimely death, and that's you. I'm not used to entertaining and intend to keep it that way. Understood?"

"Understood. But please tell me how you did it. I get that you left behind the tip of your finger but ... I mean, there was a whole body burned, a superhot fire, like ..."

"Well, I got a little warning, and I had done my prep in advance. A clerk at the post office said there had been a stranger chatting with Hazel Shaeffer, so I guessed they would be coming after me next. There was aluminum powder and oxidizing compound—homemade thermite—under the body, with more on top to melt into it to destroy it from the inside also."

"But the body ..."

"I robbed a grave and covered the fact by knocking over gravestones. It was an old cemetery, pretty much abandoned. I knew it would be awhile before the vandalism was noted and figured no one would connect the two events. The body was going to end up cremated down to ashes anyway, so they wouldn't know it was old remains."

"The fingertip?"

"It was stuck in the mouth of a beer bottle packed in dry ice, which protected it and sublimed with the heat. No evidence to find. Same with the aluminum oxide from the thermite, which just wafted away with the smoke. Besides, like most mobile homes, mine was aluminum, so traces of metal or aluminum oxide wouldn't be an issue. Same for the bullets. My assassin stepped just inside the trailer, fired two shots to the head from a .22 caliber handgun with a suppressor. As he left, he smelled gas—methyl mercaptan, part of my plan—and got inspired. He loaded a tracer shell, got clear, and fired into the trailer. I triggered my little primer remotely, and the rest is history."

"It was just some random body in the bed—right?—under a blanket, I assume. How do you know exactly what happened?"

"Because I had an infrared Wi-Fi webcam that I was recording remotely. Another insurance policy."

"And you got out just before this guy arrived, towing your roll-aboard luggage."

She gave him an open-mouthed smile. "Oh, you are good."

"Well, I noted the tracks but didn't figure it all out until just now. So, you are dead. Everyone, including your enemies, is convinced you died in that fire."

"Exactly, and that's the only way I get to stay alive—by being dead. Now it's my turn. How did you track me down?"

"I was following the trail from your husband—late husband, sorry—and from the material in your packet figured you had his laptop, must have stashed it someplace. He inherited this parcel from, well, you know . . ."

"Jeannine, his lover. You don't have to tiptoe around things with me. I actually left him before those two connected."

"I see."

"Probably not, but that's not important. So you thought a little like I did, trying to figure someplace that was not really directly associated with me. So, here I am."

"But, living out here, alone—that must be hard."

"I do miss teaching, but otherwise it's not so bad. I'm a real biologist again, doing real science. That part I love. And I don't need much more. So, sit, relax, tell me about your life while I serve us a lovely Shabbat meal. It's been cooking all day: rabbit stew with *Daucus carota*. If you remember our unit on edible wild plants that's Queen Anne's Lace: wild carrots. I hope you don't keep kosher, though. It's just so hard to find a kosher butcher in these parts, and rabbit wouldn't qualify anyway."

Clinton laughed. "No, I don't keep kosher. I'm not even Jewish. Well, I'm half Jewish."

"Hey, half-Jewish is Jewish in my book. I never really practiced except for Shabbat. Everyone should have a day of no work, a time to just be alive in the world and appreciate it. The Jews invented the weekend, you know—isn't that something?—the punctuation in the grammar of daily life. Greatest invention in human history." She walked over to the shelf, picked up a plate covered with a polka-dot hand towel, and lifted it to her face. "Smell that?" She passed the plate under his nose. "Fresh bread. Life is good. I even have wine. Rosen was always a connoisseur of good wine. When he passed, his cellar went to me. It's now down in the cellar—the root cellar." She tapped a foot on the floor. "At the rate I drink, it should be enough for years."

~ ~ ~

The simple dinner and a bottle of an Argentine Malbec kept them talking for hours. At length, she reached across the table and took his hand. "What are you going to do next?"

"Publish the story, expose them."

"I tried that route. They are not going to let the story get published. Did you ever see that old Robert Redford movie, *Three Days of the Condor*? At the end, his character and this CIA guy, Higgins, are standing on the street outside the New York Times Building. One of the last lines, by Higgins, is something like 'How do you know they'll print it?' I can now see how this poison vine has it's tendrils into everything, everywhere. If you try to publish, they'll get you. They got Rosen, and they got me. Millicent Geller is dead. Now I'm just the crazy nameless bird-and-bug lady of the Maine backwoods."

"I'll find a way."

"I hope you do." She stood up still holding his hand. As he rose, she put her arms around his waist, and they stood, embracing, for long seconds. She rested her head on his chest. "I guess there are other things I miss bedsides teaching."

He looked down as she tipped up her face, lit by the light of the waning fire and the guttering candles, to give him a warm, almost embarrassed smile. "I'm sorry," she said. "Not much human contact."

He bent to kiss her. When they stopped, she caught her breath. "I don't think this is a good idea. No. You're very sweet, but—"

He put his finger on her lips and shook his head. "I had such a crush on you. Did you know that? I hated that there were these stupid rules and that I was just a kid to you."

"It happens, adolescent hormones, crushes on teachers. Kids outgrow it."

"Not all of them."

She kept shaking her head with short pulses of laughter. "You . . . but I'm feeling so, so old. I'm old enough to be your—"

His finger was on her lips again. "No, be still."

"Not my way, being still. Let's sit back down and talk."

~ ~ ~

In the morning, she insisted on hiking with him back to his car. She scoffed when she saw the fresh dents and scratches. "My, you sure are driving one beat up automobile."

"Wasn't that way a couple days ago, but it's a long story. I'm going to have to figure out what to tell the rental agency. Right now, I should get on the road."

"Remember: no one must know. You cannot tell anyone."

"I know. I know."

She stepped up and put her arms around him. "Thank you," she said, as she held him. "Thank you for spending Shabbat with me and for . . . for being understanding."

"Thank you, for sharing a very special evening. You know something funny? I'm still learning from you; you're still my teacher. I'll be going back home with some new insights."

"You're just saying that to make an old teacher-lady smile."

"Well, I do like that smile. I used to live for that bright spot in the dark days of my middle-school angst."

"And you had to mess up the moment by reminding me of your long-ago school days." She beamed up at him.

He kissed her forehead gently. "I'll be back, I promise."

"Don't make promises like that. I might not be here." She turned abruptly and started back up the trail from the fire road.

Chapter 35

Clinton tried to concentrate on driving, but his mind kept going back to the night with Millie. That was how he now thought of her: no longer as Millicent, certainly not as Mrs. Geller. It took nearly an hour of slow going on back roads before Clinton was in range of a cell tower. Minutes later, his phone tapped out a drum solo announcing the arrival of a delayed text from Sahana. He slowed and glanced at the short message: "Home sick. Call on burner. News 4 u."

There had been no traffic, but habitual caution kept Clinton driving until he found a wide spot in the road where it would be safer to pull over to call Sahana. "Hi, what's up?"

"I was working on your request."

"I hope you were careful."

"Der. Since I couldn't actually download the files, I tried shooting a video of my monitor with my smartphone, but it was terrible, so I started thinking about what you might be interested in. Among the videos I watched were some full-face close-ups of Atchison Dougherty and some of Bertrand Lyon. I freeze-framed on the faces and started comparing them. At first they looked quite different to me—different hair, face shape, mouth—then I noticed the eyes. Lyon has slightly darker eyes, but—get this—when I zoomed in on their left eyes, they both showed exactly the same irregularity in the iris: dark inclusions at 3 o'clock and 11 o'clock. I really think it's the same guy, maybe with contacts, a little plastic surgery, hair dye, that stuff. All in all, it makes him look younger by ten years or more."

"Great work!"

"That's not all. At home I did some online research into the background of our new CEO. Everything in his official bio checked out. I was a little suspicious, because every fact was linked to a page that confirmed the claim, almost like they wanted you to click through their prepared links rather than do independent research. So, I decided to verify his birth date on my own. Sure enough, I found his Canadian birth certificate through a genealogy site.

"But, get this, I thought some of the old news stories about him linked from his bio read like they had been written by public relations people. So, I got inspired and looked for them on the Internet Archives, the Wayback Machine. They're not all there. In other words, some were created recently with doctored dates, even in the metadata."

"Wow, that's huge."

"Yes, Bertrand Lyon, the supposed head of Biontolics, is a fiction. It's really Atchison Dougherty. And whoever he is, he has the resources and expertise to plant false documents in government databases and create a fake online presence. And why this charade? Because Atchison Dougherty should have been dead long ago. He would be a centenarian by now. Do either of the men you've seen in pictures or videos look like frail, hundred-year-olds? No."

"Hmmm." Clinton let it sink in. "There is another possibility. Dougherty might have been secretly replaced by someone else, someone much younger, who now styles himself as Bertrand Lyon."

"Doesn't wash with what you told me. No, these people have bioengineered what Ponce de Leon sought in Florida. They've stopped aging, and they are determined that nothing and no one will stop them."

"Then lay low, chill out, and finish your month at the lab without drawing any attention to yourself. I'll catch up with you in California after your move."

"Do I have to wait that long?" There was a sudden change in the tone of her voice to something between teasing and petulance. "I mean, you owe me now, not only for my sleuthing. It's also your turn to buy dinner."

"I don't know. Things have gotten a little complicated."

"Your so-called research assistant? No, wait, you called her—what?—your student intern."

"Not her. Not that sort of thing. I mean it's this story I'm working on."

"And I'm not working on it, too?"

"No, you're not. You need to get on with your new job and leave this to the pros."

"Ouch."

"I didn't mean it that way. Look, it's better if you forget this whole conversation and the stuff you uncovered."

"Okay, but we have to at least have a going-away dinner before I head west."

"I don't think that would be such a good idea. I'm trying to keep a low profile, not be seen too much in public."

"Then how about dinner at my place? I'm not quite as good a cook as my mother, but she thinks I'm not bad."

"I don't know . . ."

"Friday, my place, seven o'clock. It's a date, no argument."

"Well . . ."

"Great! See you then." She disconnected just as Clinton's phone started winking that its battery was low.

~ ~ ~

He was back in the motel room, stretched out on the couch recovering from the long drive, when the call came in. "I have some news." Julia's voice on the phone was brimming with suppressed excitement.

"Me, too, absolutely amazing news. But you go first. Mine may have to wait until you get back here."

"But I thought you were coming out here, to our home turf."

"Precisely why we shouldn't be hanging out around there. Sacramento is the first place they would look for us."

"But we're no longer us. We're Jana and Collin."

"It's temporary cover to let us get back to the States, not like actual witness protection, despite what my father said. And to really stay gone, we would have to leave behind all the places and people we know. Hanging around the same haunts with the same friends is one sure way to be found. But we can hash all that out later. What's your big news?"

A sharp sigh was just audible over the phone. "Okay. I went to the bank. It's a good thing I brought my backpack with me. I almost couldn't close the zipper."

"What all was in the safety deposit box?"

"Money, that's all. Nothing but dollars: over a hundred thousand in twenties and fifties. I don't think I ever expected to see so much cash in one pile in my life. We're rich."

"Well, I wouldn't call a hundred K rich, but it certainly would do as the down payment on a house. Wow. Not bad.'

"Now, what about your news."

Clinton resisted the impulse to blurt out anything about his discovery in the north woods. "Bertrand Lyon is really Atchison Dougherty. The same guy is still the head of Biontolics. He is actually over a hundred and doesn't look a day over fifty."

"How do we know this?"

"My contact at Biontolics analyzed some photos." There was a long silence over the phone. "Pretty neat, huh?" he said. "She was able to show the eyes are the same."

"Right, pretty neat, I guess. Look, I gotta go." There was another extended pause. "What should I do with the money? Open a bank account?"

"No! Absolutely not!"

"You don't have to yell at me."

"Sorry. Look, we can't deposit it. Large cash deposits are reported. We'd have to be able to explain where we got it. The feds would assume it was drug money."

"Well, that's what I'd assume, too."

"Yes, of course, which is why we will just have to hold onto it and only use a little at a time. We can split it up when I get out there."

"So, at least you still trust me."

"What's that supposed to mean?"

"Oh, whatever … just forget it. I'll figure out some place to stash it. You just go and have fun with your … your inside contact. Cheers." She disconnected.

Chapter 36

"Sir, this is Zhu Huang. I located Holzinger. He's dead. I located Rodrigues. He's gone." The voice on the phone barely hinted at the frustration Zhu was experiencing.

"That's not good, really not good." Lyon ran a hand through his hair. "What's our next move? Rodrigues and his girlfriend are high value targets."

"It was a different Rodrigues. This one was in the building with Holzinger. He was shot. Left the hospital in a wheelchair. I checked the airport. No recent wheelchair passengers on commercial flights, no medivac flights. He's here or he left by boat."

"You said it wasn't the right Rodrigues."

"Oh, it was the right Rodrigues, just not the one you were looking for. Someone, some organization with real resources, got to him first. They posed as Interpol and took him away under armed guard."

"Was he wanted by the government, some government?"

"Yes, but I doubt that was who took him. Others have an interest in him and his work. He owned the apartment building where Holzinger died. Burned. There was a drug lab."

"So . . . organized crime."

"Probably. I suggest we let him run. I have another angle. With your permission, I want to head for the Ipswich lab. The security breaches there were never resolved. I have a hunch."

"Okay, Zhu. Bring this business to the right conclusion and you can have Holzinger's old job."

"One job at a time, sir."

"Okay. And Zhu . . ."

"Yes?"

"Be careful."

~ ~ ~

For the rest of the week, Clinton's world was bounded by the motel and by his own circadian rhythm set adrift by time-zone transitions and tension. He took his once-a-day meals just as room service was closing down for the night and would awaken from a few hours' sleep when the maid knocked on the door in the morning. Five days of frenzied research and writing was fueled by coffee, cola, and barbecue chicken pizza.

Taking his cue from Sahana, he started systematically checking information about the heads of Biontolics by comparing current web pages against earlier versions and data recorded in the Internet Archives. In some cases, he was able to find multiple revisions of the same biographical tidbits that arranged themselves in a neat timeline of successive doctoring. He made dozens of quick phone calls to libraries, schools, newspapers, and professional associations to triangulate his findings and get quick quotes for use in an article. As the anomalies piled up, he began typing up his notes in the first draft of a five-part exposé: "Archivist Talia Brucher confirmed by telephone that records showed Llewellyn Andras Cass, M.D., had been Board Certified in Oncology in 1986, but a hardcopy of the *Directory of Medical Specialists in Massachusetts* dated 1980 listed L. Andras Cass as having been Board Certified in 1972. When asked about the conflicting information, Brucher said she would 'look into it'."

After a week of erratic hours, Clinton almost forgot his promise to Sahana to come for dinner on Friday. At the last minute, he realized he had no clean clothes. With the clock ticking, he sprinted to the shopping center up the road and bought a French-blue dress shirt and a pair of khakis at TJ Maxx. On the way back, he stopped at a package store and impulsively purchased an expensive bottle of a German auslese Riesling that he thought might do as an aperitif.

He was nearly an hour late when he pressed the buzzer outside Sahana's apartment. She greeted him at the door dressed in a red-print sari with gold-thread trim. "Please come in."

"I'm so sorry I'm late. I was trying to find the right way to wrap up an article and just lost track of time."

"It's not a problem. South Indians have their own sense of time, one that's not slaved to either the clock or the sun. Welcome to my place."

The apartment was spacious, furnished in a sophisticated blend of contemporary furniture with traditional Indian wall hangings and bric-a-brac that suggested Sahana had an artistic side to complement her scientific talent. Dinner started with an appetizer of small pancakes served with an assortment of chutneys and sauces. "These are *dosa*. Perhaps you remember them from that restaurant, only I'm using them as appetizers. They're not hard to make, but for the authentic version, like these, the batter has to be fermented."

Dinner stretched over a leisurely several hours of talk about trivia and transcendence, with Sahana serving a succession of Indian delicacies between disagreements over the risks and rewards of weak ethics in science and the state of investigative journalism in America. After a full week of pizza and Pringles, Clinton's taste buds were savoring the onslaught of spices. "How did you manage all this? You must've cooked for days."

"Not quite, but I did take today off. I've accrued a gazillion sick days and weeks of vacation time. Besides, things have gotten weird at work. They've hired a new woman in the Neuroscience Section, supposedly my replacement. She's Chinese, speaks English with a British accent, but if she has a doctorate in neuropsychology from Oxford, as she claimed, I'll eat my sheepskin from Stanford. She does a good job of faking it, but it doesn't all hang together. She's always hovering around me and Nina Bracken. Asks lots of questions, not all of which make sense from a scientist."

"Maybe she's not a scientist. This could be more snooping to follow up on your earlier brush with exposure."

"But I haven't done any more of that stuff at work. Besides, I'll be out of there soon enough. Look, can we not talk about that sort of stuff tonight?"

"Sure."

"Thanks." She reached over and refilled his wine glass. "And are you ready for desert?"

"Desert? I'm not sure I have room for—"

"It's non-fattening, I promise. Wait here." She slipped back into the kitchen with the last of their dishes. When she emerged a minute later, she was unwrapping her sari, just exposing a glistening mat of jet-black pubic hair. Clinton held his breath as she let the sari fall to the floor. She narrowed her eyes as she approached. "I think it's time we expand your understanding of the culture of India, starting with the meaning of the much misunderstood word *tantra*."

Chapter 37

Bright morning sunlight reflected off the water and rippled on the ceiling. Clinton stared at the light show above him and realized he had only slept a couple of hours. Beside him, Sahana lay, one brown leg bent atop a pillow and the other half wrapped in the silk sheet. The night had been a slow swirling blur that had seemed to stretch on like a wormhole through the dark.

Clinton attempted to slip from under the sheet and out of bed without disturbing her, but she stirred just as he stood and began searching for his clothes.

"They're in the living room," she said. "But don't go yet. It's Saturday morning; there's no hurry."

He gave her a cockeyed smile. "Not for you, maybe. You don't have to worry about pleasing your boss anymore. I, on the other hand, have work to do."

"And who is this boss who expects you to work weekends?"

"Immediate supervisor or top boss?"

"What?"

"Well, the former is a real taskmaster and the latter is the ultimate in guilt-trip manipulators."

"Who are you talking about?"

"Whom. Well, me, in the first instance: I'm a really tough taskmaster. And ultimately, it's all my mother's fault. She used six thousand years of Jewish perfection of the art of guilt tripping to inculcate me with a work ethic that never slacks off. I can hear her in my head even as I excuse myself to use your shower before I duck out of here."

"Well, we're going to have to do something about that over-inflated work ethic, mister. I'm a hard worker, too, but I don't bring it home with me. If we're going to make this relationship work, there will have to be some rules."

Clinton stopped in his tracks at the words "this relationship." "I ..." He reached for a response, then gave up searching for words. "I think I better take a shower and be going," he said, without turning around. "I really have a lot on my plate right now. Maybe some other time." He walked into the bathroom and closed the door behind him.

When he emerged, the bed was made, and his clothes were neatly laid out on the side closest to him.

~ ~ ~

Back at the motel, Clinton turned the room key and pushed the door open. It banged against the taut security chain. "What the ...?" He heard soft footsteps approaching, then the door slammed shut in his face. The chain rattled, and Julia opened the door halfway.

"Oh, it's you," she said.

"I thought you were in California. I ..."

"I was. I decided you were right. We should be staying clear of the home turf for a while. I took the red-eye from San Fran to Boston. I wanted to surprise you. Guess I did. Did you have a nice night?"

"I ..."

"That good, huh? She made quite an impression on you, I take it. Left you speechless."

"I don't know what to say."

"Not a good sign for a journalist in pursuit of a Pulitzer. You need to have some sound bites ready for awkward moments like this."

"I just wasn't expecting you."

"That much we've established. Anyway, I get the picture. After all, who am I to you? I'm just some kid who hitchhiked a ride on your breakthrough story, a college student with a dream who thinks . . ." She was fighting off tears. Clinton put his arms around her, and she hugged him for a moment before pushing him away. "Don't you goddamn patronize me."

"I wasn't, I was trying to—"

"And don't be sweet either. That's even worse. It just makes it all the harder for me to get over you." She turned away from him and growled into empty space. "Shut up, stupid little girl."

"You're not stupid, and you're no little girl. Sit down and talk for a minute."

"I don't want to talk. I feel betrayed: stupid and betrayed. I want to get on the next plane back to San Francisco. But I won't. I'll be a professional and finish this work with you. It's a job; we've a job to do. That's all." She was suddenly aware that he was still just behind her. When she pivoted into him, he embraced her again, this time resisting her half-hearted efforts to pull away.

"If you won't talk, I will," he said. "It's . . . it's more than a job, more than mentoring. We, you and I, . . . It's a total mismatch, completely impossible, maybe wrong, but I want to find out. Do you understand? You terrify me, but I don't want you to leave. I don't want you to go back to California—not without me."

"What are you saying?" She looked up at him, and he kissed her tears before giving her a slow but very chaste kiss.

"I'm saying I don't want to rush into anything that we might regret, but I'm willing to follow you."

"Why? Why now? Why this sudden, like, change of heart? What about your sexy scientist?"

"It's not what you think. Hell, it's not what she thinks. I wish I could explain, but I don't really understand it myself. In any case, it's over. For now, let's just say I've been learning a few things. In time, I'm sure we'll talk more, but for now let's leave it there. Okay?"

"Okay." She hugged him harder and put her head against his shoulder. "Maybe we both will have second thoughts later, but right now, right now I could stay like this forever."

"Forever will have to wait. We have work to do. Let me bring you up-to-date."

Zhu Huang sat in the empty offices in Ipswich as she finally finished going through the recent activity logs for all the workstations in the Neuroscience Section. The only discordant note was from Nina Braken. Late the previous Friday, Braken had spent a long time watching two all-hands videoconferences: one with Bertrand Lyon and one with his predecessor. The oddest thing was that, according to the badge-reader data, Nina Braken had left the building at noon and not returned that day. On the other hand, Sahana Patel had exited shortly after the videos were viewed and Nina Braken's account had been logged out. Zhu switched to the human resources system to retrieve Patel's home address. There was a note on the file scheduling an exit interview the following week. She was leaving Biontolics.

Zhu considered paying a home visit over the weekend or sitting in on the exit interview. Time was not on her side, but if she moved too quickly or aggressively, it could frighten her target. She thought for a moment, then updated the HR record to move the exit interview up to Monday.

~ ~ ~

Clinton and Julia spent the rest of the weekend holed up with take-out food, motel coffee, and their research and writing. Julia kept arguing that Clinton's approach was doomed, that he was writing an article that could never be published.

"I have to write it. I have to get the whole story down. There must be somebody I can send it to who will act on it. Once I finish, I can send it off to everybody on my contact list. Maybe

Millie's mistake was using snail-mail to deliver paper copies; I could send it all by email."

"Look, those people were able to infiltrate the US Postal Service. What says they haven't penetrated Yahoo or Google or whoever provides your email? Hell, maybe they have access to everything the NSA vacuums up."

"That's Star Wars thinking; this is the real world. They can't be everywhere and track everything." Even as he said it so emphatically, he was thinking of what happened with Millie. "In any case, we need to move fast, finish the story with all the documentation, and figure out how to get it out there. We don't need all your negative attitude."

"My negative attitude? Who flew the red-eye from SFO to get back here to help you while you were banging that Indian super-scientist."

"Oh, we're back on that, are we? I thought I made it clear: it's going nowhere."

"You didn't make anything clear." Each word was louder than the last. "And you're still keeping me at a distance."

"Distance? What do you want: a fuck? I told you—"

"No, I don't want a fuck. From you, I don't want anything. It was a mistake coming back. You're right. It's all wrong. I don't know what got into my head that you were something special. You..."

He was standing by the door, his hand on the knob, shaking. "What is it with us? The same thing happened last night: a big blow-up after midnight, one or both of us reduced to tears, you stomping off to the bedroom while I go fetal on the couch."

"Isn't it pretty obvious?"

"No, not to me."

"Is it men who are so clueless or, like, just older people like you?'

He smiled and wiped at his eyes. "I've got a double handicap. Are you going to enlighten this clueless older male or not?"

She stood across the room, clearly uncertain whether to be the first to say it.

"Okay," he said, "I'll go first. I think I'm falling in love with you. No, wait, I don't think it; I am. No, that's not quite it either. Rewrite: I'm not falling; I've already fallen. There, I said it. And that's what scares me, because we are skating on the edge of the void here, and the thought of anything happening to you is unbearable."

She stared back at him, not moving, tears welling up and spilling over her cheeks. "I love you, Clinton, and I want you. And the thought of anything happening to you is unbearable. But, we're in this together. Look, if you're not ready for more, could we just sleep together tonight. I mean just sleep, just hold each other, because I've always been this tough street kid and now you're in my life and I'm so scared." Her shoulders shook as she broke into sobs.

"Me, too. Yes. We're both tired. Let's go to bed."

~ ~ ~

It was after ten in the morning when they were awakened by the ring of Clinton's burner phone. Half-asleep, Clinton padded out of the bedroom to find his backpack and fish around for the phone. "Hello?"

"It's me. They moved my exit interview up to this morning. The Chinese woman was there with lots of questions, not about neuroscience either. She asked if I knew a Clinton Rodrigues. I told her I didn't recognize the name. She asked me again at the end of the interview when she stood and blocked the doorway as I was about to leave."

"Where are you now?"

"At work, sitting on a bench out behind the main building."

"Hang up, go back to work, and play it straight for the rest of the day. Is there anyone you can stay with for a while? I mean besides me."

"Betsy Whitman, maybe. She's an old friend, works down the road from here."

"Okay. Figure out how to do it without drawing too much attention, but get to her. Lay low until I contact you."

"But . . ."

"Good luck." He thumbed the phone off.

"What was that all about?" Julia called from the bedroom.

"A wakeup call. We gotta move." He entered the bedroom. Julia was sitting up against the headboard, naked. He stared at her, mouth open, stunned.

"What?" she said.

"My god, you are beautiful."

"You're not so bad yourself."

He looked down and realized he was naked. "Did we . . ."

"No, too tired, but it was damn delicious waking up with your leg over mine. It's not too late to do something about our poor performance last night." She made a point of looking down at his growing erection.

"Not now, we gotta move, and I do mean move. Get dressed, pack up all your stuff. I'm going to get rid of the car and report it stolen, then we're going to get a new one. When I get back, we'll check out. Be ready to go." He hurriedly dressed and left with the car keys.

When he returned more than an hour later, Julia was sitting on the couch, typing on her laptop. "You ready?" he said. "We have to go over to the rental place and file a report."

"What did you do with the car?"

"Drove it to another mall, one of the big ones off 128, left it in a deserted back corner of a lot where I crashed it up against a lamppost. Teenage joy riders, obviously. Also explains the dents and scratches. Then I hiked back. What have you been doing?"

"Worrying about you, taking care of some loose ends out West, worrying about you. Oh, did I mention worrying about you?"

He gave her a hand up from the couch. "Me too. Let's check out of here and get a cab to the rental place. We'll keep the replacement car for a couple of days, then switch to another company—try to throw the dogs off the scent."

"What about the police?"

"We'll go all, 'oh, we were so upset we didn't think of that' and tell the rental people we'll take care of it, like, right away."

"You know, we could get in trouble for this."

"Tell me something I don't know. Hey, we're running for our lives until we get this story out. Even then, I don't know."

She gave him a long, deep kiss. "When we check in at the new place, the first thing we do is hit the bedroom. Understood? I don't want to, like, you know, well . . . without first, you know . . ."

"You are something else, but . . . let's get there first."

~ ~ ~

It was Julia's idea to drive back to the same area after getting the new car. They took a room in a second-rate strip motel on the other side of the divided highway. "See, this way we can keep an eye out for police or caravans of black limos or whatever across the way. That way we'll have some warning."

"That is, if we spend our time watching out the front window." He pulled the curtain back enough to peek out.

"Later. Now we're going to spend our time checking out the mattress in this dump." She took his hand and pulled him toward the bed.

Chapter 39

Despite an uncharacteristic sense of panic that periodically swept over her like a rogue wave, Sahana managed to play-act through the rest of the day. When she left early, she pulled out of the Biontolics driveway, headed for town, and then turned toward her apartment, checking behind her frequently. At her building, she parked in the front lot, went up to her apartment, and hurriedly changed into jeans and a sweater-jacket. She tied her hair back in a tight bun and used a cleansing pad to remove the bindi from her forehead. To finish the transformation, she put on a head scarf and a pair of blue-reflective sunglasses. Checking herself in the mirror by the door, she judged the look to be cliché but effective.

In the parking garage beneath the building, she hopped into her silver Mazda Miata, pressed the door opener on her key-chain, and gunned the low convertible through under the still rising overhead door. Reaching the town center, she shot past Argilla Road and took the long way around via route 133. As she turned off the highway, her anxiety rose—she would still have to drive past the lab. At the last moment, she realized she better call to confirm that Betsy was still working at the Crane Estate.

"Wow, Sahana, this is unexpected. Here we work not five minutes apart, and we hardly ever see each other. What's happening?"

"Oh, you know, the usual stuff. I thought we could catch up over dinner, which is why I called. It was a long shot but . . ."

"You mean tonight?"

"Yeah. Is that possible?"

"I don't know, it's pretty short notice. My partner and I usually eat takeout on Mondays: Chinese."

"Well, I love Chinese. I know it's pretty presumptuous of me to suggest it, but you don't suppose I could invite myself to join you. I mean, if . . ."

"You're right, it's pretty damn presumptuous. But, hey, what are friends for, right? Let me call Chris and see if that's okay. I'll call you right back."

Five minutes later, as Sahana was approaching the turnoff for Castle Hill, her phone rang. She answered on hands-free.

"It's me, Betsy. Chris says sure. Do you know our address in Essex?"

"No, but look, I'm right here, you know, just down the road. Why don't I pull in there, and then I could follow you."

"Well, okay, I suppose. Just come up to the main building and ask Elliot at the entrance to point you to my office."

Sahana negotiated the long winding driveway up the hill and pulled into the gravel parking lot nearest the hilltop building. The imposing brick mansion had once been the summer residence of the wealthy Crane family from Chicago. Now the estate and the adjacent beach were administered by the Massachusetts Trustees of Reservations, and Betsy worked for them as an event planner for the property, managing private parties, Christmas craft fairs, and open-air summer concerts.

Betsy was waiting in the hallway with a warm, dimpled smile. "It's been a while, but you haven't changed a bit, Sahana."

"Neither have you. You're looking great."

"Right, still prematurely gray. Did I ever tell you how much I hated that my mother wouldn't let me dye it. I was so embarrassed, but by the time I was in college, I was used to it this way and never did get around to coloring it. But, lucky me, Chris loves my hair. You'll love her, too: big, warm, sweet. She gives my life direction; she's my true north. Oh, where are my manners? Would you like a tour of the place before we head out? Or have you been here before? From the balcony up on the rooftop, the view down the *grande allée* toward the water is just breathtaking."

"No, that's okay. I got the grand tour right after you started working here and invited all your old friends from high school to one of those summer concerts."

"Oh, right. I forgot. The whole gang was here." Beneath her permed gray hair, her round, baby-smooth face broke into an incongruously lopsided grin. "Well, then, shall we go?"

"Can I ask another favor?"

"One's not enough, huh? Well, shoot."

"Could I leave my car here and ride with you?"

Betsy was suddenly serious. "This is not about some random impulse to reconnect with an old friend from high school, is it? You're in some kind of a pickle, right?"

"Yeah, some kind."

"Okay, girl. You don't have to tell me more, at least not now. The look on your face says it all. Big mama Chris and little mama Betsy will take care of you. We got plenty of room. You can stay with us tonight, and I'll bring you back for your car when I drive back tomorrow. Let me grab a temporary parking sticker so you don't get towed overnight."

"Thanks, I don't know what to say."

"Then don't say anything. Instead, you can pay for the moo shu chicken and spring rolls tonight." Her laugh was big and loud.

~ ~ ~

Allowing for the time difference, Zhu decided to leave a voice mail for her boss even though their history made her hesitant to depart from protocol. "I've talked with our scientist-spy from the Ipswich lab. She played innocent, but was unconvincing. I'm all but certain Rodrigues is here in the area, and this woman is going to lead me to him. I'm on it and will finish the job within the next few days. I'll let you know when I have news."

Zhu sat in her car down the road from the apartment building where there was a clear view of the parking lot. Sahana's car was where she had left it, and she had not re-emerged. There was only the one road off the point and back toward town, so Zhu could relocate every so often to avoid suspicion and be ready to tail the woman whenever she left.

Sahana's cellphone was being monitored by the little box on Zhu's dashboard. The blue box was a sophisticated device that pretended to be a cell tower and could be programmed for a variety of tasks. At the moment, it was set to connect only with a specific nearby phone that was programmed into it. Zhu had read the identification off the cellphone while Sahana had left for the ladies' room at work. Now, the device listened for calls in the approaching endgame.

It was nearly ten o'clock when Zhu was suddenly blinded by a spotlight in her eyes followed shortly by sharp raps on her window. She fingered the button to lower it and looked up into a woman's face, the face of an Ipswich police officer, her blond hair neatly tucked under her cap. "Is there a problem, constable?" Zhu said.

"A resident in the neighborhood reported that a car she didn't recognize had been stopped here for several hours." The officer bent low to survey the interior of the car. "Is there a reason you're still sitting here?"

'Not particularly, officer. I was fatigued, pulled over, and fell asleep. I'm sorry. I didn't realize this was a restricted zone."

"Can I see your license and registration, please."

Zhu fumbled around in her jacket "Here. It's a British permit. The hire car agent said it was acceptable here. I don't know about the registration, since this is a hire car. Do you want to see the contract?"

"Yes, I need to see the rental agreement. And your passport please."

Zhu pretended to be flustered and confused as she first rifled through the door pocket, then opened the glove compartment. "Ah, here's the contract." She handed it through the window. "Oh, and here's my passport."

"Please remain in your car and keep your hands in full view. I'll be back." The officer left for her patrol car with the documents. It was nearly ten minutes before she returned. "I need you to step out of your car, please."

"Why? Is something wrong?"

"I need you to step out of the car." The officer took several steps back and moved her hand toward the holster at her hip.

Zhu assessed the situation and considered whether to draw her own firearm, to make a run for it, or to cooperate. She opened the door slowly, and got out of the car.

"Have you had anything to drink tonight?"

"Yes. I have a bottle of Evian in the car."

"Evian?"

"Mineral water."

"Oh. I'm going to ask you to do several things. Please follow my finger with your eyes without moving your head. Okay, now I need you to walk heel-to-toe in a straight line for nine steps away from me, then turn on one foot and return the same way. Is that clear?"

"Yes, officer." Zhu imagined herself as once again a young girl on the balance beam. She marched away, spun smartly, and returned.

"Now, I want you to stand on your left foot, raise your right foot six inches off the ground, and hold that position while you count aloud slowly to thirty."

"How many centimeters is that?"

"What?"

"Inches. We don't use them anymore. What is it, now, like fifteen centimeters?"

"The height of a Coke can, ma'am. I don't know it in centimeters."

"There. How's that?" She stood statue-still as she began to count. "I can raise it higher if you would like."

"No, that won't be necessary. Here are your license, contract, and passport. You can return to your car, but you can't remain stopped here. Please move on to your destination."

"Of course. Thank you, officer. Have a pleasant evening."

Zhu did not wait for the patrol car to depart to start her car. She was angry at herself for not thinking in terms of small-town New England rather than big city Europe. She drove to the end of the road and made a three-point turn. She gave a polite salute to the policewoman as she passed, being careful to keep her speed down until she was well away. Once back through the center of town, she turned onto Argilla Road and sped toward the Lab. She figured it was better to drop the tail than risk another interruption by local police. She could pick up the track in the morning when the subject arrived at work. In the meantime, she could catch a few hours of sleep stretched out on the couch in the reception area at the Lab.

~ ~ ~

The arrival of the day-shift guard awakened Zhu. After using the toilet, she returned to her car where she connected a cable from the blue box into her laptop and reviewed the overnight logs that were uploaded. Nothing.

Always methodical, Zhu used the downtime to review files and check that all her equipment was in order. She was just returning her Beretta to her cross-draw holster when the LED on the blue box winked at her and her laptop screen brightened. She looked around and checked her rearview mirror. No one had entered the rear parking lot. She started the car and drove around to the small visitors' parking area at the front. It was still deserted.

She got out to walk around the building on the outside chance somebody had approached on foot. Through the trees, she heard the sound of a small sports car being worked through the gears as it raced past on Argilla Road. Zhu trotted to her car, spun her tires on the gravel as she reversed, then sped down the twisting driveway. A Miata was disappearing around the far curve as Zhu fishtailed out onto the road. As she accelerated down the road, the blue box blinked again, indicating that it had reacquired the signal from the cell phone.

Zhu slowed to keep from overtaking the car. The box on her dash flashed yellow, indicating an attempt to place a call. The box itself scanned for the nearest legitimate tower and passed on the request, keeping itself in the middle of the link, decrypting and recording the call in real time. Zhu punched up the volume on her laptop speakers as the caller waited for an answer.

The voice on the phone was tinny through the small speakers on the computer. "Yes, hello?"

"Mom, it's me. I'm sorry for calling so early."

"I was awake. Your father is snoring beside me. You should be sorry that you never call your parents, not that you call so early." The voice on the line had the distinctly voiced consonants of the Indian sub-continent.

"I'm sorry, Mom. Much is happening. Did you hear? I got a new job. With a high-tech startup in San Francisco."

"And where would I hear that you got a new job, if not from you? Who could tell me that? Would the airlines call me and tell me? 'Oh, Mrs. Patel, your daughter is flying to California for her new job.' No, I don't think so."

"Mom, it hasn't been that long since we last talked. I asked you for that recipe just, like, last week."

"You asked me by email; you asked for a recipe. That is not calling and talking."

"Look, I'm sorry, Mom. I'll try to call you more often."

"From San Francisco you'll call?"

"Well, that's what I'm calling about. When do you and Dad head south?"

"The same time as always. Your father and I never leave before Thanksgiving. We've been leaving for Florida for the winter the week after Thanksgiving every year for the last seventeen. Why do you ask? Do you want to visit your poor mother and father?"

"Yes, I want to visit you, but that's not why I'm asking. If it's all right with you, I'd like to stay in the condo for a few weeks. Is that okay?"

"You're in Florida? I thought you were in California."

"Not yet, Mom. I'm taking a little break before starting the new job."

"In Florida? There's nothing but old people down there. You need to be meeting people your own age. You're not getting any younger . . . or prettier."

"Thanks loads, Mom. Look, just don't start."

"You know, you should have let us arrange a marriage for you while you were still, well, you know . . . of the best age. But, no, you had to be modern and get your degrees first. We should have had a son. Is our unmarried daughter who is moving away going to help us when we are old?"

"Thanks, Mom, for your support and approval. I remember the one match you tried to push me into. Even back then, I made more than that orthodontist you picked. What a . . ."

"He was a third cousin and everyone considered him to be a good match. He—"

"Mother, he was a little boy with little-boy fantasies about sex and marriage, an absolute weirdo. But, please, just for once can we not talk about the fact that I'm not married? I'll get married when I'm ready and when I find the right man."

"Are you seeing anybody?"

"Mom!"

"A mother can ask, can't she?"

"Yes, you certainly can, Mom, like pretty much every time we talk."

"Which is very seldom."

"Mom, just tell me if I can stay in the condo for a while."

"Of course, dear. Oh, your father is waking up. I'll have to tell him the terrible news. He'll be heartbroken."

"What are you talking about, Mom? I'm just borrowing your condo."

"No, I mean that you're leaving us to pursue some fantasy in—what is it called?—Silicon Valley."

"It's San Francisco, and it's not a fantasy, and tell Dad I love him."

"You can tell him yourself, since your call woke him up. Here he is."

The voice was grainy with sleep and two octaves lower. "*Namaste.* How is my favorite daughter? And what is this about terrible news?"

"Your favorite daughter is still your only daughter, and the news is not terrible. I'm moving to San Francisco to take a job with a startup doing brain-training apps."

"Oh, that's wonderful news. Brain training. That's good. Be sure you get some equity in your package. Are they giving you stock options?"

"Yes, they're giving me options, Dad. You taught me well."

"That's my girl. Send email as soon as you settle in."

"I will."

"Look, do you want to say goodbye to your mother? She's right here."

"No, you do it for me. Love you."

"Me, too. bye."

The light on Zhu's blue box winked out as she braked to keep from coming too close to the silver convertible. As she did, she saw the driver put a cellphone to her ear. The indicator on the blue box flashed yellow, then red. It was not a phone for which the box was programmed to intercept, but there was a way to override the programming and grab the signal anyway. Zhu reached toward the laptop on the passenger seat and tried to position the mouse pointer over the correct button. The car bounced as the right wheel left the road. Zhu looked up and spun the wheel to the left but not fast enough to avoid the tree. The car bucked and swung to the side, the airbag exploded in Zhu's face, and the engine died.

The Miata was already out of sight, making the turn off Argilla Road.

Chapter 40

Sahana was finishing her yoghurt and granola in the kitchen just as Betsy Whitman barged through the door from the garage carrying two suitcases. "I think I got everything you asked for from your apartment." She set the luggage down in front of Sahana. "Here are your keys back. The suitcases weren't quite big enough for everything, so there's still some loose stuff in the backseat of the car. You can borrow my old backpack to take up the slack. You should be good. Where did you say you were headed?"

"I didn't. It's better you don't know."

"We're talking serious paranoia here, you know. I wish you could tell me what this is about."

"I told you last night."

"Well, yes, you did. Three or four sentences worth about how you were helping some reporter with a big story. I get it that you're in some kind of danger but not why?"

"I'm trying to be smart—and to protect you and Chris. You were both so sweet to take me in like that."

"Hey, we needed somebody to pay for the Chinese takeout. You just happened to come along at the right time." She winked broadly. "And you're sure you want to leave that cute little car with us?"

"I'll get a rental when I land. You might as well enjoy it— small compensation for your help."

"Look, is there anything else I can do for you before I go back to work?"

"No, not really. I'll be gone by the time you get home tonight. Thanks again."

"Don't mention it. We enjoyed seeing you. Be careful, now. I hope you know what you're doing."

"I don't know what I'm doing, but I'll try to be careful."

~ ~ ~

Zhu watched as the wrecker pulled away with her rental car in tow. It had taken some fast talking to convince the police officer who arrived on the scene that it was not a simple single-car accident. She finally talked the policeman out of issuing a ticket by her story of swerving to avoid a dog crossing the road and her convincing picture of an adorable mutt scampering off. A traffic ticket would not have been a disaster but certainly would have complicated her task.

Fortunately, she had stashed her computer, the blue box, and her Beretta in her duffle before anyone showed up. A quick swap of identity would distance her from the messy situation long enough for her to finish the job here and get back to London. The next step was clear. Just before the crash, the box and her computer had gotten enough data to identify the phone being called from the Miata. Once her replacement car arrived, she would head back to the Lab and use the system to call the phone and locate it. Sahana Patel was not her ultimate target; Sahana could wait.

~ ~ ~

Clinton was annoyed. His burner phone was ringing, and he had told Sahana not to call it again. He picked it up and looked at it. He didn't recognize the number. Second time this morning, best to ignore it, let it go to voicemail, he thought. Then the ringing stopped. He was unsure about what to do, but if the phone was compromised, it would be better to dump it and start with a fresh one.

Julia was just returning with groceries when Clinton came back from the dumpster behind the motel. "What's up?" she said, as he held the door for her.

"Something odd with my burner phone. Just to be on the safe side, I destroyed the SIM card, wiped the phone, and dumped it out back. How are you doing? You were up late last night."

"Follow-up on some more leads, working California time, you know. How close are you to wrapping up your work?"

"Pretty close, first final draft, anyway. I'll have to stay away from it for a bit so I can go back to edit it with fresh eyes."

"Hey, what about me? I could review and edit it for you."

Clinton looked to one side and frowned. "That's odd. I hadn't thought of that. I guess I still think of you as the student, I as the teacher."

"Me as the teacher," she corrected. "Object, not subject."

"Ohmagod. You're starting to sound like me. Now you're correcting *my* grammar."

"Hey, I learned from the master." She smiled and kissed him. "Let's put away these groceries, brew some more coffee, and get to work."

~ ~ ~

The morning and early afternoon passed with Julia working away on the draft and Clinton trying to look over her shoulder. "Cut that out. I'm almost finished here," she said. "You can read through my edits when I'm done."

There was a knock on the door. Clinton gave Julia a questioning look. She shook her head, shrugged, and went back to her work. He sidled up to the door and peeked through the security viewer. A tall woman stood outside holding a tray covered with a napkin. "What is it?" he said through the door.

He could see her lips move, but he couldn't hear her answer. "What is it? What do you want? I can't hear you." Again, the woman seemed to be answering but he couldn't hear. He slid the security chain into its channel and opened the door the two inches the chain allowed. "Yes? What do you want?"

"Room service."

"We didn't order room service, you have the wrong room."

"This is room 122? You are Mr. Rodrigues?"

"But," he answered without thinking, "we didn't order—"

The chain was ripped from the wall as the door was kicked open and the woman entered with a drawn handgun. "Compliments of the manager, Mr. Rodrigues." She shoved the empty tray at him as she kicked the door closed behind her. Julia quickly tapped the Enter key on her laptop, closed it part way, and pushed it aside.

~ ~ ~

Traffic was chockablock at the airport. Sahana fished in her wallet for an extra twenty as the cabbie unloaded her luggage from the trunk. He took the money, eyed the bills, and said, "Do you need change?"

"No, that's for you. Thanks."

"Thank you, miss. You have a good flight."

As the taxi pulled away, she stood at the curb watching, wondering whether she was doing the right thing. Was she running away? If she was, what was she running away from? The Biontolics cabal? Clinton Rodrigues? Men in general? Life in general? She could hear her mother's voice in her head, exhorting her to be careful—and to find a husband. It was her father who always believed in her as a scientist, but it was her father who seldom had more than a paragraph of conversation with her before he would pass the phone to his wife.

What would be the purpose of hanging around except to put herself in more danger? And what was the point? Clinton had obviously made his choice. He clearly preferred his cute little student. It was the story of her life. Maybe her mother had been right. She should have gotten married, had a baby, then gone back to school.

"You okay, miss?"

Sahana looked up to find a state trooper standing in front of her in his calf-high boots and Smokey-the-Bear hat. "I . . ."

"Can I help?" It was a professional courtesy, but there was also a look of concern on his face, as if he actually wanted to be of help.

"No, not really. I'm just thinking about getting a cab."

"Taxis can't pick up at this level. You'll have to take the escalator down to arrivals. You'll see the line down there."

"Thanks, I'll do that." She picked up her suitcases and headed into the terminal. As she approached the down escalator, she was already shifting mental gears, strategizing her next move. What could she do? She was smart enough, but she was a scientist, not some kind of clandestine operative. She knew the barest outline of the story, but now that she had been exposed at Biontolics, there was nothing more she could do there. Clinton and his student were obviously way ahead of her. She had to admit, she had none of their drive to become a knight errant out to expose evil. What she wanted to do was survive, to get some armor against becoming herself a victim of Biontolics. She figured she would need something on them, something to hold over their heads against their coming after her.

She stood at the top of the escalator, looking out through the wall of glass at the skyline of downtown Boston, with the towers of the financial district reflecting beams of sunlight her way. She had an idea.

~ ~ ~

Zhu looked over the documents spread out on the bed in the motel room. "False identities. You were registered under fake names. That's why I had to describe you to the motel clerk. And,"—she held up their new passports—"these must be what was in the package delivered to you in Madeira. How clever of you and lucky for me. It should make it all the easier for you two to disappear without a trace. An investigation will show that you left the country for Busanyu but never returned. It will become apparent that something happened to you in Africa. How tragic. People can so easily get lost or vanish in these small, unstable African countries. Now we just have to make sure you disappear completely—and soon."

She had them empty their pockets. Both surrendered their smartphones. "You're going to have to hang out a little longer here while I work out some arrangements." She had them sit down on the two kitchen-style chairs and put their hands behind them. She used zip ties to fasten their wrists and ankles to the chairs, then taped their mouths. "I'll be back later. Don't get into trouble while I'm gone."

Chapter 41

Sahana waited in the reception area of Enventia Capital, rehearsing her story.

"Mr. Templeman will see you now." The slim receptionist bent over her like an anglepoise desk lamp. "Just follow me; I'll show you in."

Felix Templeman had never been particularly handsome, but now he had the good looks that money and a surplus of time could acquire. His dark, naturally wavy hair looked as if it had just been razor cut that morning, his orthodontist-perfect teeth gleamed in his smile, and his skin had the warm glow of a recent Caribbean vacation. He buttoned the jacket of his custom-tailored double-breasted suit as he rose and came around from behind a desk that could have served as a banquet table for eight. "What a surprise. I couldn't believe it when Tonia said who was here. You are looking good, Sahana."

"Thanks. I just came from the airport, so I'm a little more disheveled than usual."

"Well, the word disheveled would never have occurred to me. You look great to me."

"Thanks again." She glanced around the office. "And you seem to be doing rather well."

"I've been lucky. I keep picking the right numbers on the roulette wheel of new ventures, I guess. I understand you've done all right for yourself, too, with a PhD in neuroscience and a position at Biontolics. I'd love to get a piece of Biontolics or a company like it, but it's closely held, and they make it hard to see exactly what they are up to. I don't suppose you could enlighten me."

"Maybe I could. Maybe you could enlighten me."

"Now this is beginning to sound interesting, almost as if this were not some random visit."

"It's not. Just how good are your financial research skills, Felix? I mean, can you really get the real scoop on companies you might be interested in?"

"My skills? Well, they're not bad, but I have an amazing staff that does the real leg work. They put together the research and then I sniff the report. I have a nose for what makes sense and what doesn't."

"Have you ever taken a whiff of the Biontolics empire?"

"Well, as I said, they're a closely held corporation, and they do not seem to lack for capital. So, no, other than casual curiosity, I haven't spent a lot of time looking into them. Should I have?"

"Maybe. If a big privately held company like Biontolics were to suddenly find itself in deep trouble, what would be the consequences? Would there be ripple effects on other companies?"

"If the company is big enough and critical enough, a collapse or crisis could trigger tsunamis in the financial markets. Look what happened after Volkswagen got caught cheating on emissions. Think of what would happen if, say, the Koch brothers empire went south. Everything is connected to everything else in the global economy."

"Would it be worthwhile to a venture capital firm to know if some such company were, shall we say, at risk for being compromised?"

"Whoa, there. I do hope we're not talking about insider trading."

"Biontolics stock isn't traded, and this information doesn't need to come from inside. I'm talking about what your brilliant staff could do on their own."

"This is starting to sound really, really heavy. Are you sure you want to continue?"

"I don't know. I'm trying to figure that out right now. Other than the fact that we shared the platform at graduation from Newburyport High, we don't really know each other."

"And I always regretted that."

"Really?"

"Really. But my parents kept me on a tight leash during high school. I didn't get to date a shicksa until I got away to college. Of course, I did end up marrying a nice Jewish girl I met at Wharton. It pleased my parents and hers, but it was a mistake."

"So, you're . . . ?"

"Divorced. Happily so. No kids. And we had a prenup—at her insistence, by the way. She was so self-deluded, convinced she was going to be a billionaire. So here I am: not quite a billionaire but on the path." He spread his arms.

"I see. But look, as you quickly concluded, I'm here for a reason, and I'm still trying to figure out whether I can trust you."

"Fair enough. So let me earn your trust: first by showing you what I've been doing with Enventia and second by taking you to dinner. Then after dinner, if you don't trust me, I'll put you in a cab and wave goodbye. If you decide you do trust me, we can come back here to start some research wheels rolling before we go for a nightcap. How does that sound?"

"It sounds like you move pretty fast."

"I do. It's one of the secrets of my success. I don't dither or delay over decisions. If I find myself wavering or temporizing, then I know that whatever it is, it's a no-go. Consider yourself warned. By the end of dinner, I'll know whether I can trust you and whether I can let you trust me. So, permit me to start by telling you about our investments in solar, hydroponics, environmental remediation—a fancy term for cleaning up chemical disasters—and genomics." He tapped at an iPad on his desk and a wall-size display sprang into life with the opening slide of a PowerPoint deck.

The maître d' at the restaurant recognized Felix and greeted him by name. "A private table, Mr. Templeman? But of course. We're fully booked for the evening, but I am sure I can get Luigi to prepare a table for you in the wine cellar, and you can have the place to yourselves. The usual?"

'Yes, that would be splendid."

"Excellent, I'll alert the staff. They'll be delighted. If you care to have a seat in the bar, I'll get everything ready for you, *subito*."

Sahana smiled at Felix as they slipped into their seats in the small bar tucked into a corner. "Very impressive. I take it you're a regular here?"

"Now and then. But they know me. I helped finance Montero when he started Firenze Sempre. Now he owns three restaurants and three homes, a sort of domestic parity."

"And the usual? What is that?"

"Oh, you're in for a treat, a succession of small plates and perfect Italian wine pairings to enjoy while we get acquainted. Or reacquainted. What did you think of this afternoon's corporate tour."

"Very corporate. I always wonder about the reality behind slick slogans and polished PowerPoint."

"Yes, I noticed that. You are a skeptic and have a knack for asking the right questions, usually rather pointed ones."

"I hope I wasn't too aggressive. I know I can be off-putting at times."

"On the contrary, I rather liked that. I trust you found my answers direct enough."

"And then some, though I would like to hear more about—"

She was interrupted by the arrival of the maître d'. "Your table is ready, Mr. Templeman. Please follow me."

~ ~ ~

After spending the afternoon finalizing arrangements, Zhu Huang returned to the motel. When she unlocked the room and turned on the lights, she found her prisoners on the floor, still strapped to their toppled chairs. "Just in time, I see. What did you think you could do, squirm your way out of here? You want to leave, do you? Okay, that can be arranged. First we'll separate you from those chairs and cuff you again. Then let's go for a ride."

The small boat bobbed in the swells of a wind-driven incoming tide. Clinton knew from the sounds that they were at a pier in some harbor. They had been blindfolded during a car ride that had taken what seemed like hours, with two unexplained stops along the way. Given the time, they could be anywhere between Portland and Providence, but some instinct told Clinton that they were actually somewhere on the North Shore, Cape Ann, maybe even Gloucester. There was something familiar about the pattern of turns they had made near the end of the ride.

The edges of the zip-tie around his wrists were cutting into his skin. The smells of fish and diesel were heavy in the air. Suddenly, the incessant seagull cries were submerged in the rattling of the boat's engine being started. It coughed and sputtered before settling into a deep throated rumble. They moved slowly at first, but after some minutes, the pitch of the engine rose sharply and Clinton could feel the pounding as they sped over an increasing chop.

He lay on his side on the floor, leaving just enough room for Julia with her back to the wall and her knees doubled up. She had been still, but once the boat was up to speed, he could feel her moving against him. Suddenly, his blindfold was yanked off, and he blinked in the dim light of a cabin below deck. The tape over his mouth was suddenly and painfully ripped away. "What the . . ."

"Sshh. Keep it down, sport," she said.

"How did you get loose?" he whispered.

"Brains. A trick from the street, you twist and flex your wrists when the zip-tie is put on, gives you enough slack to later slip out. At least that's the idea." She held up her bloody left hand. "Sometimes you leave a little something behind."

"Are you all right?"

"Not yet, not until we get out of here, and not by the route our Chinese lady has planned. Turn over."

"What are you going to do?"

"Cut your zip-tie. Unless you want to do as I did and end up scraping off half your hand."

"How are you going to cut anything?"

"With the edge of this drawer handle I just acquired. Try to keep your wrists out of the way. This is going to take a while."

Many minutes and several bloody nicks later, Clinton was able to snap the last narrow strand of plastic and free his arms. "Wow, you are pretty clever.'

"What have I been telling you?"

"What next, oh clever one?"

"There's two on board: China-girl and some guy. I heard them talking. It'll take one of them to handle the boat, so we only have to deal with them one at a time, starting with whoever comes down here."

"And how do we get *whomever* to come down here?"

"Just follow me." She tried the handle of the cabin door; it turned. "I had guessed she didn't lock it, probably didn't see the need, what with us tied up. Look, you get over there, in the shadows, just behind that ladder thingy coming down. I'll make a racket, and you find something to use to bean *whomever* climbs down."

Clinton looked around and spotted a fire extinguisher on the wall. He pulled it from its bracket and flattened himself up against the bulkhead beside the ladder.

Julia used the drawer handle to bang on some pipes running along the side, but the light clanking was drowned out by the throb of the engine and the slap of waves as the boat raced out to sea. She rummaged around in cabinets along the side until she found a set of tools. She grabbed a heavy pipe wrench and raised it to bang on the pipes again, but Clinton stopped her. "We don't want to break anything connected to anything important. This is our transportation back, too, you know."

She looked around, shrugged, and took a swing at the ceiling. She kept hammering away until she had smashed a hole in the wood overhead. There was no response. She picked a spot closer to the bow and started hammering out a pattern of thuds that Clinton recognized as a crude SOS.

As the hatch above was lifted, Clinton signaled her to stop. A man wearing a sailor's watch cap peered down through the opening. Topside was almost as dark as below deck, but the man was silhouetted against the retreating sky glow from on shore. As he waved a handgun back and forth as if it were a flashlight, Julia pulled back toward the bow as far as she could. He hesitated for a moment, then started to lower himself down the ladder. Just short of the bottom, he spotted Julia and brought his gun up. Clinton came out from behind and swung the bottom of the fire extinguisher against the man's side, causing him to drop the gun. He turned and caught Clinton's second swing in the side of his face. He pitched forward and sprawled on the deck.

Julia held out the wrench to Clinton. "Here, better than that thing." She knelt and picked up the gun, checked to make sure the safety was off, and waved Clinton up the ladder. She climbed up behind him, squatted beside the open hatch, and pointed toward the bow where the Chinese woman was at the helm. As Clinton started forward in a running crouch, the man's grizzled head emerged from the hatch. "Huang," he shouted, "look out!"

Julia swung her foot around, slamming his head against the side of the hatch. He tumbled down the ladder and thudded onto the deck below.

Clinton was nearly to the wheelhouse, when Zhu Huang turned and fired at him. As Clinton fell, Julia took aim. The pitch and roll of the boat threw her off, and the shot went wild, slamming into the controls beside Zhu. With one hand on the wheel, Zhu turned the other direction to fire at Julia. Julia dropped to the deck and flattened herself. With a two-handed grip on the pistol, she pressed her wrists against a fitting on the boat and fired, emptying the magazine in a steady pulse of paired shots. Zhu slumped, clinging to the wheel as she dropped to the deck, sending the boat into a wide arc.

"Get to the controls!" Julia yelled at Clinton.

Clinton swayed as he tried to stand. He staggered the rest of the way to the wheelhouse and pulled himself up the several steps. He shouldered the woman's body aside, grabbed the wheel, sussed out the controls, and pulled back on what he guessed was the throttle. The boat pitched forward, slowed, and chugged at a crawl through the water.

Julia climbed up beside him. "Is she dead? Did I get her?"

"Looks like it. Also looks like you killed a lot more than just our kidnapper." He swept his hand toward the control panel, which was decorated with broken glass and bullet holes. "We don't know where we are, and I don't think we're going to find out. I'm guessing this is the radio. Well, if it was the radio, it looks dead now."

"Do you think we can use a phone out here?"

"We're probably out of range from any cell tower. Besides, who has a phone?"

"I do." She smirked. "Maybe she does, too."

"You have a phone? But she took ours away."

"Not the little burner phone I had tucked in my underwear. She patted us down, but not very good."

"Not very *well*."

"Oh, for God's sake. Just can it, at least until we're back in civilization. Which is where?" She turned in a half circle.

"West. If we can figure out where west is. The compass seems to be among the victims of the slaughter."

"Der. Which way do you see the sky still faintly glowing after sunset? What we don't know is where we would reach shore if we sail toward the receding sun. It's already pretty dark, and even us California girls have heard about the rock-bound coast of New England."

"Well, what about that phone of yours?"

She flipped it open and looked down at it. "Nothing, no bars. We're too far out."

"See if our kung-fu kidnapper has a phone."

Julia finally found a phone in a pocket of the woman's vest. A bullet had smashed through one corner. Julia pressed buttons and tapped the screen. "It's dead, like literally dead."

"Okay," he said. "I've an idea. We head slowly back, roughly westward, until we do get a signal on your phone. Then we call the Coast Guard."

"And the number of the Coast Guard is . . . ?"

"9-1-1. At least that's a start."

Clinton slowly brought the bow of the boat around until it pointed toward the last faint glow on the horizon. "Okay, we're going to take it slow. You keep checking for a cell signal."

They were underway for only a few minutes when the engine slowed, coughed, and finally died. Clinton figured out which button was the starter, but the engine stubbornly refused to turn over. Without the generator, the main lights had cut out, and they were left with only emergency battery lighting.

"We're adrift, in the dark, in an area crisscrossed with ship-ping lanes, and . . ."

"Thanks for the cheery pep talk." She gave him a sour-face look. "For real, what are we going to do?"

"See if we can find flashlights or maybe battery powered lights below."

"Like, in the dark, we're supposed to find these?"

"Do your best, I'll keep trying to start the engine."

~ ~ ~

Julia emerged from below with a hand lantern she had found, and Clinton had figured out where the emergency flares were stowed in the wheelhouse. "We need to save these until another boat comes near. Keep listening."

As the last glow of dusk left the sky, they sat huddled to-gether in the partial shelter of the wheelhouse as a cold wind picked up. Clinton studied the overcast sky, searching for a break through which he might spot some familiar constellation, but the cloud cover was solid.

"Look, Julia, you go below out of the wind, see if you can find something to keep warm. I'll keep watch up here."

"Don't pull that macho crap on me, mister. We're in this together. You can have first watch, one hour, but then we switch. Okay?"

"Okay."

"If . . . if we don't . . ."

"Just get below. We're going to be fine. None of that if-we-don't shit."

"Okay. Come get me in an hour."

~ ~ ~

Clinton let an hour go by as the wind continued to pick up. He was about to go below when Julia emerged from the hatch wearing a heavy man's jacket. He recognized it as the one worn by the assailant they had dispatched. As she came up beside Clinton, she pointed astern. "Are those lights? And look at the sky; it's noticeably lighter, like sky glow from a city."

"You're right. The wind must be coming from the east. It's blowing us toward shore."

"That's good."

"Or not. Remember what you said about the rocky coastline in New England."

"Well, then let's hope we can reach the Coast Guard before we reach the coast."

Ever so slowly, the lights along the horizon were becoming more distinct and separate as the breeze stiffened. Suddenly, Julia started bouncing. "I got a signal. It's one bar. Should I try it?"

"Go for it."

Julia started entering a number.

"What are you doing? That's more than three digits. 9-1-1. That's all you need. Who are you calling?"

"Just in case we don't make it, I've another call I need to do first. Be quiet; it's ringing." She listened. "Answer, damn it."

"Hullo?"

"This is Chandrise."

"You mean . . . ?"

"Yes, Roger, it's a go. Just do it."

"Right. Are you okay?"

"Just do it. Now." She disconnected and looked over at Clinton.

"What was that all about?"

"Insurance. Now, let's try the Coast Guard."

~ ~ ~

At first, the operator did not believe her, but eventually Julia convinced the man to patch her through to the Coast Guard.

"So where are you, ma'am? Please tell me your coordinates."

"I don't know. The navigation equipment is . . . well, dead."

'Do you have GPS on your phone?"

"Nope. It's a cheapie."

"Well, if you're calling us by a cellphone, you can't be too far off the coast, but there's a lot of coastline in New England. You really have no idea where you are?"

"Not a clue."

"Can you see anything around you?"

"Yeah, we can see lights on the horizon. Like, one of them seems to be blinking on and off very slowly."

"Okay, that's good. It could be a lighthouse or an airport beacon. What else can you see?"

"Well, a little to the left of the blinking light is a pretty bright blob of light."

"How far to the left? Like on a clock face."

"Well, we're still pointing roughly to where the sun set, I think, sort of west, so the blinking light is like eleven o'clock and the bright blob is maybe ten-thirty. Does that help?"

'It does, because we just heard from Verizon with the identity and location of the cell tower that you are linked through. Do you have running lights on?"

"Er, no. Clinton, can you turn on some lights?" Clinton tried a number of switches. "Oh, there. Now we have lights. At least while the batteries last."

"Okay, sit still. We have a rough idea where you are. We're sending a cutter to search for you."

~ ~ ~

They were on the Coast Guard cutter headed back to shore and into police custody when Clinton leaned over toward Julia and asked in a soft voice what her first phone call had been about.

"You'll find out soon enough if it worked. If not, we're dead."

Chapter 43

As Roger Belknap finished the final edits on his blog post, the smartphone on his desk vibrated. It was a text message with one word—"Yo!"—the last of the confirmations from his team. Operation Chandrise was cocked and ready. Thirteen students were now poised at their keyboards, waiting for his signal. It was a scattershot exercise in which near simultaneity was essential. His tweet would be their shot heard 'round the world, triggering the first wave. A second wave, powered by sock puppets, would follow in ten minutes, then hundreds more reinforcements at random intervals over the following hour. Each of the team would be recruiting others on the fly to multiply the effort. If one medium or channel didn't succeed, there were others. His favorite was a hilarious video from two film-school students: "The International Geriatric Beach Volleyball Tournament." Nothing like California girls in bikinis to spice up YouTube. It had a shot at going viral. He started laughing just thinking of it.

Roger was both anxious and relieved to have gotten the go ahead. He wasn't sure how much longer he could have kept everybody in check without a leak. He switched over to Twitter, pasted the preplanned text, and clicked to send it off. "Game on!" he said to his sleeping roommate.

~ ~ ~

Sahana and Felix were finishing dessert accompanied by a small glass of Brachetto when he put the question to her. "Are you ready to trust me with what this is really about?"

"Is that fair after all this wine?" She blinked hard.

"If you're the person I think you are, you already made the decision by the time the first appetizers arrived."

"Before."

"Me, too. In fact, before we left the office, I had already asked a crack team in my London office to start working overtime on Biontolics. I just got a text message that said they were already finding interesting things: interesting being a code word for details that couldn't be shared over open communications. I'm going to fly over tonight, want to tag along?"

"Slow down. You are exceeding the speed limit here."

"Business, I'm just moving at the speed of business."

She looked at her watch. "I had no idea it was this late. I didn't think there were any flights out at this hour."

"There aren't. I have my own jet. Well, it's actually a time-shared Gulfstream—makes more economic sense—but we can be ready to take off in an hour or so. What do you say? You told me you just came from the airport, and you had my receptionist stash your bags, so what's to stop you?"

"Nothing. Let's do it."

Chapter 44

Ferguson's helicopter wobbled in the urban crosswinds before settling down on the helipad atop the Sellian Atlantic Building in London. Despite the unseemly early hour, the plaza below was already crowded with the media and the curious. Overhead, a SkyNews chopper circled. Hustled into the building by his security team, Ferguson was greeted inside by a tall man, as gray as the polished granite of the building façade. "Morning, sir, I'm Kevin Wellbern, Acting Head of Security. I'll brief you on the way down."

"Are the others here?"

"Dr. Mandelova is already waiting in the ninth floor conference room; Mr. Quarry is on videoconference from America. I'm afraid Dr. Lyon is still in hospital."

"Not good. Make sure security is upped at the clinic."

"Already taken care of, sir. I've had the facilities cordoned off, barricades are in place, and we've created a pretense to close the lane at either end."

"Excellent. Now, what the hell is going on?"

"It's a social media blitz. The Information Technology team has been working with us, but we haven't identified the original sources yet. That can take a very long time. It appears that a number of near-simultaneous postings, largely from America, were responsible, starting sometime between midnight and one GMT. It had to have been an orchestrated attack by numerous agents through a wide variety of channels: YouTube and Vimeo videos, posts on Twitter and Tumblr as well as several smaller and more specialized networks, pictures via Instagram and photo sharing sites, and posts and comments on Reddit and elsewhere. The topics were trending within an hour and went viral before dawn here. Our MediaTrax system detected the trend on references to Biontolics shortly before things went viral, and the tech team triggered takedown orders, but the curves were running against us. By the time IT people alerted us, some posts had been retweeted sixty thousand times."

"What are they saying that spreads that fast."

"You'll see in the briefing, but one of the YouTube videos is built from newspaper file photos and other sources. It has face shots of Douglas Atchison Doherty slowly morphing over time, eventually becoming Bertrand Lyon. Underneath, claimed chronological age is displayed. It finishes with a question: How many centuries will this man live? Then it gives the Biontolics main telephone number and Dr. Lyon's company email address. The telephone lines were jammed within hours and our email servers had to be taken down. The main hashtags on Twitter have been #AgelessBiontolics and #FontOfYouth. The most retweets are for a message with an animated GIF. The animation shows side-by-side headshots of Dr. Doherty and Dr. Lyon with their birthdates. The animation zooms in on the left eyes, which are seen to be identical. The text below says: 'Just how old is the #AgelessBiontolics CEO? Has #Biontolics found #FontOfYouth?' There are others, including links to stories about that African dictator and hints of criminal activity."

"Is Twitter cooperating to stifle this?"

"They were until the live social media like SnapChat picked it up. Live broadcasts are much harder to take down because by the time we know about them, the sources are done. Then the American authorities stepped in. It seems that not long after the social media blitz started, an extensive exposé was posted on half a dozen somewhat obscure blogs. Unfortunately, by the time our people tried to remove the articles, they had already been re-blogged in hundreds of places. Huffington, Wired, Daily Dot, The Register here, and dozens of online publications are already doing their own stories with links to copies of the original blog on their own servers."

Ferguson stared ahead and didn't move as the doors of the lift opened. Prudence Tanner was waiting and handed him a thick folder before leading the way into the conference room. "Coffee and tea are on the credenza along with bangers, toast, whatever you like. I'll leave you to it." She turned to leave.

"Prudence, I think you should stay. I want somebody to take notes and handle things as they come up."

"Of course." She took a seat away from the conference table and opened an old-fashioned steno pad.

Ferguson nodded to Ysabel Mandelova and gave Xander Quarry's image on the videoconference screen a tip of an imaginary hat as he seated himself. "Okay, what do you two think."

Ysabel pursed her lips but said nothing; Xander arched his eyebrows. "If you have to ask," he said, "then you don't know what is happening ... has happened. We're fucked. The party's over."

Ysabel turned toward the videoconference screen and let her sour face express her disapproval to the camera.

"What's that for, Ysabel? You don't like my saying it or the way I said it?"

"I think you're wrong. It will take some time and resources, but we'll get this under control again. We've squelched things before."

"You have your head up your fucking corn hole, Ysabel. This time it's everywhere. I don't think you understand how the digital world works. The whole goddamn world knows all about us.

It's Pandora's fucking box. Once it's out there in cyberspace, it's out there forever."

"Let me guess, your daughter is away from the ranch."

"She is. Why?"

"Just noting your language is suddenly saltier. She doesn't tolerate you using the F-bomb."

Xander snorted out of the corner of his mouth. "I'll fuckin' F-bomb as much as I like. Those kids, those students here in sunny California, absolutely gazumped us. They screwed us six ways from Sunday, them and their goddamn teacher."

Ferguson leaned forward. "I thought we didn't know who did this. Our head of security—what the hell is his name, Prudence?"

"Wellbern, Kevin Wellbern."

"Right. Well, he said the original source ... sources had not been identified."

Xander looked heavenward and shook his hands. "You're not fully awake, yet, Chas. They identified themselves. Hell, this Rodrigues chap has his byline right at the top of a 25,000-word article. There's another, shorter piece, from one Hidalgo Spinoza e Laredo in, of all fucking places, Busanyu. And the student network that handled the media campaign have claimed responsibility. This one kid, Roger Belknap, is already an Internet celeb, and it's still the middle of the night here.

"Un-be-fucking-lievable. A group of kids, undergrads from Sacramento State, journalism students, takes down one of the most powerful, secretive companies in history. They had an advance copy of the Rodrigues piece and did more footwork on their own. They put together this multimedia, multichannel campaign with graphics and videos and the works, then sprung it all at once all over the place. Some of it is pretty slick."

He laughed. "One of the videos to go viral is a fake ad for Biontolics. It starts with a wide shot of this wrinkled old crone partially silhouetted as she's walking naked along a beach. As the camera slowly dollies in, she gets younger and younger. The camera finishes with a head-and-shoulders shot, and she's this beautiful twenty-something. She turns toward the camera and whispers: 'Thank you, Biontolics.' Then there's a telephone number and an email address. Because of the nudity, YouTube took it down, but not before it got downloaded, duplicated, remixed, and spread all over the Internet. It didn't hurt that they picked some real hard-body goddess for the close-ups."

Ferguson swiveled in his chair. "Prudence, get Media Relations to set up a press conference for this afternoon. Between now and then, no one is authorized to speak to the media, and any questions are to be met with 'no comment.' Understood?"

Xander was laughing onscreen. "What the fuck are you going to say in a press conference?"

"I don't know. That's what we pay people for. In the meantime, we all just say 'no comment' and leave it at that."

Ysabel sighed. "You know, this could drag out for years, with parliamentary inquiries, congressional hearings, special prosecutors, God knows who or what. It's over. You think you're going to be able to keep up treatments for members of The Club with this going on? We're dead, quite literally."

Prudence touched the Bluetooth earpiece in her right ear. "Excuse me for interrupting, but there's word from the clinic. Dr. Lyon wants to speak with you. Shall I route the call through the conference phone?"

"Yes, do that." Over the speakerphone in the middle of the table came a buzz and a click and then the sound of medical monitors beeping in the background. Ferguson unmuted the mic on the speakerphone. "Hello, Bertrand. Are you there?"

"Mostly." The voice was weak and hoarse. "I just wanted to tell you that the singularity is real. It's just not the . . ." A fit of coughing and spitting lasted several seconds, and the voices of conferring medical staff could be heard in the background. "It's not the one I expected. Should have. We all face it: the ultimate singularity. And you were right, it comes sooner than we expect or wish."

"Look, Bertrand, we'll pull you through this somehow. We have the best medical people on the planet."

"That may be, but I'm done here. I don't want to go out like Edgar or Rosen, dissolving into a stew of my own tissue and fluids. I'm grateful parliament finally passed the Compassionate Termination Act. I'm all set. All I have to do is have them start the drip. I just wanted to say my farewells and acknowledge my failures first. I don't know what I should have or could have done different, but I do know I went down the wrong road."

"Maybe not, Bertrand. Ysabel thinks we might still be able to stuff the djinn back in the bottle."

"Ysabel, dear Ysabel. She is a dour optimist with never a good word or idea but an eternal faith that things will somehow work out. They will not."

Ysabel opened her mouth to speak but Ferguson gave her a cautionary shake of the head as more coughing came over the speakerphone.

"It's time, Andras, old friend. Your turn will come soon enough. Llewellyn Andras Cass will follow Atchison Douglas Dougherty down the discontinuity. The staff here will brief you on the situation—two other members of The Club are already here, nearly as far down the slope as I—but I have neither the energy nor the time." There was a pause filled with several audible breaths. "Start the drip, please."

"Douglas!"

"The one true singularity, but it's private and personal, and we . . ." The voice faded and trailed off.

"Douglas?" There was no answer. A steady chirp in the background turned into a long, steady tone, then silence as a monitor was turned off.

"This is Dr. Phradip, acting Head of Service here at the clinic. I have just pronounced Dr. Dougherty . . . I mean Dr. Lyon, dead. We should schedule a consultation in person at your earliest. Please excuse me now, as we have other patients in need of attention."

Chapter 45

By the time Felix and Sahana landed at London City Airport, the Biontolics story was monopolizing the news. "Orange juice for you?" Felix asked, once they were settled into the waiting limo. He handed her a glass from the bar. "I hope you don't mind me channel surfing on the way into the city, but it's obvious the big surf is up and I want to catch the wave."

"I don't mind. I'm just as interested as you are. I guess the question of going public or not is academic now."

"We may have some flotsam to add to the waves. We'll meet with my London team after breakfast and strategize our next moves, but I don't think either of our lives are on the line over this any longer. Your reporter friend and his crew have blown things wide open. After this drubbing, I don't think Biontolics will have room to sneeze, much less pursue ex-employees."

"You're probably right."

"This is life, not statistics, sweetie; no probably about it." He thumb-typed another message on his iPhone.

"What are you up to?"

"Giving some marching orders to my private investment team, making sure we're ready to take advantage of some volatility in big pharma and life extension. Their stocks will take a hit, then slowly rebound. We'll buy at the bottom and then move out when enthusiasm is highest just before new government regs and reality set in. Hop aboard, Sahana. We're on track for an exciting ride."

"You think so?":

"Oh, I know so. The train is leaving the station, and I'm the engineer."

"This looks more like a limousine than a train. Do you always talk in management-speak metaphors?"

"Pretty much, yes. Yes, I do. Sorry. But hey, looks can be deceiving. Don't you feel the rockin' rhythm of steel wheels on steel rails?" He pantomimed lightly bouncing to a steady clickety-clack. "Wait a minute. Did you see that text crawl on the news? Somebody from Biontolics just died. Turn up the sound."

They listened to the news flash about Bertrand Lyon dying at a private hospital outside London. "Lyon was the CEO of Biontolics Holdings, a corporate conglomerate now under siege after revelations of irregularities and secret longevity treatments. Speaking off the record, because she was not authorized to address the public, a source at the clinic said the man's symptoms resembled those of the late Dr. Edgar Jabari Mbutsu, President-for-Life of the African nation of Busanyu. Unsubstantiated allegations posted anonymously on the Internet have claimed that Mbutsu had also been receiving treatment from medical personnel associated with Biontolics. The clinic, a research facility known to locals as Saint Sophia's because it had once been a teaching hospital, is owned by Sellian Atlantic, yet another part of the Biontolics empire.

"Now we switch to a live report from our affiliate, KOCA TV in Oakland, California. Reporter Sabrina Sadler is at the famed Quarry Ranch south of San Francisco where flamboyant billionaire Xander Quarry has called a surprise middle-of-the-night press conference. Xander Quarry has also been linked with the Biontolics firestorm that has swept through the Internet in recent hours. Bring us up-to-date, Sabrina."

"Yes. One-time playboy Xander Quarry, who has been implicated in the Internet imbroglio you mentioned, is said to be ready to confirm the allegations regarding Biontolics. A spokesperson for the London-based corporate giant has declined to comment except to say that Mr. Quarry is not authorized to speak for the company. As you can see behind me here at the luxurious Quarry Ranch, swarms of reporters and news crews are waiting for Mr. Quarry to appear. Ah, there he is now, looking uncharacteristically dapper in a suit and tie."

The camera panned away from the reporter and zoomed in on a grinning Xander Quarry standing with his arm around his daughter. He began without waiting for the buzz to die down. "Ladies and gentleman. My remarks will be brief, but I will take questions. My name is Alexander Roman Quarry, and this is my daughter, Nadia. She's here for moral support—and she knows how much my morals need support—and because she is soon to take over Quarry Industries. For the past forty-plus years, I have been an underwriter of the enterprise that came to be known as Biontolics Holdings International. Biontolics has kept me and a select group of people alive—and young—through an elaborate intervention scheme that its principals devised. God-awful expensive treatments, I should add. They have kept the technology to themselves for their select inner circle of mostly obscenely rich bastards like me.

"Well, if you've been following the news feeds or turned on cable in recent hours, you know that Biontolics is going down the toilet, which means all the turds with it." He looked down. "You can't see it, but Nadia just crushed my right instep. She doesn't approve of my coarse language, but in this case I think she's being a bit prudish, since I could have said that all the shits like me are going down, too.'

"Whatever bullshit denials the company may make, I can confirm, in essence, most of what has been circulating on the Internet. To my old friends Douglas Dougherty and Andras

Cass, I offer my apologies for joining in blowing the whistle, but there already was a flag on the play. And for those of you reporters who believe that journalism is more than just holding a mic and smiling into a camera, I can provide documentation from my own records to support all the allegations, including the work of paid assassins." He held up a neatly bound folder. "My people have hastily prepared a press kit that will be made available to all of you who made the trek out here in the middle of the night to help an old man, a very old man, come clean. Thank you."

The strafing of shouted questions from reporters began almost instantly.

Chapter 46

A light drizzle rattled on the roof of the car, and the air was heavy with the smell of moss, mud, and melting snow. Clinton opened the car door for Julia. "There's somebody I want you to meet."

"And we had to drive all the way to Canada to meet this someone?" She looked around. "There's nothing but dead trees and ugly rocks around here."

"We're not in Canada, at least not quite. I just hope I can retrace my steps. Otherwise, we're in for a very long meandering hike in the woods. Ah, here it is, I think. We go up this way, past that boulder."

"Which boulder? There's nothing but boulders all around. Are you now some sort of Boy Scout?"

He looked back at her and laughed. "Just follow me, and stay close."

As it turned out, he missed the shelter and ended up at a spring. He was about to head back downhill and start over again from the fire road when the sound of a shotgun being cocked behind them got his attention.

"My oh my, you two. I thought Clinton here was a noisy city kid, but together you are a regular traveling troupe of circus monkeys."

"Millie." He spun around with a wide smile.

"Clinton. And who is this you dragged into the woods with you?"

"This is Julia."

"Just Julia, no last name. Okay then, 'significant' Julia, we can surmise."

Julia turned and looked down at the shotgun. "Is this how you welcome friends?"

"Up here, it is. At least for people like me. I'm the no-name backwoods bug-and-bird lady. Now, that is. I use to be Millicent Geller, but she died in a fire in Falmouth in the fall."

"Wait a minute. You're Millicent Geller? You're the teacher who was killed."

"That's what I just said."

"But you're not dead."

"Apparently."

"So, you, like, faked it."

"Like."

Julia shook her head repeatedly. "You're as bad as Clinton."

"Or as good."

Julia threw her arms up in surrender as she looked from Millie to Clinton. "I love her. But I see where you picked up some of your annoying tics."

Millie put on a look of exaggerated puzzlement. "Annoying? Tics? What are you talking about? In any case, how about coming in for some hot tea before we all get soaked."

Millie led the way down a meandering path to her tiny cabin. Once inside, she apologized. "Only got the two chairs. You take them. While I get the kettle boiling, you can tell me what brings you to these parts."

"News, we're bringing news."

"I can't say there's much news that would interest me. I hear a little now and then when I hike into town for supplies, but what I hear is never that good."

"This is good. Biontolics bought it. The whole business is exposed; there are indictments here, in the UK, Switzerland; the

CEO is dead, and the last time their head doctor was seen, he wasn't looking too good, either."

"And you call this good news? People dying, empires crumbling, humanity's hopes of immortality crushed? Doesn't sound very positive to me."

"But it means you can go home."

"I am home."

"I meant . . ."

"I know what you meant, but I'm content. Come summer, maybe I'll do some science programs for some of the farm kids, keep up my teaching chops. My research is going well. I have food and firewood. What else do I need?"

Clinton opened his mouth to speak but said nothing. Millie looked back at him as if to reaffirm his silence.

Julia filled the awkward gap. "You're a biologist. You might find it interesting what's going on with the Biontolics patients."

"I might."

"Basically, they were hoisted by their own petard. Their treatments meant that the genetic makeup of each patient kept getting more complicated and less manageable as the number of cell lines was multiplied."

Millie raised an index finger. "Let me guess. It's about the epigenetic effects of different cell lines each becoming part of the cellular environment of the other lines, everything impacting everything else in completely unpredictable ways. That's it, right? Particularly with regard to the oncogene expression that Janella Kai first found to be key in cell longevity."

"Yeah, at least that's sort of how I understand it, but I'm no scientist and not a doctor. Eventually, the treatments stop working, and there's no going back. This is one the scientists will be studying for decades, but I don't think there are going to be any more human subjects, not for a very long time. Biontolics is arguing that they have to continue treatments already underway or the patients will die the way your husband did. The news today said two of these people have committed suicide rather than face that."

"Oh, goody. More good news."

Julia lowered her head. "I'm sorry."

"Don't be. You succeeded where both Rosen and I failed. You brought this thing out into the daylight."

"Clinton and I did it, but you started it. If it weren't for the Millicent factor, we would never even have known the story."

"Can I ask a favor of you, Julia? I'm going to steal Clinton to help me bring some water back from the spring. Would you keep your eye on that kettle and use the poker to lift it away from the fire when it boils? Grab those buckets, Clinton, and let's hustle through the rain."

"Do you want me to make the tea once the water boils?" Julia asked.

"Sure. Pot's on the top shelf, tea's in the cupboard, tea ball is in the drawer . . . someplace. You'll find it. We'll be back."

Once outside, she took Clinton by the arm and steered him up the trail toward the spring. "Is this serious?" She nodded back toward the cabin.

"I guess so. Yeah, maybe."

"Real definitive, aren't you?"

"Yes, it's serious, but, well, she's my student . . . was . . . and she's, you know, a lot younger, and . . . ."

"Those issues didn't seem so important to you last time you were here."

Clinton's ears started burning and his face flushed red. "I . . . I'm sorry . . . I . . ."

"Oh, Clinton, don't make too much of it, and don't be too hard on yourself. It was a lovely evening. You got to revisit a fantasy, and I got to feel flattered and young again. That was that." She brushed back the hood of her rain jacket. "Rain's letting up. In the old days this would have been another six inches of snow, but mid-winter rain is becoming more and more common. Okay, here we are. Let me show you how to fill the buckets without stirring up all the sediment at the bottom."

They filled the buckets and started back down the trail, with Clinton struggling not to slosh the water out. Between quiet curses, he restarted the conversation. "This whole one-on-one thing is hard for me. It's always been hard for me."

"You're a man. Males grow up more slowly."

"Do you think it matters, this age thing, the difference?"

"What do you think?"

"I don't have much experience to draw on. It hasn't been that long."

"What about a twenty-year crush on an older woman? Does it matter?"

"That's different. I mean does it matter in, well, marriage?"

"I don't know. It's real, but whether it matters, well, that depends on what matters to you. One thing that the biology part means is that you'll probably die before she does, maybe long before, since you belong to the biologically inferior sex. If you stay together, you'll both need to face that reality. It's a promise, not a guarantee, and Nature does not always keep its promises, but that's how things generally work. In some senses, you will also always be ahead of her. You already know what it's like to turn thirty; she's not there yet. On the other hand, you will never know what it's like to carry and give birth to a child, while that option is open to her. Probably."

"You and Dr. David never . . ."

"No, we didn't have children. I can't. But then again, I've helped raise a lot of kids. Look, whatever lies ahead for you two, don't focus on the things that separate you or get hung up on the social stereotypes about older men and younger women; other people will do enough of that without your help. Stick with what connects you. If it's right between you, it's right, however old or young you are.

"Rosen and I fell head-over-heels in love as college students; we were just kids. I have a teacher friend who found her soulmate when she was in her sixties. There is no right way to do life or love; it's chemistry and luck and hard work, with no formula for mixing the right ingredients in the right order."

"What do you think of her?"

"And now we get to the other agenda: looking for my approval and blessing. I just met her; I don't have much to think about except she obviously adores you. You are going to have challenges, though. That much is obvious."

"What are you talking about? You mean the age difference?"

"More than that. In case you hadn't noticed, you two are an interracial couple. Things are a hell of a lot better now than they were fifty years ago, but that doesn't mean it will be easy."

"Funny, in a very real sense, I hadn't noticed. I mean, it's not like I'm blind, but I think in my head I think of us as both being Portuguese-American."

"You think you think? You think in your head? You wax so eloquent, Clinton. You must be in love. Oxytocin tends to tangle the tongues of males."

"Oxytocin?"

"The bonding hormone. Heavy in the air between you two. Trust me, I'm a biologist; I know about these things."

With the rain stopping after they returned, Millie suggested they take their tea outside. "It's such a mild day. Bring the chairs out." In front of the cabin, Millie upended a log and sat on it. "Now, tell me more about the big news. I want to know how you actually did it, exposing Biontolics." She turned expectantly toward Clinton.

"Don't look at me," he said. "It was Julia who really pulled it off. She and her friends—"

"Your students," Julia interjected.

"—my students. They used social media to spread the word at the speed of the Internet. She helped set it all up in advance without consulting with me, even passed on a pilfered copy of my magnum opus for posting on the class blog—and everywhere else in the world, it seems."

"It wasn't pilfered," she said. "You gave it to me to edit, remember. I just passed on a copy of the final edit to Roger and the rest of his team."

"Right, but I never saw that final edit until it was posted online, and now I have to come up with another 20,000 words or so because the *Sacramento Bee* wants to publish the complete, full, unexpurgated story. They have their eyes on a Pulitzer, I think, and they expect me to deliver it for them."

Millie patted his knee. "Marvelous. I always knew you had it in you. You were one of my favorite students. It does a teacher's heart good to see a student finally coming into his own."

"Well, I couldn't have done it without Julia. Not only did she do a lot of the leg work, but she saved my skin—more than once." He reached for Julia's hand and gave it a squeeze.

"Okay, you two, none of that. Now I want a report: the full, blow-by-blow account of your travel adventures. Clinton told me you went to Africa together. Fill me in."

~ ~ ~

It was late afternoon before Clinton and Julia finally left. As the car bucked back down the rutted fire road, Julia was the first to speak. "I get what you saw in her. She is something else. Always teaching, even in casual conversation."

"Yeah, she's pretty special. But I hate leaving her alone up here in the woods."

"Oh, she can take care of herself. You, on the other hand, you wouldn't last a week up here, not without me, you wouldn't."

"Well, I guess I better hang on to you, then."

"I do hope you aren't thinking of doing the back-to-the-land scenario. Remember, I'm a California girl, and frankly, I am eager to get back to sunshine and surf."

"I have bad news for you. There's no surf in Sacramento."

'Details, details. I just want to get home. Well, with you, anyway."

Chapter 47

A landscaping crew was busy converting the front lawn at the nursing home to xeriscape, replacing water-wasting turf and shrubbery with rock gardens, succulents, and desert perennials. Julia took Clinton's hand and led him up the zig-zag path through the work-in-progress and to the main entrance.

"She's not going to remember me," he said. "She never does, and your being with me will only confuse her more."

"She's your mother. You're going to visit your mother. Do you understand?"

"Yes, ma'am, I understand. I'll just follow you, since you already know the way."

Julia frowned at him. "Don't you yes-ma'am me, mister, if you know what's good for you."

"Oh, that part I know. You're good for me."

"You got that right." She smiled broadly as she held the door open for him.

~ ~ ~

Sarah Toledano did not turn from the window when they entered her room. "Do you see that bird out there?" she said. "I am trying to remember what it's called. At first I thought it was a cat up there in the tree, but it wasn't. It was a bird. It must be a catbird, then. What do you think?" She turned abruptly and faced them. "Oh, you again."

"Yes, Mom, it's me again: Clinton."

"Oh, not you. I mean her, the pretty one. I think I know you." She stood up.

"You do. I'm Julia. Remember? I brought you the chocolates."

"Oh, I love sweets, so you must be sweet, too. Ha ha. But who is he?"

"He's your son, Clinton."

"Is that so? Then that man who keeps calling must be his father, but I don't remember his name."

Clinton shot an I-told-you-so glance at Julia. "Angelo," he said to his mother. "Your husband's name is Angelo, Mom, but it must be someone else who calls you."

"I had a husband, but I don't think his name was Angelo. Are you sure?"

"Yes, Mom, I'm sure."

There was an intermittent buzz from the direction of the night stand. It stopped after a while, then restarted. "I think something is buzzing in that drawer, Mom."

"Oh, that's him. He calls about this time every week. Or maybe it's every day; I wouldn't know."

"It's a phone? Are you going to answer it?"

"Oh, I can never figure out those things. It's not actually a phone. One of those—oh, I don't remember the word—like a phone but not. I always let the nurse do it."

The buzzing started up again. Julia opened the drawer "Here, let me take care of it."

"Are you a nurse? You have to be a nurse to do it, I think."

Julia held up a pink smartphone. "I think I can manage this, even without a nursing degree." She answered the call and switched to speakerphone. "Hello?"

"Is this Roberta? Can I speak with Sarah?"

"She's right here. Who is this?"

"It's Angelo. Who else would be calling on this phone? You don't sound like Roberta. Are you the new nurse Sarah told me about?"

"No, this is Julia. And Clinton is right beside me. How in hell . . . ? And where in hell are you?"

"Not in hell, thank you very much. Not in heaven either, that's damn clear. But I'm okay."

"How . . . ?"

"It always helps to have friends, especially friends with funds. Mine sprung me from the hospital. They can't spring me from this damn wheelchair, but they did set up an amazing wheelchair-accessible lab for me. I've been doing some great chemistry for them, and they treat me like a prince, although I'm pretty much confined to quarters. I guess I can't complain. It's a lot better than what your Biontolics buddies had in store for me." There was the sound of forced laughter. "Is my Sarah there?"

"She's right here, smiling."

"Hi, Sarah. It's me, Angelo. I love you."

"Well, I don't know any Angelo, but I suppose I probably love you, too. And you should see these two lovebirds visiting me. I don't know who they are, but they are such a cute couple."

Clinton feigned embarrassment. "She's learning to bake challah, Mom. It's pretty good."

Sarah's eyes and mouth opened suddenly with surprise and delight, as if someone had just turned the electricity back on in an empty house. "I remember making challah, kneading and braiding, that wonderful smell that would fill the kitchen as it baked before the start of Shabbos."

Clinton looked puzzled. "You never made challah, Mom."

"Silly boy, before you came along, when I was a girl. Momma taught me: your *bubbe*. You never knew her. She could be . . . sometimes . . ." Her voice faded and her face slackened. "What were we talking about?"

"Challah. Julia is learning to make challah."

"Clint, you should help her, help her learn."

"That's exactly what I'm doing, Mom, and she's teaching me how to make *feijoada*.

"And speak a little more Portuguese," Julia added.

Sarah reached for their hands. "You should see them, Angelo. You really should."

"I know, perhaps again someday."

"They look happy, happy and in love."

"That was us, too, Sarah. Once."

"I know, Angelo, I know."

Quiet recognition overtook them for a moment, then Julia whispered, "Alone, together, in the silent finite present."

Clinton looked at her. "What?"

"One of Hidalgo's poems, 'Internet Pause.' I saved it on my phone." She found it and started reading.

> *Bound by skeins of gossamer glass,*
> *Digital veins of captive sunbeams cast*
>   *across the seas,*
> *Bright bit-streams passed*
>   *between the rejoined absent:*
> *Alone, together,*
>   *in the silent finite present.*

For that moment they were all there, all four, in the room, in the silent finite present.

~ ~ ~

~ ~ ~

Fiction by Lior Samson

The Homeland Connection
Bashert ~ The Dome ~ Web Games
Chipset ~ Gasline ~ Flight Track

The Rosen Singularity ~ The Millicent Factor

The Four-Color Puzzle

Requisite Variety: Collected Short Science Fiction

Acknowledgements

In addition to the crack editorial team I depend on for help with every book, I always turn to specialists: subject-matter experts who can steer me right on matters of technical detail where my own research may have failed me. This time around, I owe special thanks to biostatistician Tamar Sofer at the University of Washington, and to fire forensics expert Joseph LeFevre at Fox Valley Technical College, himself a writer. They not only helped me within their own areas of expertise, but made other suggestions that improved the story and its telling. I also want to thank Devan Lockwood for his advice about the finer details of contemporary social media. There were others, too, who asked not to be named but whose contributions are no less appreciated.

A special note of deep appreciation goes to North Shore Boston artist Dianna Daly for granting permission to use her painting "Passages" for cover art. The watercolor—one of a series inspired by a photograph taken at the Crane Estate in Ipswich—was on temporary display at The Lone Gull, my favorite coffee shop in Gloucester. It seemed to fit, even before I read the title and learned of its provenance, so connected with this story.

The core crew was there for me again, beginning and ending with Lucy Lockwood, who took time away from her graduate studies in marine biology to give me the benefit of her wise counsel and sharp editorial skills. And to Janet Lemnah, copy editor extraordinaire, who wields a red pencil with precision and panache, goes another round of my heartfelt applause.

About the Author

Lior Samson is the pen name of an emeritus academic who has won awards for both fiction and non-fiction writing as well as for his innovative work in interaction design. He is the author of more than two dozen books, including nine novels and a collection of short fiction. As a consultant and teacher, he has traveled the world and has served on the faculties of major international universities.

He lives in Massachusetts with his wife and two children where he cooks creative fusion cuisine and composes serious choral music. He describes himself as a full-time novelist, part-time journalist, and full-time tech support and taxi driver for the three students in his life—and readily acknowledges that his time sheet doesn't add up.

He regards the readers who write with questions, kudos, and criticism as vital parts of the dialogue he hopes to spark through his writing. He enjoys hearing from readers and appreciates those who take the time to post reviews on Amazon and elsewhere. He can be reached by email at: lior@liorsamson.com